CW00541141

LOVE AT FIRST SITE

PHOEBE MACLEOD

Phoebe
xx.

B

Boldwood

First published in Great Britain in 2023 by Boldwood Books Ltd.

Copyright © Phoebe MacLeod, 2023

Cover Design by Head Design Ltd

Cover Photography: Shutterstock

The moral right of Phoebe MacLeod to be identified as the author of this work has been asserted in accordance with the Copyright, Designs and Patents Act 1988.

All rights reserved. No part of this book may be reproduced in any form or by any electronic or mechanical means, including information storage and retrieval systems, without written permission from the author, except for the use of brief quotations in a book review.

This book is a work of fiction and, except in the case of historical fact, any resemblance to actual persons, living or dead, is purely coincidental.

Every effort has been made to obtain the necessary permissions with reference to copyright material, both illustrative and quoted. We apologise for any omissions in this respect and will be pleased to make the appropriate acknowledgements in any future edition.

A CIP catalogue record for this book is available from the British Library.

Paperback ISBN 978-1-80426-292-4

Large Print ISBN 978-1-80426-293-1

Hardback ISBN 978-1-80426-291-7

Ebook ISBN 978-1-80426-294-8

Kindle ISBN 978-1-80426-295-5

Audio CD ISBN 978-1-80426-286-3

MP3 CD ISBN 978-1-80426-287-0

Digital audio download ISBN 978-1-80426-288-7

Boldwood Books Ltd
23 Bowerdean Street
London SW6 3TN
www.boldwoodbooks.com

To my fantastic boys, Matthew and Charlie.

1

Ella,

I'm just putting together the slide deck for the final presentation to the trust tomorrow. Can you send over your project plan for the initial phase, including costs, as soon as possible so I can integrate it into our overall proposal?

Thanks

Lee

I close down the email and, with a sigh of pleasure, open up the project plan to give it a final once-over before sending it to Lee. It's not surprising that project plans give me joy; I'd be a pretty rubbish project manager if I couldn't take pleasure in a well-honed plan, and this one is a doozy. I've lost count of the number of times I've been through it, both on my own and with other people in the company. As I study the Gantt chart, looking for any tiny holes I may have overlooked, I'm filled with confidence that this really is a work of art, as project plans go.

I've always liked order, and my sister Ava used to tease me relentlessly when I was doing exam revision at school, because

I'd spend nearly as long putting together my colour-coded revision plans as I would doing the actual revision. Having assembled the plan, I'd print it off and stick it on my bedroom wall, meticulously ticking off the tasks as I completed them.

'This is borderline OCD,' she'd remarked when she first caught sight of my A-Level schedule, 'but you've missed something.'

'What?'

'There's nothing here about organising your knicker drawer. How will you cope if your knickers get out of sequence?'

'Piss off,' I'd replied as she'd sauntered out of my room, grinning.

Since joining Orchestra, the somewhat bizarrely named payroll and accounting software firm in Leeds where I've worked for the last five years, I've put together countless project plans, but this one matters more than any of them. We're down to the final two in a bid for a contract with a cluster of NHS trusts across the north of England. Not only does this deal involve pretty much all of the components of our software suite, but it could also become a template for deals with other NHS trusts going forwards if the project is successful, so to describe it as 'massive' would be something of an understatement.

The other reason that this deal matters so much is that our opposition is a company that goes by the equally bizarre name of Harmony. Harmony was founded roughly ten years ago by a couple of disgruntled Orchestra consultants who left to set up on their own. It's widely believed that they chose the name of their company as a deliberate snub to their ex-employers, but this all happened before I joined, so I don't have any firm evidence. However, most of their products have similar names to ours. For example, our database component, which all the other applications sit on top of, is called 'Maestro', and theirs is called

'Conductor' – go figure. To begin with, they didn't pose much of a threat, but Lee tells me that their offering is now on a par with, and in some ways better than, ours, so this deal really could go either way. Needless to say, this is as near to 'personal' as business gets. Everyone in the company is rooting for us to shut Harmony out and close this deal.

Having gone through the plan one last time, I convert it into a format that Lee can embed into his presentation and attach it to my reply.

Hi Lee,
Plan attached. Trust me, a lettuce leaf has more fat on it than this plan does. I've already included contingencies, so you can use the numbers in the attached spreadsheet as they are.
Good luck for tomorrow!
Ella

I attach the spreadsheet with the costs to back up the plan and press send. My part in the sales pitch is now done; it's up to Lee, as the Customer Relationship Manager (basically an upmarket term for salesman), to bring everything together into a compelling argument to put to the trust tomorrow.

'Have you seen Lee's email asking for the project plan?' my boss, Jonathan, asks, plonking his backside on the edge of my desk and manspreading. I don't think he does it on purpose, but it's definitely a subconscious power play because he never does it when he's talking to people at the same level as, or above, him. Today, he obviously feels a special need to assert himself, because he's spreading so wide that I'm having to tuck myself into the corner of my desk to prevent my arm from coming into contact with his thigh.

'Yes. I've just sent it,' I tell him.

'Oh.' He looks momentarily annoyed. 'I thought you were going to walk me through it before you committed it.'

'I did. That's what we did this morning, remember?'

His face clears. 'Of course. I'm sorry. Baby brain, I'm afraid. Even though Lucas is six months old now, we're still not getting any sleep. So, are you excited? There's a lot riding on this deal for you, isn't there? I'll be sad to lose you from my team, but I think you'll really flourish as an account manager. I'll put in a good word for you, of course, when the time comes. I'll tell them what a model of efficiency you are, and how much you deserve the job.'

'I'm not counting any chickens,' I tell him firmly. 'Let's see whether we manage to close this deal before we start celebrating my possible promotion.'

He is right, though. Although I really am trying very hard not to think about it in case I jinx it, I really need this deal to go through too. Nothing has been promised, but there have been heavy hints that Orchestra will need a new account manager, among other positions, if we land this, and I've been left in no doubt that my name is in the frame. Having delivered his speech, Jonathan obviously feels that our little motivational chat is over and strides off back to his own desk. As he does so, I look up and meet my friend Ruth's eye. She's grinning broadly and surreptitiously forms a T with her hands. I grab my mug and we head for the kitchen.

'I couldn't see everything, but it looked like we were quite high on the manspread scale just then,' she giggles as soon as we're safely in the kitchen and out of earshot of the rest of the office.

'Oh, yes,' I reply. 'I'm calling a solid nine as he pretty much had me pinned against the side of my desk.'

'Surely that's a ten?'

'No. Wrong trousers for a ten. You only get a ten when he's

wearing the dark blue ones that emphasise the crotch bulge. Come on, Ruth, that's elementary.'

'You're right. I'm so sorry. How were we on the fertility score?'

'That's a disappointing eight, I'm afraid.' I try to arrange my face into an expression of regret, but I'm not really succeeding. 'He didn't mention the baby until the third sentence.'

'Ah, well, better luck next time,' she sympathises. 'Are you sure you want this promotion? Who am I going to play the game with when you're gone?'

'I haven't got it yet, remember? And, even if Lee knocks their socks off tomorrow, it'll still be ages before they announce who's got the contract, so I'm not going anywhere for a while. Plus, assuming all of that comes off and I get the position, I'm still going to be in the same office as you.'

'You won't be, though. You might drop in occasionally, but you'll be on the road, schmoozing clients and having lavish dinners on expenses.'

'Fair point, but I think you overestimate the glamour,' I laugh. 'It'll mainly be dinners for one in various Holiday Inns.'

'Well,' she replies, expertly flicking her used teabag into the bin, 'good luck anyway. I'm rooting for you, even if I will miss you. Let's hope they replace you with someone interesting who'll keep me entertained. Otherwise, I'll have to resort to wearing low-cut tops and breaking my computer just to torment the IT guy.'

'You wouldn't! That's so cruel.'

'Of course I wouldn't,' she laughs. 'What do you take me for?'

I'm ashamed to admit that I only learned that the IT guy is actually called Ian a few months ago. He's always just been 'the IT guy'. He's good at what he does, there's no doubt about that but, if his lack of social chit-chat is anything to go by, he's generally happier talking to machines than he is to people. Until recently, he also had a frankly creepy habit of staring at women's chests whenever he thought he could get away with it. Unfortunately for him, he wasn't very subtle about it and someone made a complaint around six months ago. Rumour has it he got a verbal warning from HR and, ever since then, he makes such a point of looking into your eyes when he's speaking to you that it's possibly even more creepy than having him stare at your chest; you'd almost wish he went back to his old ways. Ruth is, to put it tactfully, generously proportioned in the chest department, so a low-cut top on her would probably be more temptation than poor Ian could bear.

I take my cup of tea back to my desk and spend the last hour or so of the working day replying to emails and making sure all the documentation I've prepared for the NHS trust project, including my beautiful project plan, is uploaded to the relevant internal SharePoint sites. I'm full of nervous energy; even though I won't be in the final pitch meeting tomorrow and there's nothing more I can do, I can't seem to sit still. The next month is going to be agonising.

'I know it's only a Thursday, but do you fancy a drink before going home?' Ruth asks, as I'm packing up at five-thirty. Our office is in one of those redeveloped commercial areas, with herringbone-patterned brick walkways and lots of trendy bars and restaurants catering to the office crowds. There's a fancy cocktail bar just around the corner, and a group of us often head that way after work on a Friday. Jonathan used to be one of the ringleaders until his son was born, but now he just paints on an expression that's a weird mixture of smugness and disapproval when we invite him, and makes some excuse about priorities changing when you have a family. The way he talks, you'd have thought nobody else in the office had ever had a baby.

'I think that's a genius idea,' I reply. 'Are we inviting anyone else, or is it just going to be the two of us?'

'Jonathan won't come, obviously, and the others have left already, so I think it's just you and me. Will you be able to cope, do you think? I know I'm awfully dull, but I'll make a special effort, I promise.'

'Oh, do shut up!' I laugh. 'It's a work night, so I'll only have one, though.'

'Of course you will. There's no chance whatsoever that you'll end up having "just one more" about three times and falling into an Uber,' Ruth giggles as we make our way outside.

She may have me bang to rights, but I'm determined to stick to one cocktail tonight. It doesn't matter if you over-indulge on a Friday, because you've got the whole weekend to get over it. But I've got to be on the ball tomorrow in case I'm called upon to talk Lee through any of the finer points of the plan before he goes into the meeting.

The bar is much quieter than I'm used to, and we have no problem getting one of the booths that are normally rammed full on a Friday night. There's also none of the usual jostling for attention to get served at the bar; we're encouraged to take our seats and a barman comes over to take our order, which is a novelty.

'So, there is a bit of a hidden agenda to our Thursday night drinks. I have news!' Ruth trills, grinning widely as soon as the barman has set down our porn star martinis.

'Oh, yes?'

'Wade's asked me to move in with him.'

'Oh, wow! That's a big step for him. What did you say?'

'I said yes, dummy! What did you think I was going to say?'

'Hey, look. No judgement from me, but you've always said you wouldn't move in until he'd given you a ring.'

'Yeah, well, he doesn't seem to have got that memo, despite some pretty heavy bloody hints from me, so I've decided to compromise. It's still a big step forward in terms of commitment and, if I'm living with him, I'll have more opportunities to nudge him in the right direction, don't you think?'

'I can see the logic. When is this going to happen?'

'I have to give my current landlord notice, so not for a couple of months officially, but I'll probably move most of my stuff over in the next week or two. I don't want to give him the chance to change his mind.'

'I'm delighted for you. I hope you'll be very happy together.'

'Thank you. Anyway, enough about me. What about you? Anything happening on the dating front?'

'No,' I tell her, with a smile. 'When I have Jonathan as a role model, somehow nobody else measures up, do you know what I mean? He's so fertile, I have to be careful not to pass him too closely on the stairs in case I accidentally get pregnant.'

'You're right, of course,' she replies. 'That was the one thing that I found myself wondering when Wade asked me to move in. "Am I accepting second best here? What if he's not as fertile as Jonathan?" I've encouraged him to manspread as much as possible at home, to give the boys some ventilation, but it's still a risk.'

I smile, pleased at having deflected the conversation back onto her. I love Ruth to bits and I'd like nothing more than to tell her the truth, but my true relationship status has to remain a deeply guarded secret, especially from her.

2

_____

It's only a couple of short bus rides from the office to the flat so, despite a detour to pick up a few groceries, it's only just gone seven o'clock when I get back. I'm expecting to find my boyfriend sitting at the breakfast bar, still poring over his laptop, so it's a bit of a surprise to find him relaxing in front of the TV.

'What's this?' I ask him. 'Slacking off? That's very unlike you.'

'To be honest, Els, I've been over this bloody thing so many times, I don't think I can tweak it any more. I've decided to let it rest.'

After dumping my coat and laptop bag in the cupboard by the front door and putting away the groceries, I pour us each a large glass of the red wine I know he likes and take them over to the sofa, planting a kiss on his head as I sit down.

'Are you confident?' I ask, as I lean into him and he puts his arm around me. Even after a long day, he still smells delicious.

'As much as I can be,' he replies, wearily. 'You know what it's like. I could go through it again, and I'm sure I'd find something I want to change. I reckon I'm at the stage now where I can't polish this turd of a presentation any more. It's time to roll it in glitter and put it to bed.'

'I hope it's not a turd!'

'No, but you know what I mean.'

'I bought steak to give you stamina, but I'm going to grab a quick shower first and wash the day off. OK?'

'Good idea. I'll go in after you,' he replies as I pick up my glass of wine and head for the bedroom.

You may be wondering why Lee and I have to keep our relationship secret. After all, he's not married or seeing anyone else, so there's no logical reason why we should have to skulk about under everyone's radar. The truth is that Orchestra has very firm views about office romances. On the day I joined, the HR person responsible for my 'onboarding' took me through a long list of company policies, one of which included the policy on employees dating each other, which was basically a no-no.

'Listen,' she'd told me when I'd raised my eyebrows. 'Obviously we can't *dictate* how you run your personal life, but it's better for everyone if office relations stay firmly platonic. If you were to form a romantic attachment with a colleague, and that relationship were to turn sour, I'm sure you can understand that a toxic break-up in an office environment poisons more than the two people directly involved. What I'm trying to say,' she'd continued when I had evidently looked completely nonplussed, 'is that we can't forbid you from having a relationship with a colleague, but it would be very severely frowned upon.'

'If you don't mind me saying, that seems slightly draconian. I'm not planning on dating anyone at work, but surely my private life is just that?'

She'd sighed. 'You're right, of course. The reason we have this policy is that there was an incident a couple of years ago that left a nasty taste in everyone's mouth. Management therefore decided to implement this policy to try to prevent anything similar from happening again.'

I'd nodded my understanding and we'd continued working our way through the rest of the company policies, which were totally predictable. Being drunk at work was out, as was being high on drugs. There was a long list of things that could lead to instant dismissal, and an even longer list that could lead to disciplinary action. I happily signed on the dotted line, confident that there would be no problem.

And there wasn't, until Lee turned up halfway through my first week.

When I was at school, my friends and I used to amuse ourselves by finding sex scenes in books and reading them out loud to each other, often shrieking hysterically in the process. One thing that was guaranteed to set us off was when a man was described as 'smouldering'. We used to draw little stick men with smoke coming off them to emphasise how ridiculous a description it was. I still believed it to be a nonsense, right up to the day I met Lee. I can clearly remember the first time I laid eyes on him.

You know how, if you look out of a window without moving your eyes for a long time, and then squeeze them tightly shut, you can still see the image? My first impression of Lee is burned into my mind like that. He was wearing a charcoal-grey suit that fitted him so well, it was like a mould he'd been poured into, black Oxford shoes that had been shined almost to a mirror finish, a crisp, white shirt without a single crease, and a blue and yellow silk tie. He'd walked over to the hot desk opposite mine and hung his jacket carefully on the back of the chair, before leaning over the partition to introduce himself. His voice was deep and rich, causing my insides to resonate in a most unsettling manner as he spoke. And all of this was before I had a chance to properly take in his face. Oh, yes, Lee Johnson definitely smouldered. His eyes were so dark, they were almost black, and there was a mesmerising intensity to them; when he looked at you, it felt like you were the only person in the world besides him. His high cheekbones and strong chin framed a mouth that you just knew would be heaven to kiss, but would also leave you filled with regret the next morning. His handshake was warm and appropriately firm, and a whiff of expensive aftershave trailed behind him wherever he went.

I took an instant dislike to him.

I knew his type all too well and it was obvious that a man who dressed and looked the way he did would be incredibly arrogant and full of himself. Thankfully, the nature of his job meant that he rarely came to the office, but I couldn't help noticing that he sought out the hot desk opposite mine every time he did. To begin with, I assumed he just liked that particular desk, but when I went through a phase of moving around, sitting at different desks for a bit of variety (sad, I know) he still sat opposite me whenever he could.

'Are you stalking me?' I'd asked him one morning, as he hung his jacket on the back of the chair and began settling himself into the desk opposite me again.

'I'm sorry?'

'Every time you come in, you sit opposite me, even when there are a number of other desks available. Do I need to be worried? Are you going to start following me home?' I'd smiled to try to indicate that I was teasing him, but I don't think he got the memo.

'I'm sorry,' he'd replied, looking deadly serious. 'I'm not trying to make you uncomfortable. Would you rather I sat somewhere else?'

I'd thought about it. Deep down, part of me wanted to say that yes, I would prefer him to sit somewhere else, but it sounded petty when I tested it in my head and there was no way that I was going to admit that I found him a little distracting, so I'd just smiled again and told him he was fine where he was and did my best to ignore him.

'I'm going down to the coffee shop, would you like something?' he'd then asked, mid-morning. I was somewhat taken aback; apart from our earlier conversation where I'd accused him of stalking me, we'd hardly spoken to each other since he'd first introduced himself. I wasn't sure how to respond. On the one hand, I didn't want to be in his debt, but I also didn't want to turn him down and appear even more rude than I had at the start of the day.

'I can never decide what I want. I tell you what, I'll walk down there with you,' I'd replied eventually. My plan was simple. I'd pay for my own coffee (a skinny latte – I'm a creature of habit, but he didn't need to know that) to avoid being indebted to him, and I'd also manage to avoid being rude at the same time.

'I really am sorry about making you uncomfortable,' he'd said as we walked out of the office. 'To be honest, I don't really know many of the people here, but you've always looked friendly so I guess that's why I've gravitated to you. I'll make sure I sit somewhere else next time.'

'It's fine, really. It just struck me as odd, that's all. I shouldn't have said anything. You're quite within your rights to sit wherever you want.'

He was as good as his word, though, and the next time he came to the office, he deliberately chose a desk pretty much as far away from where I was sitting as possible, which of course made me feel terribly guilty, so I'd invited him to get a coffee to try to offer a bit of an olive branch.

After that, we kind of got into the habit of wandering down to the coffee shop together every time he came into the office, and a

tentative friendship started to develop. I began to believe that he
wasn't quite the arsehole I'd initially thought he was, although I
was right about some of it because he's definitely got a ruthless
streak. I asked him about it once, after he'd left the estate agent
practically in tears when we were negotiating over the flat, and
he'd unapologetically told me he wouldn't be able to do his job if
he didn't have a killer instinct. Anyway, the coffees turned into
the occasional after-work drink and then, one summer evening
about six months after I'd started at Orchestra, Lee kissed me for
the first time.

It was a typical evening at the bar; by this time, we were very
comfortable with each other and, despite my best efforts, I'd
realised that I was very attracted to him. Although there had
never been anything between us beyond friendship, we always
went to a bar on the other side of the city from the office, to
minimise the chance of anyone seeing us and drawing any
unwanted conclusions. On this particular evening, we'd come out
after our usual couple of drinks to find that it was absolutely
pouring with rain. Not the miserable, freeze-you-to-death rain
that we're so used to in England, but a totally unexpected warm
summer thunderstorm that was doing its best to cut through the
humidity of the day. Lee had tried to shield me with his jacket as
he escorted me to the bus stop, but it was no good and we were
both soaked through and laughing hysterically by the time we got
there. He'd waited with me until the bus arrived and, just as it
sploshed to a halt, he wrapped his arm around my waist, pulled
me into him, and kissed me deeply.

'I'm sorry, Ella, but you have no idea how long I've wanted to
do that. If you slap me and tell me you never want to see me
again, it will still have been totally worth it,' he'd sighed when
we broke apart. For a moment, I was too surprised to say or do
anything, but his kiss definitely awoke something in me. Instead

of slapping him, which I probably should have done, I'd held his gaze and leant back in. I missed the bus, but that was the start of our relationship. We moved in together three years ago, being careful to explain to HR that we were just flatmates when we gave them the same address and, to date, we've got away with it. Sometimes I wish we could be open with everyone, but neither of us wants the hassle, so we keep it a secret. It seemed like a good idea at the time, but it is becoming increasingly difficult. I know Ruth feels slightly put out that I've never invited her round, and our social media accounts are strictly curated. We have the privacy settings on our Facebook accounts set to the highest levels to make sure nobody at work can stumble across anything they shouldn't, and everything work-related goes on LinkedIn, where we don't share any relationship information.

I take my time in the shower, shaving my legs, washing my hair and generally having a bit of a tidy up. Once I've dried it in a towel, I blow dry and brush it carefully until it falls onto my shoulders in soft, blonde waves. To look at, Lee and I couldn't be more different. Where he is dark and brooding, I'm fair with large, blue eyes. A lot of people assume that I colour my hair, but it's entirely natural, a fact that Lee delights in pointing out with various coarse remarks about how my collar and cuffs match. I limit my make-up to a touch of lipstick and a little bit of eyeliner, before spraying the lightest mist of perfume at the base of my neck and putting on some of the lingerie that I know Lee likes under my jeans and T-shirt. He's going to want sex tonight. He always does before a pitch; he says it helps him to relax and focus. The one time I wasn't able to oblige, due to a highly inconvenient case of cystitis, the pitch hadn't gone well and the deal had gone to the competition. Even though Lee had been quick to reassure me that the two things were completely unrelated when I'd mentioned it, I still felt vaguely responsible and, thankfully, it hasn't happened again.

'All yours,' I tell him as I walk back out into our open-plan kitchen/dining/sitting room. When we decided to live together, we spent ages looking for the perfect place and, despite the cost, Lee persuaded me that this was where we wanted to be as soon as he saw it. It's a penthouse apartment with two bedrooms (useful if HR decide to check) and panoramic views over the city.

'Great,' he replies, turning off the TV and running his hand through his hair. 'I'll be as quick as I can.'

'Do you want me to have a quick glance at your presentation before I start dinner, just in case there are any spelling mistakes or things you've missed?'

'No, don't worry. I've run the spell checker and if I've missed anything important, it's too late to change it now. Do you know what I'd like?' he asks, raising his eyes and looking at me appreciatively.

'I have no idea,' I smile.

'Does this give you a clue?' he murmurs as he wraps his arms around me, letting them fall onto my bum and pulling me against him.

Called it.

3

A month has passed since the NHS trust pitch and, despite things in the office seeming normal on the surface, there's definitely an undercurrent of nervous tension. Rumour has it that the trust will announce their decision either today or on Monday. The only person who seems totally unaffected is Lee, which is odd, because he's normally like a caged tiger by this point. I'm not entirely sure what his commission would be on a sale of this size, but I reckon it'll be enough for him to treat himself to a new car, and I might be able to con a holiday out of him as well. If it's particularly good, we might even go somewhere long-haul; I've always fancied a trip to the Caribbean.

At half past three, my phone pings, and my heart leaps into my mouth when I see it's a message from Lee. He must have heard the decision and decided to let me know before it's announced officially. I shove my phone into my handbag and make for the loos. I don't want anyone to look over my shoulder and see that I'm getting special treatment.

My hands are shaking a bit as I push the cubicle door shut, slide the lock across and sit down on the seat. The last thing I need is to drop my phone into the loo, so I carefully keep it to one side as I unlock it and read the message. My heart sinks.

Don't forget we're going to my parents this weekend. Are you OK to leave at 5?

I want to kill him. Of course I haven't forgotten about the bloody trip to his parents, but he must know that isn't what I thought the message was about. Keeping my phone well away from the loo, I type back.

I'm already packed. Thought you were texting about the deal, you bastard. Any news?

I can see he's typing and I'm aware that I'm chewing my lip, which I always do when I'm nervous.

Nothing yet.

Swallowing my disappointment, I shove my phone back into my bag and exit the cubicle, taking care to flush first so as not to arouse suspicion. After washing my hands, I head back to my desk.

'Are you all right, Ella?' Ruth asks quietly as I pass her desk.

'Yes, fine. Why?'

'That's the second time you've been to the loo in the last half hour,' she tells me in a whisper. 'Don't worry, I know what it's like. Nerves go straight to my bladder too.'

At four o'clock, I file into one of the meeting rooms for a project retrospective with Jonathan. These are normally fairly feisty meetings where the project manager (me in this case) and the consultants desperately try to convince him that any delays or problems on the project we've just finished are nothing to do with us. The way it works is pretty simple; if you're not in the room, you're copping the blame. The project we're looking back on today was a fairly simple implementation, and we (broadly) stayed on time and within budget, so it's thankfully not too difficult. All eyes are surreptitiously on the clock, and I notice Jonathan is particularly eager to make sure we wrap up quickly so we can get back to our desks.

It seems to take forever for five o'clock to come around but, when it does and there's still no news, the atmosphere in the office changes completely. It's now obvious that we won't hear today, and I'm not the only one making a quick getaway.

'I've got to dash tonight,' I say to Ruth as we head for the door.

'Hot date?' she asks, smiling.

'You wish. Have a good weekend, won't you.'

'And you,' she calls after me as I hot foot it across the car park towards the bus stop. 'Don't do anything I wouldn't do!' Despite my rush, I can't help but take a moment to turn around and stick my tongue out at her.

* * *

'Is this everything?' Lee asks me, waving my case at me as soon as I get through the door.

'I think so. Give me five minutes to get changed and use the loo, and I'll be ready.'

'I'll wait for you down by the car.'

He's doing this to pressurise me, I know. He waits in different places depending on how much of a hurry he's in. If there's no pressure, he'll lounge on the sofa. Waiting by the front door means we're a bit short of time, and waiting by the car is tantamount to telling me every second counts.

'Why the rush? You're not normally this desperate to see your parents,' I tease him once we're out of the underground car park and on our way.

'It's not that I'm desperate to see them, and they'll be working anyway. I just need to get out of the city and breathe some country air. It's been a bit like a pressure cooker at work, don't you think?'

'I'm sorry you didn't hear anything. I'm sure they'll let us know on Monday.'

'Yeah, I expect so.'

We lapse into silence for most of the rest of the journey. Lee's parents own a pub in a village called East Morton, which is only about half an hour from Leeds on a good day, but will take considerably longer in the Friday rush hour traffic. He's never particularly talkative when he's driving, so I allow myself to daydream about Caribbean beaches to pass the time. I'm just mentally sipping a rum punch when he turns into the car park of the Farmer's Arms.

'We're here,' he states unnecessarily as he reaches for his phone and wallet. One of the things I like about Lee is that, although it took me a while to get used to how fast he drives, he is actually quite careful on the road and never lets himself be distracted when he's behind the wheel. The phone is always locked away in a cubbyhole between the front seats and, while that means there's often a delay when we arrive somewhere because he has to deal with emails and stuff, I definitely prefer it to the alternative. His face clouds over as he checks his messages, and I know this is going to be a delay day.

'Are you OK to go in ahead of me?' he says. 'I need to make a couple of calls and then I'll be with you.'

'Is it about the deal?'

'No. Just other work stuff. I'll be as quick as I can, I promise.

Don't worry about your bag; I'll bring it with me.'

He leans across and gives me a quick peck on the lips and, with a sigh, I open the door and step out into the cool night air. The Farmer's Arms is a fairly typical gastropub; Lee's parents bought it twenty years ago when it was a run-down boozer on the verge of closure, and they've transformed it into a thriving business. If the fullness of the car park hadn't already given it away, the hubbub of conversation as I step through the door indicates that tonight is a typically busy Friday night. I make my way towards the bar, where Lee's younger brother Nathan is busily pouring drinks and placing them on a tray ready to go to one of the tables.

'All right, Ella?' he says as I settle myself on one of the bar stools. 'On your own tonight?'

'Lee's just making a couple of calls. You know what it's like.'

'Yeah, the cutthroat world of sales never stops. Sauvignon Blanc?'

'Lovely, thanks, Nathan.'

I've barely taken my first sip before I'm enveloped in a very familiar hug.

'Hello, Ella darling. Have you brought my son with you, or have you finally reached the end of your tether with him and left him in a bloody mess somewhere? Do I need to call the police?'

This is pretty much the greeting Lee's mother uses every time he sends me on ahead, and I sometimes wonder what she'd do if I said I had attacked him.

'No, he's fine, Kate. He's just making some calls.'

'You both work too hard,' she sighs.

'Says the pub landlady!' I laugh.

'Touché. We're completely full tonight, so are you OK to have something to eat at the bar? I'll send Rosie over once Lee surfaces.'

'Do you need a hand?' It's rare for an entire weekend here to pass without us being dragged in to help either behind the bar or serving tables.

'I think we're OK for tonight, thank you. I can't promise that we won't need you tomorrow, though.'

'That's fine. I'm always happy to help, you know that.'

'Aww, bless you. Hopefully we'll be over the worst by around nine-thirty, and then we can have a bit of a catch-up, if my son has deigned to make an appearance by then.' With that, she disappears back into the maelstrom of Friday night service.

I'm about two-thirds of the way down my glass when Lee appears and settles himself on the bar stool next to mine.

'All OK?' I ask him.

'Yes, sorry about that. I've just found out I've got to go away next week and my laptop's playing up, so I needed to sort that out.' He sounds a little distracted, but that's nothing new.

'Where are you off to?'

'Potential new client. I'll be there for the whole week. Listen, would you mind very much dropping my laptop off with the IT guy on Monday?'

'How are you going to manage without a laptop for the week?'

'They're going to courier another one over, don't worry. Hey, Nathan,' he raises his voice. 'What does a guy have to do to get a drink around here?'

'Ha ha,' Nathan replies, placing a pint of Lee's favourite bitter in front of him. 'Tell me, do you have a book of bar-related clichés that you're working through? When are we going to get to "a pint of your finest ale, Landlord, and be damned quick about it"?'

'I don't know. When you're the landlord, I guess,' Lee quips. Lee and Nathan get on fine on the surface, but there's always a subtle undercurrent of competition between them, and it seems this weekend will be no different.

'Do you want more time to look at the menu, or do you know what you want?' Rosie, one of the servers, has appeared by Lee's side. In typical gastropub style, the menu is chalked up on various blackboards around the place. I decided what I wanted while I was waiting for Lee, but I'm fairly certain he hasn't even glanced at the options yet.

'Oh, I don't know. What would you recommend, Rosie?' he asks, flashing her a megawatt smile. Rosie blushes scarlet and mumbles that the crab and avocado starter is proving popular, as is the chicken and ham pie.

'Then that's what I'll have. What about you, Els?'

I give Rosie my order for calamari and grilled seabass, and she scuttles off towards the kitchen.

'You're very bad,' I say to Lee. 'You know she's got a massive crush on you, and it only makes it worse when you flirt with her like that.'

'Nonsense, I've just made her day. Her week, probably. Not feeling insecure, are you?'

'Behave, or I'll set your mother on you.'

He feigns horror before laughing and taking a big mouthful of his beer.

It's not something I would ever want to do full-time, but I do enjoy my visits here. Not only do Lee's parents seem to like me, but the pub is like a whole little world in itself. Lee's dad is in charge in the kitchen and, although his is the name above the door, he's almost never seen front of house. Lee's mum runs the restaurant like a well-oiled machine and Nathan looks after everything to do with the bar and drink side of things. I didn't know anything about pubs when I first started going out with Lee, but I've learned that the Farmer's Arms is what is known as a 'free house', meaning that they aren't tied to any particular brewery and can therefore have a constantly changing rota of beers. Some are permanent fixtures, like the bitter that Lee loves, but most of them come in for a few weeks before being replaced with something else. I've tried a few, but I really can't get into beer in the way that Lee and Nathan do, so I generally tune them out when they're having what I refer to as one of their 'beardy' discussions about real ales and stuff like that. I sometimes wonder why Lee didn't go into the family business. I get the impression that his parents try to be supportive of his decision to make his own way, but there is definitely a bit of disappointment there. I raised it with him once and he told me he'd rather cut his own throat than go into the pub trade, so it looks like Nathan has nothing to worry about, inheritance wise.

After our 'freebie' dinner on Friday night, Lee's mum is true to her word and gets us both working on the Saturday and Sunday lunchtime services. We do get downtime to catch up, but I always get the impression that they're not fully engaged because they're already thinking about the next round of service. Much as I love his family, we're both a little relieved when we climb into the car to start our journey home on Sunday afternoon.

'Duty done for another month,' Lee says to me as we pull out of the car park.

'They do love seeing you, though,' I counter.

'Do you think? I sometimes wonder whether they'd notice if we didn't turn up one month. I love them, but their world is very small and insular, isn't it?'

'Thinking of the world,' I venture, 'if we close the trust, how do you fancy a trip to the Caribbean? White, sandy beaches, warm sea to swim in, rum on tap. What's not to love?'

'Yeah, maybe,' he says, suddenly distant. 'Let's see, shall we?'

His sudden change of tone rattles me, and I glance across in concern. His face is a mask, though and, for the first time, I wonder if there's something he's not telling me.

4

One of the downsides to spending the weekend with Lee's family is that it's hardly restful, so it's a bit more of a struggle than normal to drag myself out of bed on Monday morning. Lee is long gone; I vaguely remember him getting up at around four-thirty to head off to see his new client. It's only when I've had a shower and a cup of coffee to wake me up properly that I realise he hasn't told me anything about them; I don't even know where they are. I pull out my phone and type out a WhatsApp message to him.

Good luck with the new client. Are you somewhere exotic and sunny? xx

I watch the screen for a few minutes but his phone must be off, as there's only one grey tick. That probably means he's on a plane, but that's about as much sleuthing as I can fit in for now as I need to get ready for work.

I like to get in early on a Monday morning if I can. It gives me the opportunity to catch up on any emails from the weekend and start to think about the week ahead while the office is relatively quiet. I've got a couple of weekly update meetings today on projects that I'm managing, and I ought to check in with the consultants first to make sure that there haven't been any problems that might put us behind. I always think it's better to be upfront with a client if there's an issue, but also to have the plan to fix it already agreed so there's no uncertainty for them to worry about. One of the few good things about my double life is that it forces me to compartmentalise. The only person at work who knows anything about the fun side of me is Ruth; I suspect the others would all describe me as quiet, efficient and ambitious but also a little bit dull. They'd be horrified to see the Ella that emerges when I'm away from work and can let my hair down.

There are just a couple of people in the office before me: a woman called Linda who is part of the accounts team, and a consultant I've only seen a couple of times before. I think he's called Tim, but I can't be completely sure. I tend only to get to know consultants when I'm working on a project with them, and we haven't done that yet. Linda looks up and nods a greeting as I unpack my bag and set up my laptop on the desk opposite hers. Tim, if that's his name, appears to be completely absorbed in what he's doing and doesn't even look up. My morning ritual is pretty much the same every day. After plugging in and turning on my laptop, I head to the loos for a quick wee, picking up a coffee on the way back before settling down to work through my emails. I launch the email program and take a sip of coffee while I wait for it to connect to the network and start downloading my messages. It seems to be taking longer than usual today, so I also take the opportunity to check my phone. Still only one grey tick on my message to Lee.

After a few minutes, the email program still hasn't connected to the network, so I launch the browser and try a few websites, just to check that it's not the internet connection. Nothing connects.

'Linda?' I ask, and her head pops up over the desk partition.

'What's up?'

'Is the network playing up, do you know? I can't seem to connect to anything this morning.'

'It's working fine for me. Tom, are you on the network OK?' she calls to the consultant.

'Yeah, all fine, why?' Tim, who I've now learned is called Tom, replies.

'Ella's having trouble.'

'Try turning it off and on again,' he offers, before lowering his head to his screen.

By the time I've finished my coffee, I've rebooted the laptop twice but it's still firmly refusing to connect to anything. There's no sign of the IT guy; he's a strict nine-to-fiver and it's still only half past eight, but thankfully I do have offline copies of my current project plans, so I open them up and start to update them. As soon as the IT guy gets in, I'll take Lee's laptop over and ask him to have a look at mine too; the plans should sync up automatically once I'm connected again. I've got an online meeting with the project team at nine-thirty, so I hope it's something simple, otherwise I'll have to call them individually to postpone.

The office is filling up now, and I spot Jonathan arrive out of the corner of my eye. As soon as he's set up his computer, he rushes off to one of the meeting rooms, where he's joined by the woman from HR who did my onboarding when I started; I think she's called Sharon. I'm trying to concentrate on my project plan, but I am a little distracted, as it's clear that tensions are running high. Jonathan keeps jumping out of his seat and pacing around the room, running his hands through his hair. A knot of worry forms in the pit of my stomach. If Jonathan's not happy, and he certainly doesn't look it, does that mean that we didn't get the contract? Why would HR care about that, though?

My thoughts don't get an opportunity to progress much further, as the meeting room door flies open after a few minutes and Jonathan emerges with a face like thunder. He stops for a moment, gazing around the office, and then his eyes land on me and he starts to make his way over. It's obvious that something bad has happened, and my heart starts thudding uncomfortably in my chest.

'Ella, can we borrow you please?' His voice is strained.

'Sure.' I try to keep my voice light, but the thudding in my chest has intensified. I lock my laptop screen and follow him over to the meeting room, where he closes the door behind me.

'Please take a seat, Ella,' the HR woman instructs frostily.

'What's up?' I ask. My hands have started to sweat, so I place them in my lap and try to wipe them as surreptitiously as I can on my skirt.

'You live at the same address as Lee Johnson, do you not?' she asks.

'That's right.' Whatever I was expecting, it wasn't this, but I have no choice but to follow along and hope the reason for my summons becomes clear soon.

'Describe your relationship with him.'

'I'm not sure I know what you mean?'

'You are in a romantic relationship with him, aren't you.' It's a statement rather than a question.

I have no idea how to reply to this. It's never occurred to me that the company would find out, and I'm desperately trying to think what gave us away. The HR woman obviously takes my silence as defiance, as she brings something up on her screen and turns it so I can see.

'These are your holiday bookings for the last three years,' she tells me. 'As you can see, they match up nearly perfectly. Suspicious, don't you think? Flatmates who always go on holiday at the same time?'

Something about her triumphant tone, as if she's Hercule Poirot solving a particularly tricky murder, gets under my skin, and I raise my eyes and stare at her defiantly.

'He's my boyfriend, yes. So what?' I snap.

'Apart from the fact that I made it clear to you that the company actively discourages workplace romances, it means that you're implicated in a serious breach of conduct.' She smiles thinly, as if she's been waiting for me to wander into her trap and I've just obliged.

'I'm sorry, what?'

'Don't try to pretend you don't know what I'm talking about.'

'I honestly have no idea. Why should I?'

She sighs theatrically. It's obvious she doesn't believe a word I'm saying.

'Fine,' she breathes. 'I'd hoped you would be more forthcoming, but I can see we're going to have to do this the hard way. As well as embarking on a clandestine relationship, you and Lee worked together on the NHS trust proposal, didn't you?'

'I drew up the project plan, but I do that for a lot of projects. Lee was the Customer Relationship Manager.'

'Don't be pedantic. You and Lee both worked on the proposal.'

'Yes.'

'And where is Lee now?'

'He's away for the week, seeing a new client.'

'Is that what he told you?' Jonathan laughs bitterly. 'Unbelievable.'

'Just tell me what's going on,' I plead. 'What am I supposed to have done?'

'We got the email from the NHS trust at seven o'clock on Friday evening,' Jonathan tells me. 'We didn't get the contract. They've awarded it to Harmony.'

I'm not sure what to say. Just that news on its own would normally be enough to ruin my day, but it's obvious that this is just part of something much worse.

'By eight o'clock on Friday, I'd received Lee's resignation, with immediate effect,' the HR woman continues.

'What?'

'You're either a very good actress, or your boyfriend has pulled the wool over your eyes extremely well,' she observes. 'As far as we know, Lee is starting his new job as we speak.'

'At Harmony,' Jonathan slots in the final missing piece of the jigsaw.

'No. I don't believe you. He said he was visiting a new client. He'd have told me if he knew we hadn't got the contract.'

'Did he ask you to bring his laptop in today?'

'Yes, he said it was playing up and the IT guy was going to look at it.'

'Interesting. In the email to me, he said he would give it to you to hand in on his behalf.'

A lot of memories are clashing together in my mind and a horrible picture is emerging. Lee spending so long in the car before coming into the pub on Friday night. Was he sending his resignation while I was sitting at the bar chatting to Nathan? Why the hell didn't he tell me? I just believed him when he said his laptop was playing up, but then why wouldn't I? It never would have occurred to me that he would do something like this. One thing is for sure: we are going to have a very uncomfortable conversation as soon as I can get hold of him. As I'm putting

together the sequence of events, I realise that there is still a part
of the story they haven't told me.

'You mentioned a breach of conduct?' I ask.

'Look at the facts, Ella,' Jonathan says, wearily. 'You and Lee
are a couple. You and Lee worked together on the proposal.
We're up against Harmony and, within an hour of Harmony
securing the contract, your boyfriend announces that he's
leaving us to work for them. It stinks to high heaven, wouldn't
you agree?'

'Lee wouldn't...'

'You can't say that. The evidence to the contrary is over-
whelming. He must have been talking to Harmony during the
sales process, lining up the job, attending interviews and so on.
His motivation for us to win the contract would be very low, don't
you think? Maybe he inflated a few figures here and there to
make our proposal seem less attractive, who knows. I admit that
it's possible he could have played it straight, but the way he's
behaved makes it seem vanishingly unlikely, doesn't it?'

'What are you going to do?' I ask.

'We will go through his laptop with a fine-tooth comb, obviously,' the HR woman says. 'We will look at every email, every
presentation, every file, and every instant message. I had to
disturb Ian's weekend, but he assures me he will be able to
recover most of the deleted files, so we will go through those as
well. If we find even the merest shred of evidence that he skewed
our bid to make Harmony successful, we will consult with the
legal team about launching proceedings against both him and
Harmony. He may not work here any more, but he is in a lot of
trouble, trust me.'

'And what about me? You said I was implicated?'

'Of course you are. You're his lover!' She practically spits the
last word. 'You are associated with him personally, professionally,

and you worked with him on this bid. There's every probability you were in on it.'

'You must realise by now that I had no idea!' I exclaim.

'I'm sorry, but that's not enough,' she replies, and I realise the door of the trap is about to be slammed shut. 'We've revoked your access and asked Ian to go through your laptop with the same intensity. Jonathan will accompany you back to your desk and supervise you handing in both machines. Obviously, we don't want you to touch the keyboard or anything, please.'

'But how am I going to work without my laptop?'

'You aren't. You're going to hand over to Jonathan, and then we're suspending you on full pay until the results of our inquiry are available. Needless to say, if we find any evidence of misconduct on your part, summary dismissal will be the least of your problems.'

5

I'm numb with shock as Jonathan asks me to talk him through the status of my current projects and then accompanies me back to my desk, relieving me of both my laptop and Lee's. I can feel the eyes of everyone in the office on me; they're obviously desperate to know what's going on, but I can't look at any of them. I keep my eyes firmly on the floor. At least I'm not crying, although I'm sure the tears will come once the shock wears off. The final indignity is being escorted to the lobby, where Jonathan takes my pass off me, checks to make sure they have my mobile phone number and personal email address recorded correctly, and promises to be in touch as soon as the investigation is complete.

Suddenly, without quite knowing how I got here, I'm back out on the street. I glance at my watch; it's not even ten o'clock. I have no idea what I'm supposed to do, so I make my way to the bus stop pretty much on autopilot and catch the bus home. During my normal commute, it's always busy and I usually have to stand, but now it's eerily quiet. There's just me and a few older people who look like they're probably of pension age, clutching bags with the logos of some of the discount stores in the city centre. My mind is stuck on a single loop – what the bloody hell just happened?

A noise from my bag distracts me. It's my phone, pinging with a message. Wondering if Lee has decided to explain what he's done, I fish it out and unlock it. It's not Lee, it's Ruth.

Saw you leave the office. RU OK?

I have no idea how to respond to that, so I shove the phone back in my bag and resume staring out of the window. I can't get my head around it at all. Lee never breathed a word of what he was planning to do. Why would he keep secret something this important which, let's face it, affects both of us?

As the bus nears my stop, I can feel the initial shock starting to fade and something else taking its place. It's amazing how much energy being truly furious gives you. Once I've let myself into the building, I hurry over to the lift and stab the call button several times. The lift is near the top of the building, and seems to be taking an age to come down, stopping at every floor. With a growl of frustration, I make for the stairs, taking them two at a time. I'm sweaty and out of breath by the time I reach the top floor, but I don't care. My hands are shaking with anger as I push the key into the lock and, once I'm inside, I lean against the door for a moment, aware that my whole body is now trembling.

I'm not sure what I'm looking for as I march into the second bedroom, but I feel like there should be some evidence of his duplicity somewhere. I rifle through all the pieces of paper on the desk, looking for anything with a Harmony logo on it, but it's all just bills neatly annotated with the date they were paid, as well as other meaningless documents. Like a woman possessed, I yank the drawers right out of their sockets so that I can check there isn't anything incriminating sellotaped to the bottom or the back of them. By the time I've finished, there are pieces of paper everywhere, but I haven't found anything at all.

I reach for my phone and check the message I sent Lee this morning; there are now two blue ticks, so he's read it, but there's no reply. Of course there isn't. He must know that I'll have found out by now what he's done. Even if HR hadn't worked out that we were seeing each other, the office is incredibly leaky and everyone would be talking about his sudden resignation. He'll also know that I'm going to be mad as hell at him, so I imagine he's trying to buy time by ignoring me until I've calmed down a bit. I don't think so. I start typing another message, only to delete it after a few words. This is too big for WhatsApp.

I dial his number, but it goes straight to voicemail, so I hang up. What to do? He'll have no excuse not to call me this evening, but I can't wait until then. I stab the redial button and wait for the tone to tell me to start leaving my message.

'Hi, darling,' I begin, my voice almost saccharine in its sweetness. 'I know it must be very exciting and everything on the first day of your secret new job, but I wonder if you could give me a call when you're free. You see, Orchestra unsurprisingly have a bit of a problem about you jumping ship the way that you did, and they've worked out that we're not just flatmates, so I'm very slightly in the shit.' I'm aware that my voice is hardening, but I press on. 'In fact, they've suspended me because they think I'm probably in cahoots with whatever stunt you've pulled here, and I'm frankly a little surprised and pissed off that you didn't think to talk to me about any of this before you did it.' There is no sweetness any more, my voice is coldly furious. 'So give me a call and talk me through it, would you, you *fucking bastard*!'

OK, so I'm shouting now, but I'm so angry, it's not surprising. Every part of my body is humming with fury; I don't think I've ever been this mad with Lee before. For a moment, I wonder if I've missed something, a clue or a conversation, but the more I think about it, the more typical of Lee this is. He wanted something, so he went and got it and sod the consequences for anyone else.

I throw the phone down on the sofa as the tears finally come. I'm so full of emotions, I'm amazed it's taken them this long. I'm terrified that I'll somehow lose the job that I love even though I know I've done nothing wrong, I'm furious with Lee for putting me in this position, and I'm overwhelmed by the shame of being escorted out of the office in front of everyone, like a criminal. I can just imagine the rumour mill going into overdrive; perhaps there's been a meeting where the HR woman has tried to gloss over what's happened. That will really fan the gossip flames. As if on cue, my phone pings from the sofa. My eyes are blurry from crying, but I can still read the message clearly enough. It's Ruth again.

You and Lee are an item???? IT guy says you're both working for Harmony now. WTAF Ella????

I stare at the message in disbelief. I know she's going to be hurt and feel betrayed because I never confided in her about Lee and me, but how do I convince her that the rest of it is wildly off the mark, given my current circumstances? It's certainly too complex to solve by text, but I'm not ready to talk to her. She'll want to know everything, and I don't feel like I know anything at the moment. I force myself to try to think rationally. A glance at my watch shows it's just after eleven. There's the faintest chance that Lee might call at lunchtime, but my guess is still that he'll save it for the evening, especially after the tirade I've just left on his voicemail. My phone pings again. Another message from Ruth.

I thought you were my friend, but right now I feel like I don't know you at all. :'-(

'Oh, *fuck off*, Ruth, for God's sake!' I snap at the phone. 'Can't you see I've got bigger things to deal with than your bloody feelings right now? I'm in the middle of a shit storm, honey, so you'll just have to wait your turn.' A wave of guilt washes over me. Ruth has always been an open book about her life, and she is right that I haven't been a very good friend by hiding something this big from her. It was also Ruth who filled me in on the juicy details behind the 'incident' that led to Orchestra putting the ban on office relationships in place. I can still see her eyes glittering over the rim of her glass when I asked about it at one of our first after-work drinks.

'It was a huge scandal,' she'd stage-whispered. 'One of the directors was having an affair with the receptionist. It was an open secret in as much as everyone in the office knew what was going on but nobody said anything.'

'What happened?' I'd asked.

'The receptionist wanted him to leave his wife. He said no, so she tipped off the wife anonymously to up the ante. All hell broke loose. They both ended up having to resign, which was particularly tricky with him being a director. After that, it was made clear that we were expected to keep our private and professional lives strictly separate.'

'I'll bear that in mind,' I'd told her and, at the time, I'd meant it. She has every right to be royally pissed off with me, but I can't deal with her right now.

The strangest thought comes to me. While it's true that I am in the middle of a shit storm, possibly the biggest one of my life to date, I'm completely powerless to do anything about it. My boyfriend has gone rogue, my job is hanging by a thread, but there is no action I can take, no email I can write; I am literally in the eye of the storm and all I can do is wait. That thought terrifies me most of all. What on earth am I going to do while I'm suspended?

One thing is for certain: I'm not going to sit around here in my work clothes all day waiting for the phone to ring. I need to do something, otherwise I'm going to go mad worrying about whether there's anything on my laptop that they might think is suspicious. I know there isn't, but it's like when you go out somewhere and start to worry that maybe you didn't lock the door properly or you left a ring on the hob on. Even if you're sure you locked the door and everything was off, you worry about it until you get back. Was I rigorous enough about checking how many hours the consultants were booking? Did I build too much contingency into a plan, or maybe not enough? Did I say something in an email that could be misconstrued?

'Enough, Ella,' I tell myself out loud. 'Do what you're good at. Make a plan.'

After getting changed into a pair of jeans and a comfortable hoodie, I make myself a cup of coffee and carry it through into the bomb site that is now the study. I tidy up the mess and, in the absence of a laptop with project-planning software, settle myself at the desk with a blank piece of paper. I write the days of the week across the top and draw column lines between them. Then I write 'AM' and 'PM' on the left-hand side and draw a line across. I have no idea how long my suspension will last, but I reckon it's got to be at least a week.

Half an hour later, I'm still sitting there with a mug of cold coffee and I haven't managed to fill in a single box on the grid. It's not as if there are even any menial tasks that need doing. The laundry is up to date, we have a cleaner who comes every Thursday so the flat is spotless, and we do the shopping at the weekend because it's easier to bring it home in Lee's car than on the bus.

In the end, I decide to go for a walk. That's what people do when they have stuff they need to work through, isn't it? You always see people in films saying, 'I'm going for a walk to clear my head.' I dig out the walking boots that I bought to take on holiday to the Lake District last year, slip my feet into them and lace them up securely. There's a little bit of dried mud caked on the soles, which immediately flakes off onto the floor, and I stand there for a minute, staring at the flakes stupidly, as if unsure what I'm supposed to do about them. In the end, I leave them where they are and let myself out of the flat; I'll deal with them when I've 'cleared my head'.

I walk for around an hour, pounding the streets around our flat. I know them well from seeing them out of the bus window, but I've rarely walked them. I feel a bit like a tourist; everyday life is going on all around me, but I feel completely disconnected from it. I discover a library that I never even knew was there, as well as a couple of playgrounds with small groups of haggard-looking mothers desultorily pushing their preschool children on the swings.

By the time I get back to the flat, I am feeling a little calmer and, once I've swept up the mud flakes with a dustpan and brush, I sit at the breakfast bar and ponder my situation while I eat my packed lunch. There's nothing from Lee, but I decide to try to appease Ruth a little by replying to her. I type:

I'm really sorry about Lee. I really wanted to tell you, but you know the company rules. I'll tell you everything when I see you next, promise.

And no, I haven't left to work for Harmony – IT guy is making stuff up. xx

The ticks go blue straight away, and I can see she's typing a reply.

It's a pretty massive secret to keep from someone you call a friend, no? It hurts that you didn't trust me TBH.

OK, so she's still pissed off. I'm not sure what else I can say, so I just send:

All I can say is how sorry I am, and how I wish I'd been able to tell you myself.

The ticks go blue, but she doesn't reply. Great. My best friend at work hates me now, even though I haven't actually done anything wrong. I get that she's upset, I do, and I would have told her about Lee and me in a heartbeat if I could have been completely sure that she'd keep it a secret, but she knows herself that she's prone to the occasional indiscretion. There was one particularly awkward time, when she was first going out with Wade, and she completely forgot he was sitting next to her and started demonstrating his orgasm face to me. It took him a long time to get over that, from what I remember. I think about sending her a message to make this point, but I realise that it will probably do more harm than good at this stage. What a mess.

Lee's mum's regular joke may yet prove to be prophetic. The idea of murdering Lee has never felt more appealing.

6

Lee finally calls just after eight. I've spent most of the afternoon slumped in front of the TV. I can't tell you any of the programmes, but it's been strangely comforting to have a background noise to my maelstrom of thoughts. I've pretty much convinced myself that there's an email somewhere they'll have found that somehow points the finger at me, even though I know I'm completely innocent. At one point, I was sitting in front of some drama set in a doctors' surgery and I actually tried to understand the story, in case I lost my job and this was going to be my life now. I carefully waited until half past seven before pouring myself a glass of wine; whatever happens with work, daytime drinking is not a path I want to start down. I've actually been feeling fairly calm since taking the first soothing mouthful, but the jangle of the ringtone sets all my nerves instantly on edge. I can see that it's Lee, but I can't think what to say to him. 'Hello' doesn't seem appropriate, and there's no way I can go for my usual 'Hi, love', so in the end I swipe to answer and say nothing.

'Ella? Are you there? It's me, Lee.'

'I know who it is,' I reply, flatly.

'I guess you've heard I'm working at Harmony now?' If I was expecting remorse for my situation, it seems I am to be disappointed. He actually sounds excited. 'I'd have called earlier and told you myself, only I've been in back-to-back meetings and then the guys wanted to take me out to dinner to welcome me on board. It's an amazing company, Els. Totally different to Orchestra. There's a real energy about them, like they're going places, you know? Anyway, you sounded a bit upset earlier. Is everything OK?'

A bit upset? I'll give him 'a bit upset'.

'Oh, everything's peachy here, sweetheart,' I tell him, sarcastically. 'I mean, it was a bit of a surprise finding out from the HR department that my boyfriend, you know, the one I share a flat with and everything, had changed jobs without saying a damned word to me about it but yeah, I'm cool.'

'I'm so relieved,' he replies, completely misreading me. 'I was a bit worried about how you'd react, but I couldn't say anything because it all had to be completely secret, and I didn't want to put you in a difficult situation. I knew you'd be OK, though, once you understood, and I think this could actually be really good for us. I was getting disillusioned with Orchestra, you know? The software is seriously out of date, and it was getting harder and harder to believe in it. The Harmony stuff is all web browser-based, it sits on top of a Snowflake database and you just subscribe to the modules you want when you need them. It's the future, Els. I'm so excited, and I feel like this has given me a whole new lease of life. They're even talking about a "welcome on board" bonus, so we might be able to look at that holiday in the Caribbean once I've completed my probation.'

He's unbelievable. 'Do you have any idea what you've done?' I ask.

'What?'

'You heard me. You see, while you've been skipping about with your web-enabled this and your Snowflake that, a truckload of shit has been dumped on me.'

He does at least have the decency to turn off the excited puppy voice. 'Oh, no. Why?'

'Didn't you listen to my voicemail?'

'Of course I did. Well, I sort of did. I was in a short break between meetings so I kind of speed-listened to it. I got that you were upset about something, but you just said it was OK now.'

I'm on the verge of losing my temper again, so I take a swig of wine to try to calm myself.

'What is it, Ella? Tell me what happened.' He's trying to sound concerned, but something's distracting him, I can tell. I can hear faint voices in the background.

'Who else is there?' I ask, sharply.

'Just a couple of guys from work; we're about to head to the bar.'

'OK, well, don't let me keep you,' I reply, so sarcastically now that even he surely can't miss it. 'I mean, I'm glad you're having a good time with your new colleagues. I may be about to lose my job because of you but don't let that spoil your evening, will you?'

'Wait, what?' I've finally got his full attention and I hear him telling the other people to go on ahead. 'What do you mean? Why?'

'It's the silliest thing,' I begin, the ice in my voice impossible for even Lee to ignore, 'but you resigning with immediate effect to join our main competitor an hour after they beat us to a contract you were negotiating has left a nasty taste in the mouths of a few people at Orchestra.'

'I did nothing wrong.' He's on the defensive, I can tell. 'People change jobs all the time and it's normal to leave immediately if you're joining a competitor.'

'They're saying you deliberately did something to ensure the contract went to Harmony. Did you?'

'Of course I didn't!'

'Here's the thing, though. They don't believe that. They're going through your laptop with a fine-tooth comb to see if they can find any evidence you weren't putting 100 per cent into the Orchestra bid.'

'They can't touch me.' Is it me, or does his defiant tone have a hint of uncertainty in it? A niggle of doubt is forming in my mind. He was surprisingly relaxed the night before the bid. Was it because he knew Orchestra wasn't going to win?

'I don't really care whether they can or they can't,' I say. 'What I care about is them coming after me.'

'I don't get it. What's it got to do with you?'

'Let's see. I worked with you on the bid, I'm your girlfriend and we live together. Somehow, from all of that, they assumed I might know something about it and they've taken away my laptop and suspended me while they investigate whether I'm up to my neck in this with you.'

'Did you tell them we were together?'

'Of course not!' I snarl at him. 'They figured it out from our holiday patterns. They've probably known for ages. Anyway, because of that and the little midnight flit that you never bothered to tell me about – thanks for that, it really helps me to love and trust you – I'm in a lot of trouble. So yeah, I'm a little bit upset.'

'Shit, sorry. It never occurred to me that they'd think you had anything to do with it. How long have they suspended you for?'

'Until further notice.'

'But you haven't done anything wrong!'

'I know that, fuckwit, but they don't, do they? Can you blame them for being suspicious?'

'It'll be fine,' he blusters. 'They'll go through your computer, find nothing, and that will be that. In the meantime, you've got some extra holiday time, think of it like that. They haven't stopped your pay, have they?'

'No.'

'Phew. The rent on the flat is due in a few days, so that could have been awkward. So, you've got some time off at their expense. I'd call that a bit of a win, myself.'

'Are you for real? You think I'm just going to be able to swan about as if I'm on holiday without a care in the world, while they go through my laptop in forensic detail, looking for the faintest whiff of malpractice so they can sack me? Why the fuck didn't you tell me what you were doing?'

There's a pause before he answers, and his voice is distant when he finally replies.

'What difference would it have made?' he asks.

'I'm sorry?'

'Think about it. What difference would it have made if I'd told you at the beginning? I'm sorry they've suspended you, I really am, but you knowing earlier wouldn't have changed anything.'

'You should have told me because I'm your bloody girlfriend, and that's the kind of things couples tell each other!'

'But it's nothing to do with you. I know you're my girlfriend and everything, but the way I see it is that I have my work life and my personal life. You're part of my personal life but, as long as I pay my share of the bills and stuff, I don't think my work is any of your business, do you? Listen, I've got to go. Think about what I've said, yeah? You haven't done anything wrong and they'll find that out soon enough. In the meantime, make the most of your time off. Why don't you go and visit your sister for a few days? I'll be back on Friday and we can have a proper catch-up then. I'll book that Italian place you like, OK? Love you.'

And, with that, he's gone. I don't know how long I sit there, staring at my phone in disbelief, but I feel like I've just been talking to a complete stranger. I unlock the phone a couple of times and my finger hovers over his number, but I'm so shocked by his attitude that I don't have any rational words to say to him. In the end, I plug the phone into its charger and top my wine glass right up to the rim.

* * *

The alarm goes off at six the next morning, and I reach across automatically to shove Lee awake so he can go into the shower before me in the first part of our carefully choreographed morning routine. His absence brings the events of the previous day crashing in, and it dawns on me that I have no reason to get up, so I turn onto my back in the semi-darkness and stare at the ceiling. The good news is that I don't have a hangover, despite nearly finishing the bottle of wine last night. I played out all sorts of scenarios in my head as I stared blankly at the TV. There were some where I lost my job and some where I was welcomed back with open arms, but what surprised me were the number that involved me telling Lee we were finished. The dismissive way he said, 'It's nothing to do with you,' as if I were nothing more than a cameo in the great story of his life, was like a slap in the face and I'm still smarting this morning. What he's shown me is that, when he wants something, he'll think nothing of riding roughshod over everyone, including me, to get it. That's a really ugly trait in a person, and I'm not sure I want to be with someone like that. I knew he had a ruthless streak – he's never hidden it – but this is the first time it's been turned on me, and I don't like it. I don't like it at all.

My body is too conditioned to my normal routine to make

going back to sleep a possibility so, after contemplating how I feel about Lee for a while, and coming to broadly negative conclusions, I get up and wander out to the kitchen to make a cup of coffee. It's like I'm seeing the flat with new eyes this morning, and I realise for the first time how little of me there is in it. The colour scheme is all muted creams and greys, with none of the bright colours that I would naturally choose. The big, squashy, leather sofas in front of the widescreen TV are pure bachelor pad. The collection of mismatched mugs and crockery that I grew up with and loved as a child would look horrendously out of place among the sleek and sterile designer crockery that Lee insisted on.

You don't belong here, the flat appears to be whispering to me, and I shake my head to shut out the new doubts that are trying to force their way in. I decide to take advantage of my (hopefully) temporary status as a woman of leisure by running a long, hot bath and revelling in a good soak. I'll shave my legs and generally give myself a good pampering. That should use up a chunk of the morning, and maybe I'll have a flash of inspiration on how to fill the rest of the day.

By half past seven, I'm as fluffed and primped as I can be. I've exfoliated, depilated, moisturised and conditioned, and I've run out of ideas to pass the time. Something Lee said last night comes back to me, and I reach for the phone to call Ava, my sister.

It's just after lunchtime when I arrive at the station in Harrogate and I'm relieved to find Ava waiting for me outside, her battered Mini looking even sorrier for itself than when I saw it last.

'If this were a horse, someone would have shot it by now,' I laugh, after we've hugged tightly and she's thrown my overnight bag into the boot.

'Behave. It got me here to pick you up, didn't it?' she retorts, as the engine bursts into life with a deafening clatter. 'Plus, it's a lot more car than you seem to own.'

'I've told you before, I don't need a car. We have public transport in Leeds.'

'Very fancy, I'm sure,' she replies, arching her eyebrow. This is almost like a dance we go through every time I see her. Ava is what you'd call 'down to earth'. She works as a nurse at Harrogate district hospital and, like most nurses I've met, doesn't generally believe in sugar-coating things.

'So, explain to me again this fraud you're caught up in?' she asks, as we leave the town behind us, heading for the village where we grew up, and she still lives with her husband, Ben.

'It's not fraud!' I complain. 'Basically, we lost a contract to a rival and, an hour after he found out, Lee handed in his notice to go and join said rival. Orchestra think he's pulled a fast one and, because I'm his girlfriend, I'm implicated.'

'Mm. Too slippery by half, that Lee. I've always thought so.'

I sigh. This is another well-worn conversation. 'I know. You've never trusted him.'

'With good reason!' she retorts. 'He's dumped you right in the shit, hasn't he?'

I haven't shared my new misgivings about Lee with Ava; I just told her the bare bones of what had happened and asked if I could come and stay for a few days. She's never made any attempt to conceal how she feels about him, and I really don't want to stoke that fire now. If she spots any chinks in the armour of my relationship with Lee, she'll be straight in there with a poison arrow to try to finish him off. The feeling is mutual, to a large extent, which is probably why he suggested I visit while he's away.

'So, how long do we have the pleasure of your company for?' Ava asks.

'I don't know yet. It depends when I hear from Orchestra. Friday at the latest, I'd have thought. Is that OK?'

'Of course it is, you daft bugger! Stay as long as you like. Mum and Dad will be pleased to see you, and I'm sure Ben will be too.'

'Haven't you told him I was coming?'

'No time. He won't mind, though, you know what he's like. It's good to see you, Ella. It's been far too long.'

With a stab of guilt, I realise she's right. Although we visit Lee's family religiously every month, it must be nearly three months since I was last here, and I was alone that time as well. Thinking about it, Lee has managed to have a diary clash every time I've suggested visiting my family this year, apart from last

Christmas, when he knew he wouldn't get away with it. I didn't
notice at the time but, looking back on it, it's too regular to be a
coincidence. I'm generally fairly easy-going about social stuff, but
I'm starting to suspect that Lee has taken advantage of my flexi-
bility to ensure we only ever do what he wants to do. I file that
thought away for future consideration and return to my current
predicament.

'I'm not going to say anything to Mum and Dad about being
suspended,' I tell Ava. 'I don't want them to worry.'

'Are you sure? You'll need to tell them something, and you can
quickly get in a mess with a lie. Remember when you didn't want
to tell them that horrible girl in your class at school was bullying
you, so you said she was really nice in private, and then they
invited her to your birthday party and actually thanked her for
being there for you? What was her name?'

'Rebecca Studland.' I shudder as the memory comes back. I
can still feel the burning humiliation as she ridiculed my house,
my parents and everything about her experience to a rapt audience in school the next day. I never did have the guts to tell Mum
the truth about her, but I made sure I 'lost' any future invitations
and made up excuses as to why she couldn't come round again.
Ava is right, it did get exhausting after a while, and it was a relief
when we went to different secondary schools and I lost touch
with her.

'Maybe you're right,' I agree. 'I'll think about it. I wonder
where Rebecca is now.'

'In prison, with any luck!' Ava laughs.

A little while later, the familiar sign welcoming us to Wistleth-
waite and asking us to drive carefully through the village indicates that we've arrived.

'I'm on shift at three, so I'm going to drop you and run, I'm
afraid,' Ava tells me as we pull up outside her house and she

shuts off the engine. The sudden silence is a welcome relief, and I sigh with pleasure as I unfold myself from the passenger seat. 'Ben's working locally at the moment, so I imagine he'll be back at around half past four. Teddy will keep you company in the meantime, and you're to help yourself to anything you want, OK?'

Teddy, Ava's Labradoodle, appears as soon as she opens the door. He can't seem to decide whether he's delighted to see me or I'm a threat, because he's wagging his tail and barking furiously at the same time. He rushes back indoors, only to reappear a few moments later with one of his toys, but he's still growling, even though his tail is thrashing with delight.

'Shut up, Teddy. It's Auntie Ella, you idiot,' she rebukes him. 'Just push him out of the way,' she tells me as he completely blocks the doorway and insists on sniffing every inch of my overnight bag. Once I'm actually inside the house, he suddenly decides I'm no longer of any interest and lies down on his bed with a sigh. I reach down to scratch his ears, and he presses his head into my hand, loving the attention.

'He'll be your friend for life if you keep doing that,' Ava smiles. 'The lead and poo bags are in the utility room if you fancy taking him out. Right, I'm going to love you and leave you. I'm only covering for a few hours today, so I'll be home later for a proper catch-up. I assume you can remember where the spare room is?'

'Ha ha. Go and save some lives, or whatever it is you do.'

As the Mini disappears from sight, leaving an unhealthy black cloud behind it, I begin to question the wisdom of coming here. Ava and her husband Ben, a builder, will be at work most of the time, so I'm going to be nearly as alone as if I'd stayed at home. At least Mum and Dad will be around, as they're both retired, but I've got to work out what to say before I see them. I glance down at Teddy, who is watching me carefully from his bed.

'I tell you what,' I say to him. 'Give me a few minutes to unpack and freshen up, and then maybe we can go for a walk, what do you think? You can help me work out what to tell Nanny.'

The sound of his favourite activity and his third favourite human being galvanises him; he leaps to his feet and follows me up the stairs, watching impatiently while I unpack. I manage to stop him following me into the bathroom, but he positively dances around me while I carry my walking boots down to the utility room and put them on. When I reach for the lead and clip it onto his collar, he can't contain his joy any more and starts barking to hurry me up. I grab the back door key off the peg, and I'm only just able to lock the door behind me as Teddy is pulling so hard. Thankfully, once we've gone a little way down the street, he grinds to a halt to relieve himself, and things calm down after that. As soon as we get away from the road and onto the footpath, I release him and he bounds off in search of interesting smells, periodically checking that I'm still following him.

After turning it over in my head for a couple of miles, I realise that Ava's right. Much as I don't want to, I think telling Mum and Dad the truth is probably the best thing. If I don't, and I end up losing my job, it will be much worse. Teddy is waiting for me at the fork in the path, and looks a little disappointed when I turn right back towards the village, rather than turning left onto a loop that would add another three miles to our walk.

'I'm here all week; there will be plenty of time for that,' I tell him as he trots beside me. When we get back to the road, I clip the lead back onto him and turn in the direction of home. Mum and Dad live in the same Victorian end-of-terrace house that I grew up in, although it's changed quite a lot since Ava married Ben. Dad has 'encouraged' Ben to 'help him' with some modernisation projects, which seem to have involved Ben doing all the work while Dad sipped his tea and offered suggestions. The kitchen at the back of the house has been knocked through into what used to be the dining room to create an open-plan kitchen/diner, and there was a lot of faffing about with steel beams and so on to keep the house from falling down when Ben put in the bifold doors that Dad insisted on to maximise the view of the garden from the new kitchen. It's lovely now, but there were times when I think Mum was approaching the end of her tether. For a houseproud woman, the dust and mess created by the building work was unbearable, and she managed to murder two vacuum cleaners trying to keep on top of it all.

'Hang on, I'll be there in a jiffy,' Mum's muffled voice calls when I ring the doorbell. Beside me, Teddy is whining with excitement and he launches himself forwards as soon as the door begins to open.

'Oh, hello, Teddy love. I wasn't expecting to see you today,' Mum coos as she tries to dissuade him from jumping up and licking her face. It's a few seconds before he's calm enough that she notices me on the other end of the lead.

'Ella!' she cries, wrapping her arms around me and completely ignoring a newly frenzied Teddy, who is desperate not to miss out on any affection. 'What a lovely surprise. When did you arrive?'

'Lunchtime. I've got some time off work and so I thought I'd stay with Ava for a few days.'

'Lee not with you then?' she asks, stepping back and appraising me. 'You haven't had a fight, have you?'

'He's working,' I reassure her. I'm definitely not going to tell her about my feelings towards Lee at the moment; the uncertainty of my job will be more than enough for her to be going along with.

'Well, come along in. I was just in the middle of making some cupcakes for the school bazaar. Your father's in the garden if you want to say hello. He'll be delighted to see you.'

Leaving me to take off my walking boots, Mum and Teddy disappear into the kitchen together. As I look around the hallway of my childhood home, I feel suddenly nostalgic. Apart from Rebecca Studland's disastrous visit, I always felt safe here, and I realise with relief that coming back home was actually the best decision I could have made for this week. I'll enjoy Ava and Ben's company when they're not at work, and I'll spend the rest of the time walking Teddy and catching up with my parents.

I hate to admit it, but maybe Lee was right about this too. I'll try very hard not to think about what's happening at work, and do my best to enjoy my enforced holiday, however long it is.

8

I'm sick with nerves as the bus makes its way towards the office. The email arrived on Thursday, when I was sitting in the back garden of my parents' house, chatting to Dad about nothing in particular while Teddy dozed beside me. I tried my best not to think about work while I was away, taking Teddy for long walks and enjoying the company of my family, but every time my phone pinged with an email during office hours, my heart raced. The email itself gave very little away, which is partly why I'm so anxious now. I open my phone and read it for probably the hundredth time, begging it to reveal a clue that has so far eluded me.

Dear Ella,

We are writing to inform you that our investigation into your conduct is now complete. Thank you for your patience. We would like to invite you to a meeting on Monday at 11 a.m. to discuss the results and next steps. If you would be so kind as to confirm your attendance by replying to this email, I would be grateful.

Kind regards,
Sharon White
HR Manager

Still nothing. I showed it to Lee when he got back from his first induction week on Friday, but he barely glanced at it before reiterating that I'd be absolutely fine and I had nothing to worry about. I'm far from convinced, though. If they were just going to hand my laptop back, apologise and put me back to work, wouldn't they have scheduled the meeting for nine so as to make the most of the day? I made that point to Lee as well, but he accused me of overthinking it.

It hasn't been the most successful of weekends, really. Lee is obviously loving his new job at Harmony and didn't shut up about how great it is for most of the time, whereas I've been a bundle of nerves worrying about the meeting. Things got off to a bad start when I realised he'd totally forgotten his promise to book a table at the Italian restaurant, and of course they were completely full when he rang. He did get a Chinese takeaway and a nice bottle of wine as an apology, and he's also made a booking for next Friday, but it doesn't help with the general feeling that I'm not on his radar at the moment. I'm not sure why I'm so cross about the restaurant, because I was so stressed I hardly ate any of the takeaway anyway so it probably would have been a waste, but it's the thought (or the lack of it in this case) that counts, isn't it?

If I were being generous, I'd describe Lee's attitude over the weekend as 'insensitive', but I'm not feeling particularly generous towards him at the moment, so I'm going to go with 'bloody annoying'. Whenever I tried to explain how I was feeling, he shut me down, but I've had to endure a pretty much blow-by-blow account of his week, interspersed with rapturous descriptions of how wonderful everything is. He even expected sex, despite the fact it must have been blazingly obvious that I wasn't in the mood. In the end, I obliged him as I could see he was in danger of going into a major sulk, but it was purely functional, from my side at least. He didn't seem to notice my lack of participation, and even had the audacity to say, 'There, don't you feel better for that?' as he rolled off me afterwards. Thankfully, he's got another three weeks of induction training at Harmony's sales office in London, so I'll have the flat to myself during the week.

After five years of doing this journey, I'm on my feet and ready for my stop almost without thinking about it. The problem with having an appointment at eleven o'clock is that there are fewer buses outside the rush hour, so I've had to catch one that gets me here with over half an hour to kill before the meeting. I definitely can't face eating anything, but I reckon I could manage a sip or two of coffee, so I make my way to the coffee shop near the office. I hurry inside and join the short queue, ordering an espresso and taking a couple of lumps of sugar to make it palatable. I wouldn't normally go near an espresso, but the idea of my usual skinny latte, or any form of milky coffee for that matter, makes me want to heave. As soon as I've paid, I turn and start scanning to find a table, only to spot a familiar face.

It's Ruth, and she doesn't look pleased to see me. This is all I need, a bad omen if ever there was one. I can't ignore her, as we've made eye contact now, so I slowly make my way over to her table.

'Can I join you?' I ask.

'If you like. It's a free country,' she replies flatly. 'Are you coming back today then?' she asks once I've sat down opposite her and the initial silence has started to become awkward.

'I hope so.'

'What does that mean? Either you're coming back or you're not. They said you needed time to deal with a personal issue.'

'Did they?'

'Is that not true then?'

'Not strictly. Look, it's complicated.'

Ruth sighs exaggeratedly. 'More secrets.'

'It's not like that,' I tell her. 'I'll tell you as soon as I can, OK?'

'It's fine,' she says as she gets up. 'Really. I guess I thought our friendship meant more to you than it obviously does.'

'Don't, Ruth,' I beg her as she turns to walk away. 'I know I should have told you about Lee and me, and I'm sorry.'

'Yeah, well. I'll see you in the office, I suppose.'

I watch her as she goes, shoulders hunched in defiance. Whatever happens in the meeting, it looks like this whole debacle might have cost me a friend. Despite the sugar lumps, the espresso is still way too strong for me and I abandon it after the first sip. Instead, I just sit there until five to eleven, when I get up to make the short journey to the office. I can't think how many times I've done this walk, but I feel like I'm walking to the gallows today. I swear the receptionist eyes me with suspicion when I give her my name. I know I'm being ridiculous; there's no way she would know what I'm accused of or what my fate is going to be, but my paranoia levels are through the roof.

By the time Jonathan appears to collect me, nearly a quarter of an hour after the meeting was due to start, I'm glad I decided to wear a jacket, as I've sweated so much, my blouse is clinging to my back and I'm sure I have damp patches under my arms. I'm also relieved he doesn't try to shake my hand, for the same reason.

'Ella, I'm so sorry for keeping you. My previous meeting over-ran; you know what it's like. Do come on through.'

I get up and start to follow Jonathan, assuming that he's going to take me through the barriers to one of the staff meeting rooms, so I'm unpleasantly surprised when he leads me across the lobby to one of the meeting rooms that we normally use for visitors.

'We thought this would be easier without the whole office peering over and trying to work out what's going on,' he tells me, obviously sensing my disquiet. I'm frantically trying to get any clues I can from his demeanour. He seems to be back to normal, friendly Jonathan, which is a good sign, but he doesn't look completely at ease in the way that he usually does when he's talking to me, which isn't.

'Sharon will join us in a minute,' he says, as we take our seats opposite each other at the table. The visitor meeting rooms have nicer furniture in them than the employee ones, but this isn't helping me. The plush upholstery of the chair I'm sitting on is pressing my damp blouse against my back, reminding me how sweaty and nervous I am.

'So, how have you been?' he asks, obviously trying to fill the tense silence while we wait for Sharon.

How the fuck do you think I've been? I want to scream at him. Instead, I muster a thin smile and say, 'Oh, you know. I went and spent a few days with my family, which was nice. How about you? How's Lucas?'

His face clears as soon as I mention his favourite topic of conversation. I can't see, but I suspect the manspread is widening with pride.

'We think we've hit a milestone,' he enthuses. 'He's slept all the way through the night for four nights in a row now. Obviously, we're trying not to count our chickens, but it's making such a difference.'

'That's good, I'm really pleased for you.' I'm trying to sound bright and genuine, but my reply gets choked off as Sharon from HR joins us.

'Ella, thank you for coming in, and sorry I'm late,' she begins, as she settles herself next to Jonathan. She smiles, but I notice that it doesn't reach her eyes. At least her voice is relatively friendly; I try to take comfort from that. She's brought a folder with her, from which she removes a sheaf of papers, placing them in a neat pile in front of her. It feels like I'm about to be interviewed, but I'm aware I could also be facing my firing squad.

'OK,' she says, once she's checked through her pile of papers, presumably to make sure she has everything. 'I need to check a few things with you, and then I'll explain where we've got to and what happens next. Are you happy with that?'

'Yes.' I'm not, of course I'm not, but I don't really have a choice. She and Jonathan hold all the cards. I can't remember the last time I felt so vulnerable.

'Do you understand why you were suspended?'

'Yes. But I genuinely didn't know what Lee was up to, I promise.' I can hear the desperation in my voice, but I don't care. It's more than the job now; it's my reputation on the line.

'I believe you,' she replies, and I nearly fall off my seat with astonishment.

'I'm sorry? Does that mean...'

'Ian has been through your laptop and everything checked out. We are satisfied that, whatever Lee did, you had no knowledge of it, and you certainly weren't an active participant. I'm really sorry that we had to put you through this process, but I hope that you can understand that we needed to be certain, and that there were sufficient grounds for us to suspect you.'

I'm innocent. That's all I care about. As the knot of tension that I've carried for the past week dissipates, my head suddenly feels incredibly heavy and I lower it into my hands for a few seconds, taking a few deep breaths to steady myself.

'Are you all right? Do you need a few minutes, some fresh air?' Sharon asks.

'I'm fine, sorry,' I reply, lifting my head again. 'It's just a huge relief, that's all.'

'Let me get you some water,' Jonathan offers, getting to his feet and crossing to the small table in the corner where a jug of water and some glasses have been laid out. He pours a glass and sets it in front of me before returning to his seat. I take a sip and savour the coolness of it. I hadn't realised how dry my mouth was.

'Are you ready to carry on?' Sharon asks, gently. I assume this is the part where they will give my laptop and pass back, and I'll be free to pick up my projects and start trying to repair my friendship with Ruth, so I nod happily.

Sharon puts the top sheet of paper to one side, and moves on to the next.

'As you know,' she says, looking down at the sheet in front of her rather than at me, 'we were hoping to expand the company and carry out some internal promotions.'

My heart, which has only just returned to some semblance of normality, starts pounding again. It really would be the icing on the cake if they not only acquitted me, but also promoted me.

'Unfortunately, the loss of the NHS contract is going to have a bigger impact on us than we thought at first, and we're having to undertake some restructuring.'

OK, so no promotion then. It was a foolish hope, come to think of it.

'It's been a really difficult decision,' Sharon continues, 'but we need to ensure that the company is in the best place to recover from this and move forward with the strongest team in place to ensure our future success. The only way that we could see to do this was by making some posts redundant.'

I say nothing, so she continues.

'I'm sorry to tell you that yours is one of the posts that is affected.'

My eyes snap across to Jonathan. Surely I've misheard, or this is a mistake. Any minute now he'll say something, won't he? It takes me a moment to understand the look on his face and realise that he's not coming to my rescue. My stomach knots horribly as the words sink in. How the hell has this happened?

9

'I don't understand,' I tell them.

'There just aren't enough projects in the pipeline to support the staffing levels that we currently have,' Jonathan explains. 'The trust project would have put us back on an even keel and even allowed us to expand, especially if we started to get other NHS trusts on board but, without that, we aren't sustainable as we are. I'm really sorry, Ella.'

'Hang on a minute,' I interrupt. 'Something doesn't add up here.'

'What do you mean?'

'You must have known before today that you would have to make cuts if we didn't get the contract. You can't tell me that you hadn't made a plan for either eventuality.'

'We hoped for a different outcome, but we were aware of the consequences of the deal not going through, yes. What's your point?' Jonathan is wary, as well he should be.

'My point is that, when you called me in last Monday and started accusing me of being in cahoots with Lee, you'd already decided to get rid of me.'

'I wouldn't put it like that, exactly.' He's definitely on the defensive, which means he's trying to hide something, and I'm not going to let him off the hook. I'm angry.

'How would you put it then?' I fix my eyes on him. 'I have just had one of the worst weeks of my life, and it's all been for nothing. Why put me through all of that when you had no intention of letting me keep my job anyway? What kind of mad power game is this?'

'It's not like that at all, Ella,' Sharon intervenes, using the kind of soothing tone that is normally reserved for trying to calm lunatics.

'Then how the hell is it? Explain it to me.' I transfer my glare to her, and I'm aware of Jonathan fidgeting.

'I'll be honest with you. We did know that we were going to have to make redundancies last week, but we hadn't finalised the list.'

'I don't believe you.'

'That's your choice,' she says smoothly, 'but I'm telling you the truth. Even if we had finalised the list, we still needed to conduct the investigation.'

'Why? What difference does it make if you're firing me anyway?'

'It makes all the difference. If we'd have found that you had acted improperly, you would have been summarily dismissed with no reference, and we may even have begun legal proceedings against you. I agree that this is not the outcome that any of us want, but at least you will have a redundancy payout to soften the blow, and you will also be assured of a glowing reference for any future employers.'

'It doesn't feel like much of a consolation prize.'

'I know, and I know you won't believe this, but this is hard for us too. You're the third person we've had to break this news to so far today, and it doesn't get any easier.'

The fight goes out of me. What's the point when I've obviously already lost? Sharon obviously senses this and uses the opportunity to move things along.

'Let me explain the process to you,' she begins. 'You will initially be placed on gardening leave for a month. This is a necessary step, which allows you to consider whether there are any available roles at Orchestra for which you might be suited. We will also consider whether there is another position we can offer you.'

'Are there any current vacancies?' I interrupt.

'Not at the moment, no,' she admits. 'But someone might hand in their resignation tomorrow, you never know.'

I raise my eyebrows at her. We both know that's extremely unlikely.

'If, at the end of the gardening leave period, neither of us have found another role within the company that would suit you, then we finalise the redundancy at that point. Your redundancy package will consist of three months' full salary in lieu of notice, which I'm afraid you will have to pay tax on. We will also give you three months' full salary as an ex-gratia payment.'

'What does that mean?'

'It's a kind of thank you payment. The good news is that it forms part of your redundancy package, so it will be tax free, as will the five weeks of statutory redundancy pay that we are obliged to pay by law. We will continue to make payments into your pension during your notice period, and you will also still qualify for private medical treatment under the company scheme for that time.'

She slides a piece of paper across to me with the numbers on it. My eyes race to the bottom and widen when I see the final sum. It's enough to keep me going for several months.

'Do you have any questions?' Sharon asks.

'Why me, and not any of the other project managers? Is it because of my relationship with Lee?'

'No, that wasn't a factor. Even though we make plain our preference that employees don't date each other, we'd never be allowed to use that as a reason to select someone for redundancy. You'd have ample grounds to claim unfair dismissal in that situation. The truth is that we look at a number of factors including your calendar, your time with the company, what development opportunities there are for you and so on.'

I turn to Jonathan. 'It's not like I was sitting around doing nothing!' I exclaim. 'I had two active projects, even without the NHS trust.'

He sighs. I can tell they both want this meeting to be over.

'That's true, but you had spare capacity, as did a couple of other project managers, so we will be redeploying your existing projects to them.'

'I really am sorry, Ella,' Sharon says again. 'I know it's a horrible shock. The only thing I can say is that research has shown that people who are made redundant usually go on to a new job that they're far happier in. I hope that's the case for you. We'll be in touch in due course, OK?'

With that, she gathers her papers together and they both stand, indicating that the meeting is over. Part of me wants to refuse to leave, to stay here asking difficult questions just to disrupt their plans, but I think back to the quarter hour I had to wait, and I can't help asking Sharon one more question.

'Do you have anyone else you've got to do this to today, or am I the last one?'

'Just one more after you,' Sharon tells me. 'I can't tell you how much I hate this part of my job.'

I look at the clock. Ten to twelve, which means the next candidate for the firing squad is probably due in ten minutes. I don't want them to have to endure the wait I did, so I get up and walk out of the door that Sharon is holding open for me. As we make our way across the lobby, there's an awkward pause where it's obvious that I'm heading one way and they're heading back through the barriers to carry on with the jobs that they still have. For a moment, I hate them both.

'Good luck, Ella. I mean that. We're going to miss you.' Jonathan holds out his hand. I force myself to be rational; it's not his fault, after all.

'Thanks, Jonathan,' I reply as we shake hands. Then, before things can get any more awkward, I turn on my heel and stride out of the door onto the pavement.

As soon as I'm out of the building, the shock kicks in properly. I'm not crying, but I feel dizzy and numb, like my brain and my body have somehow disconnected from each other. I'm also disorientated and unable to decide what to do now. I don't want to go back to the flat; oppressive silence is the last thing I need. I am, I realise with surprise, ravenously hungry. It's weird, because I've hardly been able to face anything to eat since the email arrived on Thursday, but now that I know my fate and the uncertainty of the last week has gone, it's like the hunger switch has been turned back on. I consider my options and decide to treat myself to lunch at the French bistro a couple of streets away. Hopefully, it will be fairly quiet on a Monday, and a bowl of moules with crusty bread to soak up the sauce, and maybe steak and fries to follow, sound just the thing. I need to get some food into me before I can even begin to process what just happened, let alone make any sort of plan about what to do next.

I'm relieved to see that the restaurant is as quiet as I predicted, but I still choose a table away from the window to minimise the chances of being seen. I'm not ready to face anyone from the office. The waiter takes my order; I'm briefly tempted to have a huge glass of white wine to wash all the food down with, but I've never been much of a midday drinker and lots of wine on an empty stomach is a recipe for disaster, so I play it safe and stick to water. I'm just starting to think about how long my redundancy package will keep me going for when my phone pings to let me know I have a message. It's Lee.

How did you get on? I hope they offered you a massive pay rise to say sorry! Looking forward to celebrating when I get back on Friday. xxx

Argh. He's even managing to be annoying by text now. I can see the waiter approaching with my moules, so I bash out a quick reply to get rid of him.

They found nothing. Celebration premature as I've been made redundant.

I'm barely three plump mussels into my starter when he calls.

'What the fuck, Ella? How can they make you redundant?'

'They needed to win the NHS contract and didn't, so I'm out. That's all there is to it.'

'That's too bad,' he replies. 'Listen, I've got to run to a meeting, but we'll chat later, OK? Knowing you, you'll have found something else before the end of the week. You'll be fine, I promise.'

The speed with which he lost interest in my predicament is completely typical of how he is these days. I hang up and flick a pleasantly cathartic V-sign at the phone screen before turning my attention back to the mussels. By the time I pay the bill and leave, I've made my way though the mussels, an entrecôte de boeuf with frites, and a slab of tarte de pommes with cream. I don't feel better, exactly, but I do feel pleasantly full at least. The important thing I've realised is that, although I'm not working, I am still being paid for the next month, so if I get my act together and start job hunting sooner rather than later, I might even have something lined up before my main redundancy package kicks in. I decide to start updating my CV this afternoon. It will be a much better use of my time than sitting around watching daytime TV, and then I'll be ready to move as soon as I spot a vacancy I like the look of.

I'm about a hundred yards from the office on my way to the bus stop when I spot Jonathan coming the other way with a large carrier bag. I don't really want to speak to him again, but he's seen me and there's no point in being rude. He looks terrible, but I'm not surprised. Despite his manspreading, he's a good manager, and making people redundant has obviously taken a real toll on him.

'You look worn out,' I tell him as we meet. 'Are you all done? Last victim sent packing?'

'Yeah, something like that,' he replies, and I'm surprised by the bitterness in his voice.

'Are you OK?'

'Not really. You know Sharon said there was one more redundancy after you?'

'Yes.'

'It was me.'

'What?'

'Yes. Ironic, isn't it? There I am, having to rip the rug out from under my colleagues, only to have them do it to me at the end.'

'Oh, Jonathan. That's really shitty. You'd think they would

have the decency to tell you first and spare you the job of telling the others.'

'What am I going to do, Ella?' he whines. 'I've got a wife and baby to support. Gina's going to hit the roof.'

I'm tempted to snap at him that I actually have my own problems to deal with right now, and the fact that he's married doesn't make his situation any worse than mine, but I manage to bite my tongue and remain civil.

'You're going to do exactly the same thing I'm going to do,' I tell him, firmly. 'You're going to lick your wounds, and then you're going to look for another job. Shit happens, Jonathan. Today it's happened to us. Listen, I think I can see my bus. Good luck, yeah?'

'Thanks, Ella. You too.'

I have to sprint to catch the bus, but thankfully the driver is in a good mood and waits for me. As I settle into my seat, my phone pings with another message. I hope it's not Lee again. I'm in no mood for more of his bullshit platitudes. I grudgingly unlock the phone and see that the message isn't from Lee, but I would almost rather it had been. It's a message from Ruth. With a sigh, I open it.

Just been told the news. Fuck. No wonder you didn't want to talk about it this morning. I'm sorry I've been such a bitch to you. Let's meet up for a drink soon, OK?

I sit and stare at the message for a while as I try to work out how I feel about Ruth now. She's been incredibly self-righteous since the whole Lee thing kicked off, and it wouldn't surprise me if one of the motivations behind her message is to get a blow-by-blow account of my redundancy meeting so she can share it in shocked tones with everyone else in the office. I would always have described her as one of my best friends, but I realise I don't trust her any more, and there can't be a friendship without trust.

My finger hovers over the screen for what feels like an age, and then I delete her message without replying.

10

I'm sitting on the sofa, watching TV in my trackie bottoms and a T-shirt and nursing a glass of wine, when I hear Lee's key in the door. I haven't been lounging about for the whole week, but it didn't take me long to get my CV up to date, and there are surprisingly few job vacancies for project managers in Leeds currently. I've sent off one application and registered with a couple of agencies, but there's really not much more I can do at the moment. After just four and a half days without work, I'm in danger of turning into exactly the sort of stay-at-home slob that I promised myself I wouldn't become. There are already a couple of mid-afternoon drama series on TV that I've started to get into.

Lee and I have spoken a couple of times since Monday, and I can tell he's trying to make the right noises, but he just doesn't get it. To him, this is a blip that I will magically solve within a week or so, and then we'll carry on as if it never happened. All he feels he needs to do is chivvy me along and encourage me, but I'm finding his faux positivity and motivational claptrap incredibly irritating, frankly.

'Hi, Els,' he calls from the tiny space that serves as our hallway. 'I'll just dump my stuff and I'll be with you, OK? Pour us a beer, would you, I'm parched.'

'Certainly, your lordship,' I mutter under my breath as I pull myself out of the sofa and pad towards the kitchen. I retrieve one of the bottles of craft lager he likes from the fridge and pour it carefully into a glass, leaving it on the side for him before retreating back to the sofa. After a few minutes, he appears from the bedroom.

'I'm sorry I'm late; the traffic was terrible today. I'll just have a couple of swigs of this, leap in the shower, and I'll be ready to go. I'm bloody starving, I tell you.'

He leans over the back of the sofa to kiss me, but his lips have barely touched my hair before he's pulling back.

'Ella, you're not ready!' he exclaims.

'Ready for what?'

'Don't tell me you've forgotten. We're going out. The Italian restaurant, remember?'

'Oh, right. Yeah. Sorry, I must have lost track of the time. I'll jump in the shower after you.'

'Umm, no,' he replies. 'You go in first, because you need to do your make-up and all that stuff. I just need a quick rinse down and a clean shirt.'

The truth is that I'd completely forgotten we were going out tonight, and I'm not sure a celebration dinner at the Italian restaurant is appropriate. What are we celebrating? I've lost my job and my boyfriend is being a prick. At least the prick is paying; although I'm technically still on a salary, every penny counts until I've secured a new job. I have a finite amount of money and I need to make it last as long as I can. I did various budget plans during the week, and I've worked out that I could last for nearly six months if I'm very frugal, but it'll be closer to four if I maintain my normal spending. I spent yesterday evening doing an online food shop, carefully substituting the premium products we normally buy with cheaper alternatives. I haven't told Lee yet; I'd rather present him with a done deal than have to fight with him all the way round the supermarket. I was amazed how much I saved compared to our usual bill.

As soon as I'm out of the shower, I wrap myself in a towel and pad into the bedroom. Lee is lying on the bed in his pants.

'Mm,' he says, eyeing me appreciatively. 'Perhaps I should cancel the table and unwrap you instead.' He reaches out and starts tugging at the towel, trying to dislodge it.

'Get off!' I grab the towel to prevent it slipping off and pull away from him. There's nothing like being suddenly unemployed to completely shut down your libido, and sex is the last thing on my mind.

Of course, he completely misreads the signals I'm giving off, and slowly pulls off his pants to reveal his building arousal while humming 'The Stripper'.

'Cut it out,' I tell him firmly. 'We'll be late.'

'We might be,' he agrees with a wink, coming up behind me and stroking my bare shoulders. 'I've realised I'm still very hungry, but I'm not sure it's for Italian food any more. I'm sure we can find a snack for you too if we look carefully.' He prods my back with his erection as he says the last bit, to make sure I'm not in any doubt as to his meaning, before leaning down and, after moving my hair out of the way, starting to nibble on my earlobe. To be fair, I do normally like having my earlobe nibbled, but at the moment, I just want to recoil.

'Lee, I mean it. Not now, OK?'

'Fine,' he huffs as he heads for the bathroom. 'I wasn't really in the mood anyway. Coming home to find you dressed like a prison inmate was a bit of a turnoff if I'm honest. I was only trying to cheer you up.'

What is the matter with him at the moment? Has he always been like this, but I've just never noticed before? Suddenly, the weekend ahead seems impossibly long, and I'm dying for Monday to come around, just so I can be alone again. It comes to something when daytime TV seems infinitely preferable to spending time with your boyfriend. I'm seriously beginning to wonder what I ever saw in him as I listen to him singing tunelessly in the shower.

Thankfully, by the time we're dressed and in the taxi, things are on a slightly better footing. Now that I've got my head into the right place, I'm looking forward to dinner, and Lee seems to have cheered up as well. The maître d' greets us as if we're long-lost family members, even though I'm sure he doesn't remember us, and we're shown to a table in the window, which I'm pleased about because it means I'll have something to look at if Lee starts to get annoying again.

'So,' he says as soon as we've placed our drinks order, 'tell me about you.'

'What do you mean?'

'Well, what's your plan?' He steeples his hands.

'It's pretty simple, really,' I tell him while trying to ignore his faux avuncular attitude. 'I've registered with a couple of agencies, and I've applied for one job so far. I'll keep searching the job sites and applying, and hopefully someone will employ me before my money runs out.'

'Hm.' He stares at me as if appraising me, and I try very hard not to be irritated.

'What?'

'I was just thinking. I could ask whether Harmony have any project manager vacancies. I could put in a good word, you know.'

'No. Absolutely not.'

He looks affronted. 'Why not?'

'Because I don't want a job based on you "putting in a good word". That's not how it should work. Also, even though I'm really pissed off with them for putting me through the mill and then firing me anyway, I think Orchestra were right about one thing. Office romances are a bad idea.'

We're momentarily interrupted by the waiter coming to take our food order, but I can see Lee is unhappy with my response.

'Why do you say that?' he asks, once we're alone again. 'We did OK, didn't we?'

'*You* did OK,' I tell him. 'But my life would have been a lot simpler if I hadn't been going out with you when you decided to pull your little resignation trick. Yes, I probably still would have lost my job, but at least I wouldn't have had that horrible week when I was suspended.'

He leans forward. 'I know you'll say this is just the rose-tinted spectacles talking, but I never realised what a crappy company Orchestra was to work for until I started working at Harmony. You're better off out of there. I've done you a favour, I reckon.'

'Are you mental?' I ask him in disbelief. 'You got me suspended, and now I'm out of a job because we lost the contract to Harmony. How, exactly, is that doing me a favour?'

He smiles, oblivious to everything except how clever he is. I've seen this look many times before, and I've always accepted it as part of his salesman's swagger, but this time I want to punch him.

'Look,' he says conspiratorially. 'I couldn't say anything at the time, for obvious reasons, but now that you're no longer with Orchestra, I reckon I can tell you.'

'Tell me what?'

He lowers his voice conspiratorially. 'The truth is that I gave Harmony that contract on a plate. Their sales guy was so green that I could have wiped the floor with him if I'd have wanted to.'

I stare at him in horror. 'Are you saying...?'

'Yup,' he grins. 'It wasn't hard, you know. A little tweak of the presentation here, a small adjustment of the numbers there. Oh, sorry. I'd better take this.' He grabs his vibrating phone and I hear him say, 'Hi, Tom! No, not a bad time at all. What's up?' before he disappears outside.

I feel like I've been kicked in the gut. I want to get up from this table and storm out, telling him he can go and fuck himself on the way. No, I want to empty a whole bowl of pasta over his head, followed by a glass of red wine, and then tell him to go and fuck himself. How can he sit there, all smug and pleased with himself, knowing that what he's done is not only unethical and dishonest, but that it's his fault I'm unemployed?

I try out a number of scenes in my mind, each more extreme than the one before, but they're not helping. I know I'll never have the guts to actually do any of them, and they probably wouldn't play out the way I anticipated anyway, although the one where I replace the shampoo with hair removal cream does sound sorely tempting. As the heat of my rage starts to dissipate, it's replaced by something much colder, and I have an idea.

I've just put my phone down when Lee reappears.

'Sorry about that. They don't seem to be able to get enough of me. Where were we?'

'You were telling me how you handed the contract to Harmony on a plate,' I remind him acidly.

'Oh, yes.' He's just about to continue when our starters arrive. I ordered the calamari, but my appetite has deserted me. I take a swig of my wine and pop a piece into my mouth. I can tell it's delicious, but it takes me ages to swallow it. Lee is tucking into his beef carpaccio with gusto.

'So, here's the dilemma,' he tells me quietly between mouthfuls. 'I'm pitching for a job with Harmony, but I'm also up against them in a sales cycle. What to do? I can either prove what a brilliant salesman I am by mashing them into the ground, but then they'd be pissed off because they would have lost the contract, or I can let them win and take the risk that they wonder if I'm actually as good as they thought.'

'I can see how hard that must have been for you,' I say, trying desperately to keep the savage sarcasm out of my voice.

'It was,' he replies, completely oblivious to the waves of loathing coming from my side of the table. 'In the end, I decided it would be better all round to let them have the contract, particularly as they made it pretty clear they were relying on it to fund their expansion. I have nothing to prove. My history shows how good I am and, now that this trust has signed with Harmony, I can prove my worth by landing all the others.'

'So they basically told you that you'd only get the job if you scuppered Orchestra's bid? Isn't that illegal? If not, it ought to be.'

'They were very careful what they said, but yes. They made it clear enough that I knew what they meant.' He taps the side of his nose.

'So what did you actually do?' I ask him, trying desperately to keep my voice level as the scale of his duplicity unfolds.

'Nothing big. Nothing that Orchestra are going to find, anyway. The truth is that, although the Harmony software knocks Orchestra's into a cocked hat in terms of how it looks and how modern it feels, it isn't as mature. There are a couple of modules that either aren't as well developed, or simply don't exist at all yet. Normally, I'd point this out and use it to drive home the point that software needs to be more than pretty, and that Orchestra has a mature offering that's well respected in the market. I'd go pretty big on it, doing my best to instil doubt in the customer that Harmony was everything they'd been told.'

'And you didn't do that this time, I'm guessing.'

'Never mentioned it. Glossed over the slide completely.'

'Uh-huh. I admit sales isn't my game, but that doesn't sound enough to me.'

'No, you're right.'

'So what else did you do?'

'You know your project plan, with all the costings?'

'Yes.'

'I added a contingency percentage.'

'Why? I explicitly told you that I'd already done that!'

'Keep your voice down. People might be listening. Maybe you did tell me, but I must have "forgotten".' He makes quote marks with his fingers and smiles as he says it.

'So how much did you add?'

'The standard 20 per cent.'

'But that would have completely priced us out of the deal!'

'Duh!' he grins. 'That's the point. As soon as the trust saw the figures, I knew Harmony had it in the bag.'

'What did Roger say? Surely you had to run your deck and everything past him?'

'Roger may be my boss, but he doesn't really show much interest in the nitty gritty. Wow him with some pretty slides and he doesn't notice the numbers.'

'You'll be found out. They're going through your laptop, Lee. They'll see that you changed the figures even when I told you not to. They'll realise what you did and come after you.'

'They won't, because I deleted that sentence from your email.'

'For God's sake, you idiot! They'll see the original in my sent items and know you've doctored it!'

My frustration only makes him more pleased with himself. 'Only if they know what they're looking for, and they don't. It's like looking for a needle in a haystack and, even if they did find it, what are they going to do? A doctored email isn't proof of anything.'

'And did you, at any point, think that what you were doing might impact me?'

'Why would it? Look, I'm really sorry about your job. I never intended that to happen, of course I didn't. But you'll get another one, and it'll probably be better.'

I really am struggling not to punch him.

'One more question. If you'd have known that what you were doing was going to cost me my job, would you have done anything differently?'

'I don't know.' He appears to consider for a while as he finishes his starter and starts to help himself to mine. 'Probably not. Look, I was just doing what was right, career-wise, for me. I'm sorry you got caught in the crossfire, but it was Orchestra that made you redundant, not me. And, if I'm honest, I'm not sure I'd have landed the deal even if I had put my all into it, and then we'd both potentially be out of work, so I think it's probably turned out the best it could do. Anyway, I feel so much better now that you know everything. You do understand why I had to do it this way, right?'

I raise my eyes to meet his gaze. Physically, every contour of him is familiar. He looks like the Lee I've loved for the last five years. But under the skin, I realise I have no idea who he is at all.

'Of course,' I tell him.

'Great,' he replies. 'I knew you'd get it when I explained. And I meant what I said about putting in a good word for you at Harmony if you change your mind. Right, I'm just going to pop to the gents' before our main courses arrive, OK?'

I watch his retreating back and wait until he's completely out of sight before lifting my phone and turning off the voice recorder.

11

I've now been officially unemployed for three weeks, there isn't even the vaguest sniff of a new job, and I'm getting worryingly addicted to *Homes Under the Hammer* as well as a couple of daytime TV dramas. Lee's induction course has finished and he's working from home this week putting together a proposal for another NHS trust, so I've conveniently arranged a trip to stay with my parents. It's a beautiful day and I should be relishing the warmth of the sun streaming through the train window, but I'm feeling morose. I shouldn't be on this train in my jeans in the middle of the working day, escaping from a boyfriend whose job satisfaction I can't help resenting. I should be in an office, doing what I do best. A week at home is hopefully going to give me some perspective, because I know I have decisions to make, and I can't make them with all the trappings of my old life around me.

I haven't done anything with the recording. My first instinct was to send it straight to Sharon, the head of HR at Orchestra, but I realised I ought to listen to it first to make sure it wasn't just a confused mumble over the clanging of cutlery. In the end, I didn't get a chance to listen to it until the Monday, after Lee had left for work. It was all there and the sound was crystal clear but, although it still made me incredibly cross, I wasn't so sure about sending it. It sounds silly but, at the moment, I'm the innocent party in all of this. If I send the recording, which will undoubtedly make things very difficult for Lee, it kind of means I've sunk to his level, and I'm not sure I want to be that person. I very nearly deleted it a couple of times during the last fortnight, but it's still there as a kind of insurance policy if I need it.

I truly don't know what to do about Lee. I don't know if I should try to put his behaviour behind me, or even if I want to. Now that he's got his confession off his chest, he's settled back into something closer to the Lee I love, but my opinion of him has definitely taken a serious nosedive. I've got to do my bit to keep our relationship going for now because, whether I like it or not, I'm dependent on him for the time being. There's no way that I'd be able to rent another flat without a job and, although I'm sure Mum and Dad would let me move home and Ava would probably put me up as well, I feel I need to be in Leeds while I'm job hunting, not out in the sticks. Now that I'm not working, our flat suddenly feels like a massive drain on my finances, but there's no way Lee's going to want to downsize, and the least I can do is leave him the home he loves if I do end up moving out. I don't know whether he could actually afford to live there on his own, but that really isn't my problem. He should be able to, because the rental agreement is in his name and the agents must have done credit checks. When we moved in, he said it would be easier if the paperwork was in just one of our names because it would be simpler to unravel if things didn't work out. I don't think, in his arrogance, he ever imagined 'things not working out' would involve me leaving him, but I'm grateful to have my options open, that's for sure.

'Hello, sweet pea. How are you holding up?' Dad drew the

short straw of collecting me from the station today, and he squeezes me into a tight hug. I breathe in the smell of Pears' soap and fabric conditioner that is the hallmark scent of him.

'I'd be better if there was even the faintest sign of a new job,' I tell him honestly as we detach. 'It's starting to get me down.'

'It's only been a couple of weeks, love. You'll find something, I know you will. Here, let me take your bag.'

Dad's car is even older than Ava's, but where hers is definitely suffering from her total lack of care, his is immaculate. He keeps it in a garage a couple of streets away that he rents from the council, and it's washed, polished and vacuumed every Sunday, regardless of whether it needs it or not. The interior smells of pine air freshener and there are always two tins of travel sweets in the glovebox, to make sure they never run out. He's also a very careful driver, never exceeding the speed limit and creeping over speed bumps to ensure he doesn't accidentally scrape the bottom of the car. If you were planning a bank job and had to choose a getaway driver from our family, Dad would definitely not be it. Ava? Yes, she'd probably be pretty good. Although I'm perfectly able, I haven't driven for years, so I'd probably be closer to Dad than her. Mum used to have a little red hatchback that she zipped about in when she was working, but she sold it when she retired and I think she's quite happy to let Dad do all the driving now.

'Your sister is at work, but her shift finishes at lunchtime, so I think she's expecting you to pop in this afternoon,' Dad tells me as he pulls up outside the house. 'Your mother's waiting for you. Just bang on the door and she'll let you in. I'm going to put the car away.'

I get another big hug from Mum, who then holds me by the shoulders at arms' length so she can appraise me. 'Are you getting enough sleep? You look tired,' she observes.

'I'm fine, Mum. I'm just lacking a sense of purpose at the

moment, that's all. I spend all day either searching online for jobs or wandering about, feeling useless. You don't realise how much you're defined by your work until you don't have it any more.'

'Are you still only looking for jobs in Leeds?'

'No. I've widened my search to include Manchester and Sheffield, and I even applied for a job in Liverpool, but I haven't heard back from them.'

'Goodness, what would Lee do if you had to move to Liverpool?'

'I'll deal with that if it happens. I'm sure we'll figure something out.' I'm not telling her about my current problems with Lee. If she thought I was hedging my bets and keeping him on side while I still need him, which I probably am a bit, she would firmly disapprove and accuse me of being manipulative. Maybe she'd be right. I think I've earned the right to be a little manipulative, though, haven't I?

After lunch, I wander across to Ava's house, where I'm greeted by an ecstatic Teddy. Once he's finished jumping up and I've admired his latest toy, Ava and I retire to her garden with cups of tea. The garden is another thing in which Ava takes absolutely no interest. Where my parents' garden is lovingly tended with abundant flowerbeds, hers is a scrappy piece of lawn and a patch of wilderness that could probably be turned into something pretty if someone took pity on it. Maybe it could be a project for me while I'm here; it would give me something to do and get me out of the house.

'Tell me everything,' she demands as soon as we're settled. This is typical of her, no beating about the bush. As soon as I've sworn her to secrecy, I fill her in on the redundancy but I don't sugar coat it like I have for Mum and Dad. Ava gets the warts and all version, including Lee's confession.

'What an absolute bastard,' she fumes. 'You'd better have sent the recording in.'

'No. I thought about it, but I want to be the better person here,' I tell her.

'Nonsense! Why bother recording him if you had no plan to use it?'

'I'm not saying I'll never send it in; I'm just not sure now is the right time.'

'You're overthinking this. You should have sent it straight away before you had a chance to second guess yourself. I know you. You'll never send it now, and that means he's got away with it.'

'It's complicated, OK?'

'It really isn't. He shat on you, you have the evidence, but you're too much of a wimp to do anything with it.'

'Just let it go, will you, Ava? I know you don't like him—'

'With good reason!'

'I get it. I'll think about it some more. I've got bigger fish to fry right now.'

'I guess so. How is the job hunting coming?'

'Not great. I think I've applied for pretty much every job vacancy in the north of England with the words "project manager" in the title apart from one, which was on a building site.'

'Why didn't you apply for that one?'

'Because it's on a building site, obviously! I don't know the first thing about building sites, and I'd like a job where I'm taken seriously, not seen as some sort of sex object to be wolf-whistled at all day.'

'Interesting,' Ava remarks, after a moment's silence.

'What?'

'There's so much wrong with what you've just said, I don't know where to begin.'

'Eh?'

'OK, let's start with "I don't know the first thing about building sites".'

'I don't.'

'I know that, but you've always said a good project manager doesn't need to know the product; they just have to be able to manage the resources. So yeah, it's a building site, but it's still people. You're just swapping software for bricks and mortar. You don't have to know how to build a house to project manage it, Ella. That's what the trades are there for.'

I consider what she's said. 'Yes, but I still need to understand what the stages of building a house are, and I don't have a clue. Some bits are obvious, like the walls probably have to go up before you can put the roof on, but I suspect it's a lot more complicated than that. If I don't know the stages, then how am I supposed to know what order they go in?'

She grins at me. 'Ben can help you,' is all she says.

I raise my eyebrows.

'OK, so his work is mainly alterations and extensions,' she continues, warming to her theme, 'but he knows everything there is to know. If you apply, he can coach you so you go in there and sound like an expert.'

'Do you think he would?'

'Of course! He'd love nothing more than to drone on at you about building regulations and stuff for a couple of hours. I always tune him out, so he'll be delighted to have a captive audience.'

'I'm still not sure, Ava. I imagine it's a pretty macho working environment. They'd probably just stare at my chest all the time and expect me to make cups of tea.'

'That's the second thing you've got wrong. You would probably be the only woman on site, I grant you, but builders have come under fire a lot lately for catcalling and wolf-whistling. Ben says there's a zero-tolerance policy about that sort of thing on most sites now. Yes, they'll probably eye you up a bit, but think of it the other way round; there are going to be a lot of physically fit men doing manual labour around you. That's not a bad view from the office window, is it?' She waggles her eyebrows and we dissolve into fits of giggles.

'Show me the advert,' she continues when the laughter has subsided.

I open the browser on my phone and navigate to one of the many job sites I have bookmarked. After a quick scroll, I find it and hand the phone over.

'I can't read this out here; all I can see is the sunlight reflecting off your phone. Do you want another cup of tea? I'll read it while the kettle boils.'

'Yeah, why not?' I hand her my mug and she disappears inside.

While she's gone, I consider what she's said. I'm really not sure a building site is me, but she does have a point. Maybe, if Ben gives me some coaching and I can at least use some of the terms and sound like I know what I'm talking about, I might at least get an interview. I haven't a hope of being offered the job and, despite her assurances, I'm not sure I'm desperate enough that I'd take it even if it were offered, but it would be good interview practice if nothing else.

'Your phone's locked itself while I was filling the kettle,' Ava calls from the kitchen. 'What's the code?'

'Two-two-oh-three,' I reply.

'What's that?'

'Lee's birthday.'

'Nice. I must remember to send him a card,' she says sarcastically. 'I'll be out in a tic.'

When she finally returns a while later, she's beaming from ear to ear. 'What?' I ask her.

'It's got accommodation included, did you see? You'd be mad not to apply.'

'They probably won't even offer me an interview. I can't pretend I have experience when I don't.'

'They definitely won't offer you an interview if you don't apply. Go on. Give it a go.'

I sigh. 'Fine.'

She's right, of course she is. After all, what have I got to lose?

12

———

It's after nine when I wake the next morning. Three weeks out of a job and I'm getting worryingly used to sleeping in. After all, it's not like there's a lot to get up for. Ava delightedly agreed to let me have a crack at her garden, so I'll borrow some of Dad's tools and head over there in a bit. After Ava's nagging, I sent off an application for the building site job late yesterday afternoon. I'm not expecting to hear anything, but it's another iron in the fire at least.

Before heading down for breakfast, I automatically reach across and check my phone. There are two new emails, one from an address I don't recognise, and one from Sharon White at Orchestra. Sharon's is probably some boring procedural stuff to do with my redundancy, so I decide to open the other one, from Deborah Smythe. As I scan the text, I'm suddenly fully alert and sit bolt upright in bed. I read it several times, just to make sure I haven't imagined it.

Dear Ms Mackenzie,
Thank you for your application for the post of project manager with

Atkinson Construction. We have reviewed your application form and
CV and I would like to invite you to interview with myself and the CEO,
Christopher Atkinson, at your earliest convenience.
Please contact me on the number below to arrange your appointment.
I look forward to meeting you.
Deborah Smythe

I leap out of bed and rush downstairs clutching my phone.

'Mum, Dad, I got an interview! Look.' I hold the phone out excit-
edly, but of course they have to potter off to find their reading glasses
and there's a lot of humming and hawing before they're ready.

'Is that the one Ava persuaded you to apply for yesterday?
They got back to you very quickly, didn't they?' Dad observes.

'Of course they did,' Mum tells him. 'They could see she was
quality and wanted to snap her up. This is great news. Have you
called them yet to arrange a time?'

'No. What do you think I should do? I don't want to suggest a
time that's too soon in case I come across as desperate, but I don't
want them to lose interest either. Even if the job isn't right for me,
it's good interview practice, so I don't want to put them off.'

'Why don't you suggest Monday next week? That's soon
enough to be keen without being desperate. Do you know where
they are?' Dad asks.

'Ava looked them up yesterday. They're in Alwoodley. I can get
a bus out there from the flat, but I think it takes around an hour.'

'Nice. I didn't realise there were offices there, though. I
thought it was all big houses and stuff.'

'Well, I'll see when I get there, won't I?'

'You'd better ring them now,' Mum interjects. 'Get in there
before someone else. You don't know how many applicants
they've had.'

Realising she's right, I dial the number Deborah left me in her email and step out into the garden. I don't want an audience for this.

She answers after just a couple of rings. 'Deborah Smythe speaking.'

'Hello, Ms Smythe, it's Ella Mackenzie. I just got your email inviting me for interview, so I'm calling to arrange a time.'

'Goodness, I only sent it half an hour ago. You're keen,' she laughs, and I kick myself. I should have waited until lunchtime or early afternoon.

'I happened to have a gap in my diary, so I thought I'd call now,' I tell her. It's not a lie: I do have a gap in my diary at the moment. It has no defined end, but she doesn't need to know that.

'Not a problem,' she purrs. 'When are you available?'

'I've got a few commitments this week, but Monday next week looks pretty good. Does that suit you?' Again, not strictly a lie. I have promised to do something about Ava's garden this week. That's a commitment, isn't it?

I wait patiently while she consults her diary. Eventually, she comes back.

'Mr Atkinson and I could see you at eleven-thirty next Monday.'

'That's perfect, thank you.'

'We will look forward to meeting you then. Do you have the address? I'll email it to you anyway, just to confirm.'

I actually feel a bit trembly as I put down the phone. I'm excited, obviously, but I'm also nervous. It was all very well discussing this in theory over a cup of tea in Ava's back garden yesterday, but what happens if I go in there and make a complete fool of myself? I'm going to need all the help I can get from Ben, that's for sure. Ava's working this morning, so I bash out a quick message to her.

The building firm only want to interview me!!! Going to need to borrow your husband for serious tuition...

She won't get it until her next break, so I wander back indoors. Mum and Dad are looking at me expectantly.

'Well?' Mum asks.

'Next Monday at eleven-thirty. I probably should have waited a bit longer before I called. She called me keen.'

'You are keen, though, aren't you?'

'I don't know. It seemed like a good idea when Ava was talking me into it yesterday, but I'm really not sure I'm cut out for construction. Also, if I come across as too eager, it puts them in a better negotiating position. I read an article online about it. I need to play it a bit cool. I shouldn't give them the impression that I'll work for peanuts just because I've been made redundant. I'm still worth the salary I was earning at Orchestra.'

'Yes, but you don't want to miss out because you were too demanding either,' Dad says. 'You need another job, Ella, and this might be it.'

'I know. At least I've got the best part of a week to prepare. Something tells me I'm going to be spending a lot of time with Ben over the next few days.'

After a celebratory cup of tea and a bacon sandwich ('You'll need the energy if you're tackling that wilderness of Ava's'), I pad upstairs to have a shower. It's going to be a warm day, so I select a pair of shorts and a T-shirt before consulting with Dad on the best tools for the job.

'I'll come over with you,' he tells me after we've raided his garden shed. 'I'm supposed to be collecting Teddy and bringing him back here, but I could give you a hand instead if you like.'

'Are you sure?'

'Yes, I haven't got any plans today, and your mother will be glad not to have me and the dog under her feet. To be honest, I've been dying to get my hands on that garden, but Ava would never let me. She thinks I'm too old and I might have a heart attack. I don't know why I put up with the cheek of the girl. Anyway, if we get all the rubbish out of there today and tomorrow, we could maybe have a little trip to the garden centre on Thursday and get some new plants to go in.'

By lunchtime, we've made good progress, but my hands and arms are covered in scratches. Dad isn't much better, and is sporting a couple of impressive bloodstains as well. We have discovered a couple of roses in among the assorted weeds and brambles, but not much else. The stuff we've cut and dug out is starting to form a fairly impressive pile on the grass. Teddy, naturally, has been 'helping', which largely seems to have involved sniffing around the ground we've uncovered and periodically relieving himself against the pile of detritus.

'Wow, look at this!' Ava exclaims when she gets back from work. 'I didn't realise you'd rope Dad in to help, though.'

'She didn't. I offered,' Dad explains.

'Of course you did. All I'm going to say is that I'll be very cross if you keel over and die in my garden. Come on, why don't you have a break and I'll put the kettle on. Have you eaten?'

'Not since breakfast,' I admit.

'I'll rustle something up. Can't have the workforce complaining that they're not being looked after, especially when one of them has an important *interview* lined up. I've told Ben, by the way, and he's happy to help. If you're still here when he gets home, you can make a plan with him.'

'Thanks. I'm going to need all the help I can get.'

'Oho. Someone suddenly sounds like she actually wants the job,' Ava laughs.

'It's not that,' I counter. 'I just don't want to make a tit of myself in there, that's all.'

'Yeah, right. What would you do if they offered it to you?'

'I'll cross that bridge if I come to it. I expect I'll be up against people who know everything about construction, so it won't be an issue.'

We decide to sit outside to eat our slightly bizarre lunch of bits and pieces that Ava has found in her kitchen. There are Scotch eggs, crisps, slices of ham and tomatoes. Teddy sits attentively next to Dad, obviously hoping for a titbit. I realise that I probably ought to tell Lee about the interview, so I fish my phone out of my pocket and unlock it. I'm just about to open WhatsApp when I see I have a new email. It's probably from Deborah Smythe with the address, but I decide to check anyway. Sure enough, the most recent email is from her, but the mail from Sharon White is also still in my inbox. I'd completely forgotten about it in all the excitement. I open it and read:

Dear Ella,

Thank you so much for your email. I was a little surprised to hear from you, especially considering the subject matter. I have listened to the recording, and I will be discussing it with the senior management at our next meeting, in two weeks. In the meantime, I have asked the IT department to revisit both laptops in search of corroborating evidence.

Your loyalty to the company and desire to do the right thing, in spite of your circumstances, is the mark of a truly exceptional person, and I sincerely wish you every success in the future.

Regards

Sharon White (HR Manager)

I don't understand. I never sent her an email.

'What's up?' Ava has obviously seen the confusion on my face.

'This doesn't make sense. It's an email from the HR department of my old company, thanking me for sending them the recording. But I never sent it, I'm sure I didn't.'

'Oh. Right, well, I'm going to take the plates in if everyone has finished?' She starts stacking the plates and bustles off with the leftovers.

I go to my sent items folder and, sure enough, there's an email from me to Sharon, and the timestamp indicates that I sent it yesterday afternoon. The attachment is the recording I made of Lee's confession. I feel like I'm going mad. I'm certain I didn't send it, but the evidence is there on the screen in front of me. As the penny suddenly drops, I plaster a smile on my face and turn to Dad.

'I'm just going to help Ava with the dishes,' I tell him. 'You enjoy the sunshine and I'll be out in a minute, OK?'

'Suits me,' he replies and tilts his head back, closing his eyes.

As I enter the house, I carefully shut the back door behind me, so he can't hear me murdering my sister.

'What the fuck have you done?' I hiss at her as soon as we're alone.

'What do you mean?' She's trying to look innocent, but I can see the guilt in her eyes.

'You sent the recording to Orchestra, didn't you?'

There's a long pause before she answers. I can sense her weighing up various options before, at last, she speaks.

'OK, yes. Look, I'm really sorry. I didn't mean to, but I was looking at the job ad and I couldn't help thinking about what Lee had done. It just made me fume, and before I knew it, I was hunting for the recording and attaching it to an email. I thought I was doing the right thing.'

'But that wasn't your decision to make! Jesus, Ava. Do you have any idea how much trouble Lee could get into?'

I can see the spark of defiance in her eyes. 'Listen to me,' she says firmly. 'I will apologise to you all afternoon if that's what it takes. I shouldn't have taken advantage of having your phone to myself, and I have been feeling bad about it, if that's any consolation. But I won't apologise for any trouble Lee might get into. What he did was probably illegal, certainly immoral, and he screwed over my favourite sister, who is far too nice to exact the revenge he deserves.'

'I'm your only sister, so don't try and butter me up with that.'

'It's the thought that counts. Seriously, Ella, if he gets away with this scot-free, then there really is no justice in the world.'

'It doesn't change the fact that you violated my privacy.'

'You read my diary when you were fourteen, remember?'

'You shouldn't have left it lying around!'

'You shouldn't have given me unsupervised access to a phone with incriminating evidence on it.'

'Oh, no. You don't get to play that card. We're supposed to be adults now, remember? You know, able to tell right from wrong?'

'It's not that simple, though, is it? Yes, I was wrong to go behind your back, but it's completely right that someone dobs Lee in.'

'But that wasn't your choice to make!'

'You've already said that and I've already apologised. Look, I really am sorry, OK? But it's done now. She's got the recording and we can't change that.'

'How did you even know where to send it?'

Ava does have the decency to blush a little. 'I, erm, had a little scan through your inbox and found her that way.'

'Bloody hell. You are a piece of work, you know that? And I don't mean that in a nice way. What else did you do, have a little mosey through my photos to see if there were any of Lee in the nude?'

'Are there?'

'Don't change the subject. This is every bit as bad as me reading your diary. In fact, it's worse, because you acted on what you found. At least I never told Reuben that you fantasised about him when you masturbated.'

She flushes scarlet. 'You said you'd only just opened the diary and hadn't seen anything!'

'I lied,' I smirk.

'Look, I know you're cross with me—'

'Do you think?' I interrupt. 'Don't worry, I'm still going to finish your garden. I just have to decide whether or not I'm going to chop you into small pieces and bury you in it when I'm done. Teddy would love it, digging up bits of you to eat. It would be like a treasure hunt for him.'

'You're disgusting, you know that?' she smiles. Despite my best intentions, I can't stay cross at her for long and I smile back.

'One piece of advice, though, if I may?' she asks.

'It'll be a long time before you earn back the right to give me advice.'

'Fine. You're welcome to ignore me, but if I were you, I'd probably delete the recording now, and the emails between you and the HR woman. Just in case.'

'What, just in case Lee is a dirty little snooper like you?'

'Something like that.'

She's got a point. I unlock my phone and carefully delete the evidence, before changing the passcode.

13

When I arrive at the address given for my interview, my first thought is that I've somehow got it wrong. As Dad said, Alwoodley is very upmarket and, instead of an office block like I expected, I'm actually standing in front of a pair of wrought-iron gates. Behind them is a large, detached house, with a huge SUV and some kind of sports car parked on the driveway. Only the small brass plaque on the wall next to the gate with 'Atkinson Construction' engraved on it gives the game away. Having spent hours going through it with Ben, my head is now full of house-building terms such as 'breaking ground', 'watertight', 'first fix' and 'second fix'. I know the difference between a chippy, a pipey and a sparky, and I'm probably as ready for this interview as I can be. That doesn't stop the nerves, though. I hope they aren't hand shakers, because mine are slick with perspiration.

I haven't said anything about the interview to Lee; on reflection, I realised he'd scoff at the very idea of me applying for a job in construction, plus we're not really speaking at the moment. We had a bit of a blow-up last night because I told him that I was applying for jobs in other cities, and he'd told me flatly there was no way he was prepared to move, and he wasn't prepared to be a weekend boyfriend either. I countered with the fact that I'd been a weekend girlfriend more often than not, what with him doing his induction and being on site with customers, and it kind of escalated from there.

I check my watch. Five minutes early, which I think is about perfect. I'm still riddled with doubts about making a fool of myself, but I give myself a mental shake and press the buzzer.

'Atkinson Construction, how may I help?' The disembodied voice comes from a small speaker above the button.

'Ella Mackenzie, I'm here for an interview at half past eleven,' I reply, hoping there isn't a hidden button I have to press to make myself heard, like on the walkie-talkies Ava and I used to play with when we were little.

'Of course, I'll just open the gate. Come to the front door and I'll let you in,' the voice replies. Completely silently, one of the wrought-iron gates begins to swing open, and I step through as soon as the gap is big enough. I silently curse my decision to wear stilettos, as my heels are sinking into the deep gravel, so the confident stride I was aiming for is more of an inelegant totter. I breathe a sigh of relief when I reach the safe ground of the steps up to the front door, which is being held open by a woman I guess must be in her early twenties.

'Come on in,' she says, stepping aside to let me enter. If the outside of the house was impressive, the inside is amazing. I'm in a large hallway with a polished wooden parquet floor. I can just see an opulent sitting room through a set of double doors on the right, and there are muted voices coming from behind a closed door on the left.

'I'm Abby, Mr Atkinson's daughter,' the woman explains. 'I

think they're on a conference call or something. Are you happy to wait in the sitting room? As soon as they open the door, I'll let them know you're here. Would you like a drink of anything?'

'A glass of water would be lovely, if it's not too much trouble.' The combination of my interview nerves and feeling like a fish out of water in these luxurious surroundings has made my mouth dry out completely.

She leads me through the double doors and indicates an enormous, leather sofa. 'If you want to settle yourself there, I'll bring it to you.'

OK, this is awkward. I've lowered myself into the sofa, but it's one of those really squishy ones that are brilliant if you want to stretch out and watch a film, but a total disaster if you're trying to sit up straight and look like a professional. I wriggle forwards so I'm sort of perched on the edge, but I can feel myself slowly sliding back into its leathery embrace.

'Here you go.' Abby returns with a crystal glass and I instantly regret asking for a drink. The glass looks like it's probably some ultra-exclusive make that costs a fortune. It would be just my luck for it to slip out of my sweaty hands and smash on the floor, although I've lost my battle with the sofa, so it would probably just fall on my lap, and the carpet on the floor is so thick, it would cushion the impact anyway. But, oh God, the sofa and carpet are probably allergic to water and would stain horribly. I hold the glass tightly in both hands, fully aware that it makes me look like a child. Abby settles herself on the sofa opposite and I get the impression she's about to start a conversation with me, but we never get that far.

'Sorry to keep you, Ella. Would you like to come through?' I can tell from the voice that the dark-haired woman who has just walked in is Deborah Smythe. She must be fifty if she's a day, but she's hiding it fairly well with beautiful clothes and just a little too much make-up. What's more interesting is that, for the briefest moment, Abby's face transforms into a mask of pure loathing. There's obviously some history there.

'Thank you,' I say to Deborah as I try to extricate myself from the sofa without spilling any water. 'It was nice to meet you,' I say to Abby as I start to follow Deborah towards the hallway.

The room Deborah leads me into is set up as an office, with two large desks and a seating area where a man that I'm guessing is Christopher Atkinson is waiting for us. He stands and holds out his hand as we enter, and I try to surreptitiously wipe mine on my skirt before offering it to him. He looks mid-fifties but, apart from a little thinning of the hair, he's in good shape. His eyes twinkle and he has a kind face, which helps to alleviate my nerves a little.

'Christopher Atkinson,' he says by way of introduction. 'It's a pleasure to meet you, Ella. Is it OK if I call you Ella?'

'Yes, please do,' I reply.

'Excellent. Please call me Christopher. Deborah you've already met, of course. Have a seat.' He indicates a chair which is, thankfully, much more upright than the sofa in the sitting room. He and Deborah take their places in the chairs facing me. There's a small table between us, on which I carefully place the glass of water.

'Before we start, it would probably be helpful if we told you a bit more about us and the opportunity,' Christopher begins. 'My late wife and I founded the company a little over twenty years ago, starting out with house renovations before moving into new builds. Deborah joined us three years ago, just before my wife passed away. Our philosophy is simple: we find plots that are too small for the big developers to be interested in and build on them, usually between fifteen and thirty houses on each plot. We currently have six plots in various stages of development, and the one we're recruiting for is in the south of England, in Kent. Do you know that part of the world at all?'

'I don't, I'm afraid.' That's a blow. I know I was spreading my search, but I don't want to go that far. That settles it. I won't be taking the job even if they offer it to me, which is unlikely. Shame really because Christopher seems nice and he sounds like he'd be a good boss. Still, it takes the pressure off, and I can feel my nerves settling down.

'The role can work in one of two ways,' Christopher is saying. 'If you're flexible and happy to move around the country, it can be a permanent position. We have a couple of project managers who have been with us for a number of years. However, that doesn't suit everyone, and the PM on our site in Oxfordshire is a case in point. He lives nearby and is only working for us as a contractor for that one development. We will be offering the role on a contract basis initially, to become permanent at the end of the project if both parties are happy. Do you have any questions?'

'Not at this stage,' I reply.

'Great. So, looking at your CV, your background is in computer software. What makes you think you would be suitable for this position?'

By the time they've finished grilling me, nearly an hour has passed, but I reckon I've acquitted myself pretty well. There was a stumbling point when they asked whether I had a CSCS card, and I had to admit I didn't know what one of those was (apparently, it's a certification that most companies require for people working on building sites), but it seems I can get a temporary card by passing a test, and that will tide me over until I qualify for the proper card. I've put Ben's teaching to good use and I think they were impressed by my level of knowledge. Deborah has been encouraging, with lots of smiles and open questions, but I'm not so sure about Christopher. He's been perfectly friendly, but I don't think I've done quite enough to win him over. We've discussed my availability, which is unsurprisingly very good, and we're now at the crunchy part where we talk about the pay. I'm pretty chilled; I just want to see how hard I can negotiate for this job that I'm sure they have as little intention of offering as I do of accepting.

'In terms of salary,' Deborah is saying, 'we would have to take into account your lack of experience, so we'd probably make an offer in the region of £30,000 per annum.'

'I'm sorry,' I smile at her. 'But I couldn't accept that. I was earning £45,000 in my previous position, so I'm looking for something close to that.'

'I understand,' she replies. 'Don't forget, however, that there are significant perks in this role that need to be taken into account. We include your accommodation, so you'll be saving on rent, plus there are bonuses for hitting relevant milestones on schedule.'

'Even still, I'd need thirty-eight as an absolute minimum, I'm afraid.'

'We won't be able to get that high. Thirty-five would be the most we could possibly offer, if we make an offer at all.'

Although it's a lot less than my salary at Orchestra, she's right that not having to pay out in rent, plus the bonuses, would leave me significantly better off, even at £35,000. I've squeezed an extra five grand out of her too, which I'm pretty pleased with. It gives me confidence that I'll be able to negotiate a decent rate when I'm doing this for real.

The interview wraps up fairly swiftly after that and, after

running the gauntlet of the gravel driveway, I head for the bus stop. On the way home, I send a quick message to Ava.

Interview went OK. I don't think they'll offer it to me as I don't have experience or a CSCS card (who knew?), and it's in Kent so I can't take it even if they did, but say thanks to Ben anyway.

The ticks go blue straight away, and her reply is almost instant.

What's wrong with Kent? They speak English there, don't they?

I start to type a reply and then delete it. She's not going to back down, so I might as well leave it. I know why she's so keen, though. She thinks it'll mean the end of my relationship with Lee and, given last night's argument, she's probably right. I'm not so worried about Lee, though, I'm more concerned about being so far away from Mum and Dad. Out of interest, I check the train times and I'm surprised to see that the journey from Leeds to the rather grandly named Ashford International station is only three and a half hours. That's nowhere near as bad as I thought it would be.

I'm not even home when the email arrives. Expecting it to be a 'thanks but no thanks', I merely glance at it, but then I realise that they're offering me the job and the £35,000 salary and my mouth drops open. I can't believe they actually think I could do this job. There's no way I could, is there? My mind is flip-flopping madly between emailing straight back to accept, and the more realistic probability that it would be pure madness and I'd be out on my ear by the end of the first week.

'You look smart. Been somewhere interesting?' Lee asks as I walk into the flat.

'I wasn't expecting to see you. I thought you had a meeting today?' I reply.

'It was cancelled so I thought I'd work from home. So, what's with the outfit?'

'I've been for an interview.'

'Really? You never mentioned anything.'

'Well, you know how it is. It's my professional life, so it's not really anything to do with you.' I know it's a low shot, but I can't resist it.

'What do you mean by that?' he demands. 'Oh, I get it. You're still sore about me not telling you I was thinking of moving to Harmony. You need to get over yourself, you really do. So, what's the job?'

'Project manager for a construction site.'

'What? You're having me on.'

'No. I'm completely serious.'

'But you don't know the first thing about construction! I bet they had a good laugh at your expense when they realised.'

'They offered me the job, actually.'

'Really? You're not going to take it, are you? It's totally not right for you, Els. Anyone can see that.'

'I haven't decided.' His total lack of support is pissing me off more than a little.

'Oh, come on. Stop winding me up.'

'I'm not winding you up. I've been offered the job and I'm thinking about whether to accept it.'

'Where is it?'

'Kent.'

'Now I know you're taking the piss. There's no way you're moving to Kent.'

'Why not?'

'Because... because you don't belong in fucking Kent, Ella!

Look. I'm having a bit of a stressful day here so I'm not really in the mood to play games with you. I'm very pleased that you got an interview, and I get that it's good for your ego to have an offer. But we both know you're not going to accept it, so stop pretending that you're considering it.'

And with that remark, my decision is made.

14

On the journey south, I try to work out when Lee became such an absolute arse, and I'm irritated to discover that my findings don't reflect particularly well on me. I think the reality is that he's always been like this but because I've broadly fitted in with his life the way he wants to live it until now, this side of him has been hidden. It's only when I stopped being 'compliant Ella' and started to challenge him that his shortcomings really came to the surface. I've had a lot of time to think about this, because Leeds to Ashford may be only three and a half hours by train, but it's much, much longer than that by car. I've been on the road for over five hours, and the satnav says I've still got an hour and a half to go.

Even after Lee's outburst convinced me to take the job, I was still plagued with doubts about whether it was the right decision. Ava and Dad kind of ganged up on me, alternating between encouraging remarks about this possibly being a whole new start for me, and dark warnings about not looking gift horses in the mouth. Deborah sounded delighted when I phoned and told her, and she's arranged for someone called Noah to meet me at the site, show me around and then take me to my accommodation.

I'll admit that I've been avoiding Lee a bit since accepting the job offer just under a month ago. He's been very snappy and irritable lately; I'm not sure that he's finding working at Harmony to be quite the dream ticket he first believed but, of course, I'm not very sympathetic about that, so we avoid the subject. I haven't told him that I've accepted this job; he seems to have assumed that I would comply with his wishes like I have in the past, and I couldn't be bothered to have another argument about it. Instead, I've been using the time when he's been at work to get my CSCS card and compile a list of everything I wanted to take with me. I quickly realised that my clothes alone were going to be more than I could cram into a couple of suitcases on the train, so I used some of my redundancy payment to buy a car earlier this week. It's nothing fancy, a second-hand Fiat 500 that's small enough not to make me feel anxious about manoeuvring it, but big enough (just) to get all my clobber in. I picked it up this morning, after waving Lee goodbye. He's going straight from work to his parents' and wanted me to come, but I managed to make an excuse about a party Ruth had invited me to. Even though it's a lie, and I haven't spoken to Ruth since that day in the coffee shop, I think he's secretly glad to have a bit of space. What he doesn't know yet is that he's about to have all the space in the world.

I did shed a few tears when I locked the front door behind me. They weren't heartbreak tears; I think Lee and I have definitely reached the end of the road. They were more like tears of frustration, that I'm going to have to rebuild my life from scratch at the age of thirty-two. The whole of the last five years suddenly seem like they've been a colossal waste of time.

In an ideal world, I'd have left the keys behind on the side in the kitchen, but the door has a security lock that you have to set from outside, so I've carefully fed them into our secure postbox on the ground floor. As I cross the Queen Elizabeth II bridge and see the sign welcoming me to Kent, a few more tears leak out. What if Lee is right, and I don't belong here? I certainly feel like I don't belong here. It's weird, really. Out of the window, I'm still looking at the same tarmac, sky, grass and stuff, but it feels different somehow. Alien.

Before long, the satnav is directing me onto the M20 and the last stage of my journey. Around thirty minutes more and I should be there. A lead weight of unease settles itself in the pit of my stomach and intensifies as the motorway signs count down the miles to Ashford. The voice of self-doubt in my head is saying, *What are you doing here, Ella? This has got to be one of the biggest mistakes you've ever made.* If it wasn't way too far to contemplate, I'd seriously be considering turning round and driving straight back home.

It takes me a while to find the site. The satnav dumps me in the general vicinity, but I have to drive up a few roads before I pick up signs directing site traffic for Atkinson Construction. The site itself, when I arrive, looks fairly typical of developments I've seen before. There are lots of large, shiny billboards advertising an 'exclusive development of four- and five-bedroom homes' with artists' impressions of the houses, and a promise that the show home will be open soon. There are also large flags featuring the Atkinson logo on poles either side of the site entrance. Even though it's only 4 p.m. on a Friday, the gates are padlocked, so I park the car, get out and peer through the gap to see if I can spot anyone.

'Are you Ella?' a voice behind me asks, making me jump. I turn to see a man dressed exactly as I would expect a builder to look, with a hi-vis vest over a short-sleeved top and trousers that are both covered with cement dust marks. Even his sturdy-looking boots are scuffed and faded. He's squinting a little in the bright sunlight, but I can see that his eyes are deep brown. His dark hair matches the stubble on his chin and, as my eyes drop to his torso, I can't help noticing the thickness of his arms. My stomach does a little flip, and I mentally tell myself off.

'That's me,' I reply. 'You must be Noah.'

'I am,' the man replies with a smile. 'I'm the site foreman. You're not from around here, if your accent is anything to go by.' He holds out his hand for me to shake and I'm not surprised to find that it's rough and his grip is strong.

'I'm sorry I'm late. I've driven down from Leeds, and the M25...'

'Don't sweat it. I'm on overtime, so you can take as long as you want.' He grins. 'In fact, if you wanted to go and explore for a couple of hours...'

'I think I've done enough driving for one day,' I smile back at him. The whiteness of his teeth is in sharp contrast to his sun-bronzed skin and there's a definite twinkle in his eye. If I didn't know better, I'd think he was flirting with me.

'Come on then, let's get you in,' he says, pulling a large bunch of keys from his pocket. 'The main gate key is this one.' He separates a key from the rest before handing them all to me. Although the padlock is probably the biggest one I've ever seen, the key turns easily and the lock pops open.

'I'll open the gate for you,' Noah tells me. 'Just drive through and follow the signs for the site office. I'll meet you there in a sec, OK?' I go to return the keys, but he holds up his hands. 'Those are yours. I've got my own set,' he explains.

The site office turns out to be a Portacabin about a hundred yards inside the gate. I pull up in one of the spaces marked outside it and Noah strolls up a few seconds later, as I'm pulling on the steel toe-capped boots I bought after completing my training. I yank my new hi-vis vest and hard hat out of the boot and turn to face him again. I feel slightly self-conscious wearing them, mainly because I've been hiding them at the bottom of my wardrobe for the last week, desperately hoping that Lee wouldn't spot them. I don't know why I was worried – he never looks in my wardrobe – but I'm still getting used to the idea of keeping secrets from him.

'So,' he says, eyeing me up and down. 'I'm not gonna lie, the boys and me were a bit concerned when they heard the latest victim, I mean project manager, was a woman. We don't get a lot of women in this industry. I'll warn you now that some of them are a bit old-fashioned in their views and don't think a building site is any place for a woman to be. You know how women used to be considered bad luck on ships?'

My anti-sexist tirade is choked off by curiosity.

'No, why?'

'Two reasons. The first was that sailors believed women made the sea gods angry, and they would send bad weather as punishment. I don't know if this is true or not, but my grandad told me that there was an incident way back where a ship went out with a load of female passengers, hit a terrible storm, and so the sailors decided to lob the women overboard to try to appease the gods.'

'Did it work?'

'Of course not! The women all drowned and the boat sank anyway. There was only a handful of survivors.'

'Oh. What was the second reason?'

'Simple, and probably more relevant here. Captains worried that women on ships would distract the sailors. A sailor who isn't paying full attention to what he's doing is a disaster waiting to happen, as is a builder.'

'You seem to know a lot about it.'

'Yeah, well, I come from seafaring stock. Anyway, the point is that some of the boys have similar views about women on building sites. I'm dealing with it, but you just need to be aware.'

'I think we need to get one thing clear from the start,' I tell him, coolly. 'I'm not going to put up with any sexist claptrap, OK? For a start, women can't be bad luck on building sites, otherwise Sarah Beeny would have been dead long ago.'

'Ah, but is she a real builder or just a TV personality?' Noah challenges.

'She looks pretty hands-on to me.'

'Maybe she's the exception that proves the rule,' he chuckles. 'Anyway, don't worry about it. I have it in hand. Maybe I shouldn't have said anything.'

'No, you definitely should, but you can tell "the boys" that they'd better keep their medieval opinions to themselves. Thinking of which, where is everyone?'

'It's POETS day today, so the site packed up at lunchtime. All building sites pretty much do.'

'POETS day?'

'You don't know?' He grins mischievously. 'It's a building site tradition. Every Friday is dedicated to a different poet, so we pack up at lunchtime and spend the afternoon reading that particular poet's work. We may work with our hands, but we're not an uncultured bunch.'

'Really?'

'No, of course not. It stands for Piss Off Early, Tomorrow's Saturday. I had you going, though, didn't I?'

'Very clever. Are you going to show me around, or just take the mickey for the rest of the afternoon? And why did you call me the latest victim when we first met?'

'Before I answer, can I ask you a couple of questions?'

'If you must.'

'How much experience have you really got with building sites?'

Damn. This isn't a question I want to deal with right now. I'd been kind of hoping to dazzle them all with my amazing project management before they found out I didn't know the first thing about construction.

'My brother-in-law is in the trade. I've worked with him on a few projects,' I bluster.

'Really?' He looks sceptical.

'Yes, really.'

'Forgive me for noticing, but all your gear is obviously brand new. There's not even a scuff on your boots. Do you buy new gear for every project? Is that a thing for you?' Despite trying desperately not to show it, I know I'm crimson with embarrassment. Of all the ways to be caught out.

'OK, fine,' I huff. 'I don't have a lot of experience on building sites, no. But I do have a proven track record in project management, and that's what I'm here to do.'

'Hey, no judgement from me. I didn't hire you, and you'll have enough to contend with once you get started on Monday. It just helps me to know what I'm dealing with. You might want to scuff your hat and boots up a bit, and I'd recommend jeans rather than the skirt you're wearing. If you go up a ladder in that, you'll be sure to attract an audience on the ground, just saying.'

'I wasn't planning on coming to work in a skirt. It's just more comfortable for driving, if you must know. Anyway, you still haven't explained why you referred to me as a victim.'

'No, I haven't. Here's a suggestion. Why don't I show you around, help you unload, and then I'll take you to the pub and fill you in? Don't worry, I'm not coming on to you, it's just that it's half past four on a Friday afternoon, and my brain is threatening to go on strike if I don't get a pint inside me soon.'

I study him. He is definitely attractive, in a rough and ready kind of way that I find refreshing in comparison to Lee, but his constant piss-taking and his descriptions of the general sexism I'm going to be launched into have wound me up. I'm also enormously irritated by the fact that he rumbled me so quickly. On the other hand, he hasn't been unkind, and I have a feeling I'm going to need all the allies I can get.

'You're on,' I tell him.

15

'What on earth is that?'

We're standing in the site office, which is much as you'd expect it to be. Directly in front of me, an ancient-looking computer sits on a battered, teak-effect desk. I glance at the grimy keyboard and make a note to get some antibacterial wipes. Behind the desk is a moth-eaten swivel chair that has definitely seen better days. There are a couple of dented, grey, metal filing cabinets against one wall, underneath one of those yearly planners that, if I'm deciphering it correctly, seems to be tracking everyone's holiday plans. An ancient photocopier and printer stand against the other wall. At the other end of the cabin sits an equally unloved kitchen area, with multiple ring stains on the worktop along with used mugs and dirty teaspoons. There's a microwave as well, and I dread to think what's growing in there. However, the article that's caught my attention is on the wall behind the desk. It's best described as a series of flipchart sheets taped together, with what look like dates across the top, and annotations like 'No. 4 Kitchen Units' in hand-drawn boxes underneath.

'That's the project plan. Your predecessor, Andy, drew it up. Surely you're familiar with those, at least?' Noah seems bemused.

I study it for a while. 'That's not a project plan. It's just a series of events. Where is the resource allocation? How do the various elements fit together? How could anyone work out the critical path from that?'

'I'll admit that I don't understand a lot of what you just said, but the resource bit is my job. Your job is to make sure that we have the right materials for the right houses at the right time.'

'Well, I'm never going to be able to work it out from that. I'll have to start again on Monday. I'll need to borrow you for most of the day, is that OK?'

'That will depend on what crops up, but I'll give you as much time as I can.'

'Please. This is just chaos. You and I need to put together a proper plan, with resources allocated so we can coordinate the work and the people. Otherwise I can't see how anything will get done.'

'Yes, boss,' he grins. 'Would you like to see the site now?'

'Go on then. Hopefully it's in better shape than the site office.'

'We're building two styles of property on this site,' he explains as we walk. '"The Eton" is a five-bed detached, and "The Windsor" is a four-bed semi. We're building eight Etons and twelve Windsors. The show homes are over there,' he points out the houses closest to the site entrance, 'and they're nearly done. We're on second fix with those. The rest, well, we'll figure it out on Monday.'

'How do you come up with the names?'

'What?'

'The house styles. Why "Windsor" and "Eton"?'

'It's aspirational, isn't it? We're not just selling houses, you know.'

'Aren't we?'

'God, no! We're selling a lifestyle, a dream. Punters want to believe that these houses are their ticket to the good life with a couple of matching BMWs on the driveway, perfect children and no worries, rather than what they actually are, which is more space to have the same old arguments about whose turn it is to take the bin out. It's all bollocks, but they lap it up.'

'I guess you haven't put your name down then?' I laugh.

'Not bloody likely. These are way out of my price bracket and I imagine that the sheen of buying "The Eton" will wear off pretty quickly once it's just "Number Fourteen, The Oaks", which is what the show home will be.'

We come to a halt and I do a slow turn, taking in everything around me. This is a totally alien landscape, with houses in various states of build. The ones nearest the gates look broadly complete but, at the far end, there are a couple which have only just started to rise from the ground. I'm incredibly intimidated by the prospect of project managing all of this, but also weirdly encouraged by the disaster of a project plan that I saw in the office.

'Seen enough?' Noah asks. 'Shall I show you your digs?'

'Yeah. Thanks.'

'OK. If you hop into your car and follow me, I'll lead you.'

We pull out of the site and I lock the gates behind us. As I follow him, I can't help speculating on what sort of house or flat a company like Atkinson Construction would provide. We seem to be heading away from the town, so I start to imagine a little cottage with a garden that I could maybe grow a few vegetables in. When he slows and turns into a drive next to a large sign with 'Belvedere Caravan Park' on it in faded letters, my enthusiasm is only slightly dented. OK, it's not the cottage I was imagining, but I've stayed in lots of static caravans on holiday growing up, and they were fine. It might still have a bit of garden, too. As we drive through the park, I'm encouraged. Most of the caravans here look well cared for, even if they aren't exactly modern. The one he pulls up outside, however, has definitely seen better days. The windows are filthy and there is some sort of moss growing around them. The outside step has obviously broken off at some point, and been replaced with an upended plastic crate, and the 'garden' is an overgrown patch of scrubland. Above the door, a peeling label announces that this is a 'Premier Deluxe'. It's a long time since this caravan has been anywhere near premier or deluxe, I suspect.

'This is you,' he announces, handing me another key. I can sense his discomfort, as he's shuffling from foot to foot.

The source of his disquiet becomes evident the moment I open the door and step inside. If the site office was off-putting, this is in a whole new league. Andy, whoever he is, obviously didn't believe in tidying up or cleaning. The caravan smells musty and there's an acrid undercurrent, which I have a nasty suspicion is coming from the kitchen area. A quick exploration leads me to a half-empty bottle of milk that has been left on the counter, presumably since Andy left. I stick my head into the filthy bathroom and a bedroom that has patently never seen a duster or vacuum cleaner and I can feel the tears bubbling up. This has to be the most stupid thing I've ever done. There's no way I can bring my stuff in here with the state that this caravan is in. I'll be smelling of God knows what for weeks. I swallow hard and try to think logically, but I'm exhausted from the long drive, and I just don't have the mental capacity to deal with this. Glancing in the bedroom again, I notice that there are no bedclothes on the bed, not that I'd dream of sleeping under them if there were. Thankfully, despite my exhaustion, I do manage to have an idea and pull out my phone. Telling Noah that I've just received a message I need to deal with, I step outside, open the browser and, within minutes, I've booked myself into the local Premier Inn for tonight.

'Do you want a hand unloading then?' Noah asks from the doorway, as I slip the phone back into my pocket.

'No, you're OK. I'll do it later.' For some reason, I don't want him to know that I've chickened out at the first hurdle. 'Let's go and get that drink, shall we? Where's the pub?'

'Not far, about half a mile or so. I'll give you a lift if you like, save you driving.'

I don't really like. I'm sure Noah's van is going to be absolutely filthy, like everything else around here, and I also don't want to give him the impression I'm dependent on him. He seems very keen to be helpful, but I don't know him well enough to trust his motives.

'I don't want to put you out,' I tell him.

'You aren't. I go straight past here on my way home, so it'll be no trouble to drop you. Come on.' He strides off before I have a chance to answer, so I reluctantly follow him, locking the static caravan behind me.

'Sorry about the mess,' he tells me as I pull open the passenger door. 'I clean it every weekend, but by Friday, it's usually looking a bit the worse for wear.'

After the caravan, the dusty interior of Noah's van doesn't bother me at all. He grabs the empty takeaway coffee cups that have accumulated in the passenger footwell and finds somewhere to store them in the back, before removing the aftermarket cover on the passenger seat to reveal pristine upholstery beneath. As soon as he starts the engine, the radio comes on at deafening volume, and he sings along to it lustily while he drives. He's actually got quite a nice singing voice, so I find I don't mind too much.

By the time we're settled in the pub with our drinks, my curiosity is almost at breaking point.

'Come on then, tell me the victim story,' I demand.

'Have you met Deborah?' he replies.

'Are you going to deflect me with a question every time I come back to this?'

'No. It's relevant, I promise.'

'Yes, she was one of the people who interviewed me. Her and the CEO, Christopher Atkinson.'

'I don't know him. What did you make of her?'

I smell a trap, so I consider my words carefully. 'She seemed nice enough. Why?' I reply eventually.

'OK, so you probably know that she's in charge of this site, not Chris. Round here, she's known as the Evil Bitch Queen, or EBQ for short. You'll struggle to find anyone who has a good word to say about her.'

'Oh. Tell me more.'

'I'm going to make some assumptions, based on what Andy told me just before he left. She'll have screwed you down to the lowest salary she thought she could get away with, but promised you milestone bonuses to compensate. She'll also have made a big deal about your so-called free accommodation, otherwise known as the caravan of shit. Am I warm?'

'Obviously, I can't share the precise details of my contract with you, but you're not a million miles out,' I tell him. This sounds ominous.

'On top of that, everything that we do has to be approved by her, and she's negotiated a "preferential contract" with a firm in Leeds, so everything has to be ordered from them.'

'Everything? Bricks, cement, windows...?'

'Yup, it all comes from Leeds. And they're the most unreliable bunch of fuckers you'll ever come across.' He claps his hand over his mouth as soon as he realises what he's said. 'I'm really sorry,' he tells me, looking mortified.

'So you fucking should be,' I smile. 'Swearing at a lady like that.'

He laughs. 'You're OK, you know that? Anyway, the number of lorries that have "broken down", or drivers that have "gone off sick" unexpectedly has to be seen to be believed. So, the way it works in reality is this. You'll do all your clever project planning and lining up of resources and all that other stuff you talked about before, but you'll still miss every single milestone because the materials we need to actually build the bloody houses don't turn up half the time. When we do get a delivery, it's quite often the wrong stuff anyway, so we have to get it collected and reorder, which causes more delays. I know he hasn't impressed you so far, but Andy was a good guy who knew his way around a building site. He just couldn't take any more of Deborah, and that's why he left. I don't want to be rude, but don't you think it's odd that you got the job when you don't know anything about it?'

My hackles rise again, just when I was beginning to trust him and let my guard down. 'What do you mean?' I ask.

'I know for a fact that they advertised both locally and up north for a new project manager. I'd also happily bet you twenty quid that nobody applied. Everyone round here knows how toxic she is, and none of them would touch her project with a barge pole, and I expect it's the same up there. I hate to break it to you, but you were probably the only applicant.'

'So why are you working for her?'

'Because I'm on a daily rate, same as pretty much everyone else on site, so, although it's bloody annoying when things don't turn up, I don't end up out of pocket. Also, I don't have to deal with her directly because that's your job. And finally, I'm not living in the caravan of shit. Even still, if she takes on another site round here, none of us would sign up for it unless we were on the breadline. You're looking a bit shell-shocked. Do you want another drink?'

'No, I'd better not.'

'Suit yourself. Come on then, let's get you back.'

After he's dropped me back at the caravan park, I wait until his van is well out of sight before jumping into my car. It's clear to me that I've been played for an absolute fool and, as soon as I've had a decent night's sleep, I'll be heading back up north. This was going to be hard enough, but the pigsty caravan and the fact that I've obviously been set up to fail is enough to convince me that Atkinson Construction will have to find themselves a new project manager, because this one is quitting.

16

Having been absolutely certain that I'd be heading north as soon as I woke up, things look a little different this morning. When I'd got to the hotel last night, I'd checked my phone and seen a message from Lee. From the timestamp, he'd sent it at lunchtime, but I was obviously driving then.

Hi Els, just been contacted by the bank because the landlord tried to take the rent payment and there wasn't enough in my account to cover it. Your half doesn't seem to have come in. Can you sort it ASAP before it becomes a problem?

I'd read it a couple of times before carefully typing out my reply.

Hi Lee. I've moved out, so won't be paying my half any more.

I would estimate that fewer than ten seconds elapsed between me sending the message and my phone ringing.

'What the fuck, Ella? What do you mean "you've moved out"?' he'd started.

'Exactly what it says. I took the construction job down south and that's where I am now.'

'Don't be ridiculous. I've had a stressful day and I'm not in the mood.'

'I'm serious.'

'Oh, come on. You won't last five minutes on a building site and you know it. Is this some point you're trying to make because I really don't get it. Is it some kind of cry for help? You're not having a breakdown or something, are you?'

'What on earth makes you think I'm having a breakdown?'

'Well, you have let yourself go a bit. I've tried to be patient, because of your job and everything, but you've got to admit you've become a little...' he pauses to search for the word, '... unkempt lately. Are you depressed?'

That was the final straw. 'I'm not depressed, thank you, and I think I'll be just fine on a building site,' I'd told him sweetly, 'but thanks for your words of encouragement. I'll treasure them. And, just in case you were in any doubt, you and I are over, OK?'

'I'm sorry?' He evidently hadn't seen that one coming, and I'd felt a momentary pang of guilt. Five years is five years, after all, and he wasn't toxic for all of them. I'd had to steel myself to carry on.

'It's over, Lee. You've changed and I don't like the selfish person you've become.'

'*I'm* selfish?' he'd practically howled. '*I'm* not the one who's just done a midnight flit from their financial commitments, leaving me seriously in the shit.'

'No. You're the one who did a midnight flit from your employer, lost me the job I loved and then crowed about how clever you were.'

'You'll regret this. Don't expect me to be waiting for you when it all goes tits up and you want to come crawling back,' he'd snarled, before hanging up.

I'd sat there staring at the phone for quite a while, trying to work out how I felt. Part of me was sad that the final death knell of our relationship had just sounded, and I did shed a few tears, but his total conviction that I couldn't do it had stirred up something stubborn in me. The idea of Dad and Ava's inevitable disappointment when I turned up, having walked out of the job before I even started, also gave me pause for thought, as did the fact that I've blown a substantial amount of my redundancy payout on the car, so I can't survive much longer without work. I have absolutely no idea how I'm going to solve the Deborah problem, but there's a bloody-minded part of me that is determined to give it my best shot. If I run away now with my tail between my legs, she's beaten me before the game has even started.

After breakfast, I head back to the caravan park. My plan is to take a serious look at the caravan of shit and make a list of everything I need to make it habitable. On the way, I stop at a supermarket and pick up some basic cleaning supplies, including several bottles of bleach, fabric freshener and antibacterial spray, along with a couple of pairs of rubber gloves. I'm dressed in my oldest, tattiest clothes so it won't hurt to throw them away if I can't get the smell out of them. As soon as I get there, I open all the windows as wide as I can to get some fresh air going through. The rancid milk is the first item that goes into a black bin liner, closely followed by a host of other out-of-date foodstuffs I find in the kitchen cupboard and fridge. I empty a whole bottle of bleach into the toilet and leave it to soak. I take the grimy net curtains and curtains down and stuff them into bags. There's no washing machine in the caravan, so I trudge over to the site office to see if there are washing machines there, only to find that they're both out of order. Someone has helpfully left a postcard advertising a laundrette in the town, so I take a photo of it on my phone.

When I get back to the caravan and sniff, things seem a little better, but there's still a residual pong coming from somewhere. I find an ancient vacuum cleaner and mop in a cupboard, and set about sprinkling the threadbare carpet in the living area with freshener, before mopping the kitchen and bathroom floors thoroughly. The hot tap in the bathroom sink looks like it's been dripping for a while, as it's grown an impressive limescale stalactite, and there is a corresponding stain in the basin underneath it. I add limescale remover to my ever-growing shopping list.

By lunchtime, there are concrete signs of improvement. I've cleaned the fridge thoroughly, and the bleach has made a surprising difference to the toilet, to the extent that I was actually able to use it without worrying what I might pick up from it. Sadly, the same can't be said for the oven, which is going to need some industrial-strength cleaner. It looks like something exploded in there and then got heat-welded to the inside. The glass door is so badly covered in black residue that I can't see through it at all. On the plus side, I've treated all the soft furnishings with lavish amounts of fabric freshener and run the asthmatic vacuum cleaner over all the carpets, so the place is now smelling sufficiently fresh that I reckon I can safely bring my stuff in from the car.

As I'm hanging some clothes in the wardrobe, my eye is drawn to the bed, and I realise I have another major hurdle to overcome. There is no way I am going to be able sleep on that mattress. I don't know how old it is, but Andy or one of the previous occupants of the caravan must have been quite a sweaty person, because there are very distinctive human-shaped dark stains on one side. I'm revolted and fascinated at the same time. In a funny way, it reminds me of the shroud of Turin, only without the historical and religious significance. Keeping well away from the stains, I tentatively perch on the mattress, only to have my fears confirmed as it sags hopelessly.

As soon as I've finished unloading the car, I grab the mattress and pull as hard as I can to try to get it upright, so I can drag it out of the caravan. I'm not sure how I'm going to dispose of it, but I need it out of here. It's not particularly heavy, but it is unwieldy and, at one point, I end up with my nose practically pressed against one of the darker stains. I try as hard as I can to breathe through my mouth, but I can't help inhaling some of the smell, and it makes me gag. How anyone could have slept on this is a mystery.

'Hello?' I hear Noah's voice call from the doorway. 'Is anyone in?'

'In here!' I call.

'Where are you going with that?' he asks as soon as he's clapped eyes on me struggling with the mattress.

'I'm getting rid of it.'

'Right.' He sounds uncertain. 'Well, let me help you with it, at least.' I feel the mattress go light as he effortlessly takes it off me and drags it out of the door.

'Thank you,' I tell him. 'I'm not being funny, but what are you doing here?'

'I was passing,' he replies. 'I thought I'd check in to see how you were in case the caravan of shit had depressed you so much you'd decided to bugger off back north.'

I smile at him guiltily. He has no idea how close to the truth that statement is.

'No. I'm still here, as you can see.'

He sticks his head back in the door. 'Wow,' he observes. 'You must have been working hard. I don't think I've ever seen it looking so clean before.'

'Thank you. There's a long way to go, though. I need a new mattress, for starters, and I don't know if a cleaner has been invented yet that's going to put a dent in the nuclear wasteland that's the inside of the oven.'

Noah is looking at my car with a quizzical expression. 'What?' I ask him.

'I was just wondering how you planned to get the mattress in there. I assume you're taking it to the tip?'

'I hadn't really got that far,' I admit. 'I just wanted it out. I was going to figure out the next steps later.'

'I tell you what. Why don't we load it into my van, take it to the site and throw it in the skip, and then I'll give you a lift to a discount bedding store I know. They're one of those "pile it high, sell it cheap" places and they always have loads of mattresses and stuff like that in stock.'

'Are we allowed to do that?'

'What, go to a discount store?'

'No, dump the mattress in the site skip.'

'It's Atkinson Construction's rubbish, isn't it? Plus, I won't tell if you don't.'

'Are you sure you don't mind? I feel like I've already put you out quite a lot, and I haven't even been here for twenty-four hours.'

'Of course I don't mind. I wouldn't have offered if I did, would I?'

'In that case, can I ask another cheeky favour?'

'Go on.'

I show him the picture on my phone. 'Can we go via this place so I can drop off the curtains and nets?'

He glances at the screen. 'You don't want to go there. I know a much better one, run by a Nepalese family. If you're lucky, they'll turn them around for you in an hour or two.'

As we head for the site, the manky mattress safely stowed in the back of Noah's van, I can sense him pondering something, and I wonder if he's changed his mind about helping me.

'What's up?' I ask. 'If this is all too much aggro for you, you can just say. I won't be offended.'

'It's not that. I was just wondering where you slept last night. You obviously didn't stay in the caravan of shit.'

'You're right,' I admit. 'I checked myself into the Premier Inn. I couldn't face the caravan, with the state it was in.'

'I hope you're going to charge it to expenses.'

'I'm not sure I can. I haven't officially started yet.'

'Nonsense!' he exclaims. 'They knew you were coming down yesterday, so it's only reasonable that you should expect to be able to sleep in the accommodation. If you had to stay in a hotel because it was so disgusting, that's down to them and they should pay. Same with all the cleaning stuff I guess you must have bought. I'd charge the bastards for every single thing.'

I glance across at him, surprised by the strength of his feelings on the subject.

'You really hate Deborah, don't you?' I ask him.

'Honestly? I want nothing more than for someone to hand that woman her arse on a plate. I don't know if that will be you or not, but you're the only horse I've got in this race at the moment, so I'm backing you.'

I sit there for a while in silence, digesting what he's said. If I look hard, I think there might be hint of a compliment lurking in there, but I can't be sure.

17

My plan to get to work early and settle in before everyone else arrives backfires massively as, when I pull up outside the site office at eight, the place is already a hive of activity. There are people everywhere, climbing ladders, walking around the scaffolding, and there's a backing track of dozens of radios, all of which sound like they're tuned to different stations. Partly blocking the entrance to the site is a massive articulated lorry with a load of bricks, which the crane operator at the back is offloading onto the ground, and forklift drivers are then ferrying to one of the houses about halfway down.

'Afternoon,' Noah greets me with a smile as I enter the office. He's studying the wallchart with the holidays on it and adding a few annotations.

'What time do you guys normally start?' I ask him. 'I thought I was early.'

'I usually unlock the site at seven, and the guys start arriving shortly after that. The first deliveries start arriving at around eight. You're just in time for the weekly team meeting. Did you want to lead that, or would you rather I did it this time?'

Noah has definitely taken me under his wing, and I'm both grateful and a little annoyed by it. Grateful, because I now have a habitable caravan with clean curtains and bedding that isn't likely to give me a skin disease, but annoyed because all his interventions just keep reminding me how hopelessly out of my depth I am here. I've taken his advice and put on a pair of jeans this morning, but I'm acutely aware of the steel toe-capped boots. I have been wearing them this weekend to try to break them in a bit and stop them looking so new, but they still feel like bags of cement strapped to my feet, and I've had a slightly hairy journey from the caravan park as they're slightly too wide for the dainty pedals in the Fiat, so I accidentally caught the side of the brake a couple of times when changing gear.

'Why don't you run it today, and I'll take the opportunity to observe and get a feel for how things work,' I tell him, settling myself behind the desk and turning on the computer. After I finished cleaning the caravan yesterday, I snuck down here with the leftover products and had a bit of a blitz in here as well, not that Noah seems to have noticed. The keyboard is less of a health hazard, and I also cleared up the kitchen area. The computer was password protected, but I laughed to myself when I typed in the string of letters written on the post-it note stuck to the bottom of the screen and found that I was in. Cyber security was obviously not Andy's bag. I wasn't surprised, when I tested it, to find that Orchestra had cancelled my subscription to the online project-planning software I'm used to, so I set up a new subscription for myself. It's not expensive, and it will make my life loads easier. I've already filled in the bare bones of a plan, which I'm hoping to flesh out with Noah once the meeting is over.

After a few minutes, the office door opens and a bearded man that I reckon is in his fifties walks in, carrying his hard hat.

'Morning, Michael,' he says to Noah, completely ignoring me.

'John, this is Ella,' Noah tells him. 'She's our new project manager. Ella, this is John, who heads up the chippies.'

John makes no attempt to hide his disdain as he looks me up and down, before acknowledging me with a grunt.

'Don't take this the wrong way, darlin',' he tells me, 'but a building site is no place for a bird.'

I spot Noah shooting me a knowing look but, before I can open my mouth and tell John exactly what I think of his attitude, the door bangs open again and we're joined by the rest of the team. Noah introduces me, but the names and roles quickly blur into one another. I'm going to have to ask him to draw me an organisation chart so I can learn who everyone is, I realise. Thankfully, they all seem friendly enough, unlike John, who scowls every time his eyes meet mine. What's interesting is that they all refer to Noah as Michael; I'd love to find out the story behind that.

'Right, guys. Usual format. I'll go round each of the trades and get an update. John, why don't you go first?'

'Usual fucking disaster,' John growls. 'The roof trusses for plot eight came on Friday, but they're completely the wrong size and they're not the attic-style ones we need. They'd probably be OK if you were putting a roof on a bloody dolls' house, but they're fuck-all use to us. We'll have to put in a new order, which will cost us another week at least.'

'Do we know why they were too short?' I ask. 'Have we checked the original order?'

'What are you suggesting?' John demands.

'Nothing,' I say as soothingly as I can. 'But if the mistake is on their end, can't we put pressure on the supplier to get the replacement trusses to us faster than that?'

'Hah. Good luck with that one, darlin',' he harrumphs, and I realise that I may have been here for less than half an hour, but he's already written me off. Great.

The rest of the meeting has a similar tone; the wrong items have been sent or, more often than not, items just haven't arrived at all. After turning Andy's gibberish into a coherent project plan, I'm going to have to think of a way to tackle the supplier, otherwise Noah's predictions about me failing to hit a single milestone are definitely going to come true.

'Right. Let me show you what I've done,' I say to Noah once the meeting is over and he's pulled up a chair next to me. 'The top level of the plan is each plot. I think I've managed to match up the plot numbers with the type of house, but if you can just check it, that would be great. The next level down are the stages – foundation, superstructure and so on. So, what I'd like us to do is fill in the details below that, try to get some names assigned and put together a general picture of the overall flow of the project and the critical path. Once that's done, I should be able to go through the paperwork I found in the filing cabinet and work out what orders need to be placed when.'

'When were you in the filing cabinet?' he asks, and I blush a little as I realise my mistake.

'Umm, I had a bit of free time yesterday,' I admit.

'I thought as much. This office has never looked so clean. You need to get out more, you know that? You can't be coming in to work on a Sunday. The boys will never let you live it down. You know they'll have a nickname for you before the week is out, don't you?'

'I was going to ask about that. Why do they call you Michael?'

'John likes to come up with nicknames for people, but the references are always a bit obscure. So, for me, he took inspiration from the story of Noah, famous in the Bible for predicting the great flood and building an Ark.'

'I know the story. I'm pretty sure there aren't any Michaels in it.'

'No, but it means Noah was the original weather forecaster, wasn't he? So that extrapolates to Michael Fish, the weather forecaster who was equally famous for failing to predict the great storm of 1987. Most of us either hadn't been born or were tiny, so he had to explain it. Anyway, that's how I became Michael.'

'That's a bit convoluted.'

'That's how he likes them and, to be honest, I'm happier being named after Michael Fish than Helen Young. He also picks things that remind him of his youth. So, if he found out you were sneaking into the office on a Sunday, you'd probably end up with a name like Eleanor.'

'Do I want to know why?'

'Eleanor Rigby from the Beatles song – "All the lonely people…" That's probably a bit obvious for him, but it would be something like that.'

'I doubt he'll be making up any nicknames for me. He obviously hates me.'

'Oh, don't worry about him. He growls at everyone until he knows them. He's a dinosaur but he knows his stuff, and his team will do anything for him.'

'Hm. He'd better not make a habit of referring to me as a "bird", otherwise we will have a major falling-out.'

Noah laughs. 'I think I'll leave that little battle to you. Shall we fill this in then?'

By lunchtime, we've got a pretty comprehensive-looking plan on the screen. We've taken the least developed houses of each style and filled in all the blanks, and then copied that up the chain, deleting the stages that have already been done. The hardest part was figuring out the dependencies, both in terms of tasks and people, but those are all in, and I get the impression Noah is actually quite impressed.

'You've got to admit, it's a lot better than whatever that was,' I tell him, indicating Andy's panel of random scribbles. 'We've also shaved a month off, which isn't too shabby.'

Noah sits and stares at it for a while, chewing his bottom lip as he does so. Every so often, he scrolls to look at a different section, or opens up a task to look at the subtasks underneath it. I feel a little like a schoolgirl, watching while the teacher marks my homework.

'It's good,' he professes at last. 'I like it. There's just one thing.'

'What?'

'It doesn't take the weather into account. If we get torrential rain, for example, that will really set us back. What happens to all of this then? You'll be completely out of whack.'

I smile. 'Just for fun, let's say we lose a week due to bad weather somewhere. Pick a week.'

'That one.' He points at the screen.

'OK, so that would mean that this task here would be pushed out, yes?'

'That's right.'

I make the adjustment on the screen, and Noah watches in amazement as all the tasks underneath it realign themselves automatically to the new schedule.

'That's bloody genius!' he declares.

'Thank you. There's just one other change we need to make to get the best out of this.'

'What's that?'

'Your weekly meetings. We need to have them daily. If there are any issues like the ones that were raised this morning, I can't wait until the next Monday meeting to hear about them.'

He looks dubious. 'I'm not sure the lads will like that.'

'It only needs to be ten minutes or so. If I find that they aren't productive, I'll rethink, but I'd like to try it, please.'

'You're the boss.'

After he leaves, I take a while to go through the plan again. Noah's affirmation has really buoyed me up, and I decide to celebrate by retrieving my ham and cheese sandwich from the (newly cleaned) fridge. I'm halfway through when the door opens and a young lad comes into the office.

'Are you Ella?' he asks.

'That's me.'

'Umm. John asked me to come and get you. He wants to show you something.'

'Can it wait until I've finished this?'

'He said it was urgent, sorry.'

I set my half-eaten sandwich aside with a sigh and, grabbing my new hard hat, follow the lad outside. He leads me to the house that I now know is plot eight, one of the 'Eton' range, looks up and lets out a piercing whistle. Moments later, John's head appears over the top layer of scaffolding.

'Ah, there you are,' he calls. 'I need you to come up here so I can explain the problem with the roof trusses properly. Nipper will show you the way.'

I look up at him and my first thought is, *You have got to be bloody kidding me.* If there is one thing I really, really don't do, ladders would be it. I had enough trouble with the stepladder I had to use to reach the tops of the walls when I was helping Ava and Ben decorate their house, and that was only a few steps high. I'm between a rock and a hard place, though, particularly as I'm aware that pretty much everyone working on the house is watching me. If I refuse to go up, I'll never gain their respect. However, if I do actually make it to the top, I'll probably be a gibbering wreck and incapable of responding sensibly to whatever John has to say.

Fuck it. There's only one way out of this. I grab the ladder, place my foot on the bottom rung and start to climb. It only takes a few rungs before my legs start turning to jelly, and it takes all my concentration to focus on the first layer of scaffolding and not look down. After what seems like an age, I reach the first level and step gratefully onto the scaffolding boards. When I look down, my breath catches in my throat. I know I'm only one storey up, but the sensation is totally different when you're standing on a scaffolding frame as opposed to looking out of a bedroom window.

'What the hell do you think you're doing?' I hear Noah bellowing below, and it takes me a moment to realise he's shouting at me.

'Sorry?'

'You heard me. What do you think you're doing up there?' He looks genuinely angry, but I have no idea why.

'John wants to show me the problem with the trusses,' I call back.

'Does he hell. Get back down here right now and, for God's sake, be careful.'

Going back down the ladder is even more difficult than climbing, because I have to look down to make sure I'm locating my feet in the rungs properly. By the time I reach the ground, I'm shaking and it has nothing to do with the thunderous look on Noah's face.

'Don't you *ever* pull a stunt like that again,' he practically bellows. 'Are you ladder trained?'

'There was some stuff about ladders in my health and safety training.'

'It probably mentioned forklift trucks, too, but there's no way you're helping yourself to one of those either. If health and safety had turned up and seen you, they'd have shut us down so fast, we wouldn't even have had time to turn the machinery off.'

'I didn't do it for fun,' I retort. 'John sent someone to fetch me, and he told me he needed to show me something. I thought I was doing the right thing!'

'Yeah, well, you weren't. And as for John, I'm going to talk to him now.' He turns away from me and practically runs up the ladder. After a moment or two, feeling everyone's eyes still on me, I beat a hasty retreat to the office, angry tears of humiliation already burning my cheeks.

18

'Right, I think we can safely assume John knows he did the wrong thing,' Noah informs me as he stomps into the site office, banging the door behind him. 'Are you OK?'

'Of course I'm not OK!' I exclaim. 'You made me feel like a complete idiot in front of pretty much everyone. How was I supposed to know I needed to be ladder trained? I don't even like bloody ladders, but I knew John would never respect me if I didn't go up there, and then you arrived and started bellowing at me like I was a naughty toddler, as if I wasn't scared enough already.'

'I'm sorry. I knew John would try something like this to see what you were made of, and it was obvious, watching you climb, that you weren't comfortable. It was the only way I could think of to save you from having to go all the way to the top without the lads thinking I was giving you special treatment.'

'If that's you saving my bacon, I can do without it, thanks.'

'Look, I know it doesn't feel like it now, but it's actually worked out for the best. The lads all saw you climbing, and they respect you for that. For all they know, you would have gone all the way to the top if I hadn't come over all heavy-handed with the health and safety stuff. You've gone up a great deal in their estimation, honestly. Having said that, please don't do it again until you're properly trained.' He smiles.

'I'd happily never go up a ladder again in my life.'

'It kind of comes with the territory, being on a building site, so I can't guarantee you'll never have to do it. It does get easier with practice, though, but there is an online course you must do to keep the health and safety people off our backs. If it's any consolation, the lad who came to fetch you was terrified of heights when he first started, but you'd never know it now.'

He can obviously see the scepticism on my face because he laughs. 'We'll build you up slowly,' he assures me, before turning on his heel and disappearing back outside.

I'm reflecting on what he said as I dig out the order for the roof trusses and compare it to the delivery note. I'm surprised to see that they both match, which is bad news because it means I'm going to have to find John again and get him to explain to me what the differences are between the order and what actually arrived. Reluctantly, I grab my hard hat and head back towards the scene of my earlier humiliation.

'Can I help you, love?' one of the workmen asks as I approach the house.

'I'm looking for John. Is he still here?' I'd love to tell him that I'm not his 'love', but I don't have the energy for another fight today.

'We've got a few Johns on site. Which one are you after?'

'Bearded John, the guy in charge of the chippies,' I tell him, pleased to have used the correct terminology at least.

'Ah. He's gone up to the show home. Apparently, there's a problem with the skirting boards.'

Thanking him, I head up towards the show home, my relief

that skirting boards won't need me to do anything with ladders tempered by the fact that Noah has obviously bawled John out on my behalf, which will probably make him hate me even more.

'John, can I borrow you for five minutes when you're free?' I ask when I locate him in the living room of the show home. This is the first time I've been in here, and it really does look pretty much complete.

To be fair to him, he does look a little wary as he gives his final instructions to the team fitting the skirting boards and follows me into the kitchen.

'Look, it was just a bit of fun, OK? A little initiation, to see what you were made of,' he begins defensively as soon as we're out of earshot.

'It's not about that,' I tell him. 'I need you to explain the roof truss problem to me before I contact the suppliers. I've cross-checked the order against the delivery note and they match.' I spread the two documents out on the counter for him to examine.

'I'll show you. Come with me.'

'There aren't going to be any ladders involved, are there? I've been shouted at enough for one day,' I tell him as we set off down towards the other end of the site.

'No ladders, I promise.' I'm surprised to see the faintest glimpse of a smile play across his lips.

After a couple of minutes, we come to the offending stack of roof supports, which look completely normal to me. They're triangular, with supporting beams inside them in a kind of W shape.

'These are supposed to be for the Eton,' John tells me. 'You'll need to look at the plans to see the full picture, but I can point out enough to get you started. The top floor of the Eton has two bedrooms and a toilet in the roof space, with dormer windows, like the show home. OK?'

'Right.'

'Good, now look at these trusses here. These are what we call standard fink trusses. If we put these on, four hundred millimetres apart like we're supposed to, the supports would completely fill the space where the bedrooms would be. Do you see?'

'I get it,' I tell him.

'So, what is on the order form are attic trusses, which have the supports right at the edges so we can put living space in the middle. That's not these. These are, to put it bluntly, fucking useless.'

'You also mentioned something about them being the wrong size?' I'm trying to sound as conciliatory as I can. He's actually being quite helpful, and I'm keen to make the most of our truce, in case it's temporary. He pulls a tape measure out of the tool belt around his waist and runs it across the bottom of one of the trusses.

'Come and tell me what this says,' he tells me.

'Three hundred and fifty centimetres,' I read off.

'Exactly. Now look at the order form.' I spread the paper out again. 'Four hundred and twenty-five.' He points out the relevant line on the form. 'Clear as fucking day. They're almost metre too short.'

'And this happens a lot, would you say?'

'Pretty much every delivery. It used to drive Andy spare. He tried to persuade the Bitch Queen to find another supplier, or let him use local suppliers, but she wasn't having any of it.'

'I see. Thank you, John. I'd better go and see what I can do about this.'

He smiles again. 'Don't take this the wrong way, darlin', but I'm not sure what you're going to be able to do that Andy couldn't.'

As with the workman earlier, I'd love to tell him that I'm not his 'darlin'' and cut him off at the knees, but something tells me that's a battle for another day. He's being civil, which is a big improvement on a few hours ago, so I swallow my irritation with difficulty and head back to the site office. I'll get him later, I promise myself.

* * *

'Williamsons building supplies, Ross speaking. How may I help you?' The voice on the other end of the phone sounds bored, and I haven't even started speaking yet. This doesn't bode well.

'Hi, Ross, this is Ella Mackenzie. I'm the new project manager at the Atkinson Construction site in Ashford. I need to talk to someone about the roof trusses that were delivered on Friday last week.' I'm trying to sound authoritative, in the hope that he will start to show a bit more interest.

'You can talk to me,' Ross tells me disinterestedly. 'What's up?' So much for that, then.

'Two things. They're the wrong type and the wrong size. We ordered attic trusses 425 centimetres wide, and you've delivered fink trusses 75 centimetres shorter than that.'

'I see. And what would you like me to do about it?'

'I'd like you to collect these ones, refund me, and deliver what we ordered as a matter of priority.'

There's a brief pause before the voice comes back. 'You said you were new, right?'

'Yes,' I reply, unsure what that has to do with anything.

'OK, that explains it. Listen, I can't do anything about the trusses you have. You accepted delivery so they're yours now. Here's what I'm going to do for you. You tell me what trusses you think you should have had, I'll re-take the order and make a note to the factory to ask them to prioritise, and we'll hopefully get them to you in a week or two. How does that sound?'

'That's not good enough, Ross. I've got clear evidence of what we ordered, both on the order form and the delivery note. The mix-up is definitely at your end, so I'd like you to get the new trusses here this week, and collect the old ones at the same time. It's not our fault they're the wrong size, so you need to take them back and refund us.'

'No can do,' Ross replies, and I get the impression that he's actually starting to enjoy himself. 'We can't just magic these things out of thin air, I'm afraid. They take time to make and, now I come to think about it, you'll have to submit all the details again, just to make sure there aren't any more problems.'

'What do you mean?' I'm genuinely irritated now. 'Look, Ross. We're building eight identical houses in one style and twelve in another. You must already have the specs somewhere because you've delivered the correct materials at least once.'

'Yeah, but if you're saying we got it wrong, and I think that is what you're saying, isn't it?'

'Yes.'

'Well, we need to be absolutely sure that doesn't happen again. So you need to resubmit all the dimensions and specs. We will need to re-enter the specs into the system and get you to verify they're correct before we can even think about going to production.'

'And how long will that take?' I ask, exasperated now.

'Three weeks, minimum.'

'Ross, I don't have three weeks! I needed these trusses on Friday last week. There must be a quicker way.'

'Sorry, love. That's the best I can do for you. Now, are you going to send through those specs or not?'

As I end the call, I let out a bellow of frustration, just as Noah comes back in.

'What's up?' he asks.

'I've just been onto the supplier about the trusses. Some smug bastard called Ross just ran rings around me, and every time I pushed him, he found a reason to make the delay longer. He's now telling me I have to resubmit all the specs and it will be a minimum of three weeks before we get them.'

'Yeah, that sounds like them.' Noah seems unperturbed.

'He also refused to take the original ones back, even though the mistake has to be at their end, because we accepted delivery. What kind of logic is that?'

'Don't take it personally,' Noah begins. 'This is standard practice for them. They won't just let you return stuff, particularly things that are made to order. I'm sure you can work something out with that software of yours so we're not held up completely.'

'I can, but that's not the point. I'm going to call Deborah. Maybe she can exert some influence.'

Noah laughs, but there's no humour in it. 'I think I'll leave you to it. Good luck.'

'Ella, you're not filling me with confidence here,' Deborah tells me when I manage to get hold of her around half an hour later. 'This is only your first day, and already you're telling me you've delayed the project by three weeks?' She doesn't sound pleased at all.

'*I* haven't delayed it. The building supplier has delayed it by delivering the wrong materials and then being obstructive when I rang up to ask them to rectify it. From what I've heard from the guys down here, this happens a lot. Isn't there anything you can do?'

I can hear her sigh. 'Fine. I'll call them and see if I can smooth this out. But you need to get on top of this stuff, Ella. I can't be bailing you out every five minutes, do you understand?'

'Thank you,' I manage, even though I don't feel remotely grateful. Why is she having a go at me when all I'm trying to do is fix something that wasn't even my mistake in the first place?

While I'm waiting for Deborah to call me back, I go back into my plan to see what can be moved around to minimise the delay. The process is strangely soothing, and my frustration levels start to fall as I jiggle the tasks around. By the time the phone rings, I reckon I can bring the overall delay down to one week if I need to.

'Right,' she informs me. 'I've spoken to Williamsons, and they're going to do their best to get the new trusses out to you early next week. I've also apologised on your behalf to Ross, the person you spoke to. He said you were very aggressive and confrontational. Ella, if you're going to succeed in this industry, you need to learn how to treat people with respect. I'm very disappointed in you, do you understand?'

I'm having to bite the inside of my cheek. How dare Ross say that, and how dare she take his side without even asking me?

'Do you understand, Ella?' she repeats.

'Yes. Thank you,' I mumble.

'Good. I've also arranged that they'll collect the old trusses when they bring the next delivery, although I have no idea what we're going to do with them. Are there any other messes you've made in your few hours of employment so far that I need to clean up, or is that it for now?'

'Nothing else,' I tell her. I need to get off this call before I say something to her that will end my role here before it's even properly started.

'Right. I trust you've learned a valuable lesson here.'

You have no idea, I think to myself as we disconnect the call.

19

'How was the Bitch Queen?' Noah asks me when he pops into the site office at the end of the day.

'Don't,' I reply. 'I certainly saw the other side of her today.'

'I did warn you.'

'You did. Anyway, we're going to have a new rule going forwards.'

'What's that?'

'Nothing, and I mean absolutely nothing, gets unloaded from a lorry before it's been checked against both the order and the delivery note. If it's not right, it stays on the truck and goes back.'

'The drivers won't like that,' he advises me. 'They're on a pretty tight schedule.'

'Tough. I don't like being told that the wrong stuff is my problem just because we unloaded it.'

'You're the boss,' he laughs. This seems to be his new catch-phrase. 'By the way, what did you do to John?'

'Nothing, why?'

'I overheard him talking to one of the chippies just now. He said, "I may have got her wrong. She don't know fuck-all, but she's a fast learner." That's praise indeed from him.'

'Bloody hell, what a day!' I laugh. 'It says something when the highlight is a guy who pretty much took an instant dislike to me decides I'm possibly not so bad after all.'

He smiles at me. 'I'd take your victories where you can, and that's not a bad one for your first day. Got any plans for the evening?'

'Yeah. I'm going to drink some wine. I reckon I've earned it.'

'You might want to look at the ladder training while you're at it,' he says as he climbs into his van. 'I'll see you tomorrow.'

* * *

The next morning, I make a point to get in just after seven, and I'm relieved to see that the whole team assembles as requested at eight. I explain the new rule about deliveries to them and, with a little bit of grumbling from one or two, they agree that they'll come and check everything before it's unloaded. The first lorry arrives at eight-thirty and, from what I can see, they're being as good as their word. It doesn't take long, however, for the driver to hop out of his cab and come storming over to the site office.

'Who's in charge here?' he asks angrily as he bursts through the door.

'I am. What's up?' I reply.

'Your lads are saying they won't unload anything until they've checked it.'

'That's right.'

'You can't do that! You're putting me behind schedule.'

'I'm sorry,' I tell him. 'But that's really not my problem. Williamsons made it very clear to me yesterday that anything we offload basically becomes ours, even if it's not what we ordered.

So, from now on, we're going to check everything and, if it's not right, it stays on the lorry.'

'You've got no bloody right,' he storms. 'Don't you know anything about haulage? I've got a load booked to take back north. If you don't unload all your stuff, I won't have room for it.'

'You'll have to take that up with Williamsons,' I tell him mildly.

'Oh, I will. Don't you worry about that.'

'Good. I imagine you have a copy of the paperwork that you need me to sign?'

'Yes.' He slams it on the table. I'm delighted to see that it's an itemised list.

'Right, let's go and see how they're getting on, shall we?'

An hour later, an extremely disgruntled driver leaves the site with a surprising amount of the original load still on the truck. On top of that, I've gone through his list, marking every incorrect item and crossing out every missing one. Hopefully, that will send a very clear message to Williamsons, and I'm not disappointed. Barely thirty minutes pass before the phone rings. However, when I answer, I'm surprised to find that I'm not speaking to Ross, but an incandescent Deborah.

'What the hell is the matter with you?' she practically yells.

'I'm sorry?' I'm completely blindsided.

'I've just had Ross from Williamsons on the phone. He told me there's an extremely angry driver heading their way, because you refused to unload his truck and he doesn't know if he'll have enough space for his next load.'

'That's not strictly true. We just refused to offload any items that were incorrect. I'm not being saddled with another load of useless roof trusses, or whatever garbage they were trying to foist on us today.'

'Did I, or did I not, expressly tell you that we needed to keep Williamsons sweet?'

'You told me not to be aggressive with them. This isn't being aggressive, it's just refusing to accept, and presumably pay for, materials we can't use.'

'That's not your job!' she cries. 'If there are discrepancies, mark them on the paperwork and I'll deal with them when I get the invoice.'

'But they're taking the mickey, Deborah. I thought that, if we refused to accept incorrect goods, they might get the message and step up their game.'

'I've told you before,' she hisses. 'I have negotiated *extremely* favourable terms with Williamsons, and if you continue to upset them, you'll be putting other projects at risk and I will consider it a disciplinary matter. Am I making myself clear?'

I can't believe what I'm hearing.

'Perfectly,' I tell her, being careful to keep my voice calm. 'But let me reiterate what I think you've just said, so there's no misunderstanding. I place the orders, Williamsons deliver whatever the hell they like, and I just suck it up. Is that right?'

'Don't press your luck. I don't need to remind you that you're on probation, do I? Consider this a verbal warning.'

I'm shaking with rage as she disconnects. I can see clearly why Andy resigned. I'm sorely tempted to ring her back and tell her where she can stick both her attitude and her job.

'You don't look very happy,' Noah observes as he wanders into the office a while later. 'I thought you'd be in a good mood, having sent all of that stuff back.'

'The Bitch Queen rang and tore me off a strip.'

'Really? Why? What did she say?'

'Basically, although I'm the customer, I have to kiss the arse of whomever I speak to at Williamsons and accept whatever shit they choose to deliver. Oh, and she gave me a verbal warning, just to make sure I got the message.'

'Bloody hell,' he whispers. 'It does make me wonder whether there's something dodgy going on, do you know what I mean?'

'Go on.'

'Well, I've been in the trade for a while, and this is the first time we've been so tightly tied to a single supplier. It just seems odd to me, particularly when they're so useless. There are loads of building material suppliers around here. This whole town is practically a building site. Why use a single company in Leeds?'

'All I know is that I need this job. So, from now on, we go back to just unloading the trucks and doing the best we can with what we get. I might as well kiss any prospect of a milestone bonus goodbye, because I can't see how I'm going to hit any milestones with my hands and legs tied like this.'

'The boys will be disappointed. They weren't sold on the idea of checking everything to begin with, but I think they quite enjoyed seeing the truck leave with all that stuff still on it. It was like a small act of rebellion.'

'Yeah, well, the revolution is over.'

Thankfully, the rest of the week passes much more peacefully. The morning stand-ups are helping me to get a feel for where we are and who everyone is. Noah was right that the guys were disappointed my new delivery regime was crushed so quickly, but it seems like the message might have got through anyway, because the remainder of our deliveries have been broadly correct. I've done exactly as Deborah instructed, and mailed details of any discrepancies to her, although she hasn't seen fit to dignify my reports with any kind of response. That's probably for the best; now that I know what she's really like, I want as little contact with her as possible.

'Are you coming to the pub?' Noah asks me at lunchtime on Friday, causing me to give him a nonplussed stare. 'POETS day, remember? The guys are starting to pack up already.'

'I'm not sure,' I reply. 'I wouldn't put it past the Bitch Queen to ring later, just to check I'm still here. I don't want to give her any more ammunition to use against me.'

'Fair enough. Got any plans for the weekend?'

'Oh, yeah. It's going to be a rollercoaster of excitement. I've got food shopping, a trip to the laundrette and I might even have a look at the ladder training. You?'

'I'll be working on my house. I'm in the middle of repointing at the moment. Actually, I've just had an idea.'

'Do I want to know?'

'Yes. If you do your ladder training, you could come round. I've got scaffolding up at the moment, so you could practise going up and down without all the lads watching.'

'Hm. Don't take this the wrong way, but I think I'd rather drill holes in my head.'

'I'll give you the address in case you change your mind. I'll be there all weekend, and you have my mobile number if I've popped out for anything.' He grabs a piece of paper off the desk and scribbles a few lines on it. 'Are you sure you don't want to come to the pub?'

'I'd better not, but thanks.'

Sure enough, I'm working my way through some paperwork when the phone rings. I glance at my watch before answering. Half past four.

'Ella, it's Deborah,' she announces, as if I don't have caller ID. 'I just need you to check a couple of lines on a delivery note for me. I assume you're still in the office?'

'I am,' I tell her.

'Good. Can you find all the delivery notes from last month for me?'

I head over to the cabinet and retrieve the relevant file, and she spends the next ten minutes cross-checking random items with me. She's trying to sound like it's terribly important, but I know she has copies because we send them all on, so it's obvious she's just using it as an excuse to check I am where I say I am. She really is a piece of work.

'Should I be expecting any more complaints about you before I head off?' she asks, acidly, when we've finished going through the documents.

'Why, has there been more than one?' I ask. I'm trying to think who else I could have upset, but I'm coming up blank.

'Not that have come to me, which is how I like it. Dare I hope that, after your decidedly rocky start, you're starting to get the feel for how things work in this company?'

'I think I understand a lot more,' I tell her, while making a series of surprisingly imaginative obscene gestures at my phone.

'Good. Have a nice weekend,' she replies and disconnects. I dash out a quick text to Noah.

Just as well I didn't come to the pub. The Bitch Queen has just phoned to check I'm still here.

It doesn't take long for his reply to come in.

Unbelievable. You were missed. My scaffolding is always available if you need to burn off some anger.

I can't help smiling. There's about as much chance of me going anywhere near his scaffolding as there is of Deborah

ringing back to offer me a pay rise. I glance at the piece of paper
with his address as I'm shutting down the computer. Without
thinking, I hastily fold it up and stick it in my bag, before locking
the site office behind me. I've been so used to the bustle of
activity that the sudden quietness of the site is slightly unnerving,
and I'm quite relieved when I've locked the gates behind me and
I'm on my way back to the caravan.

20

This weekend seems never ending, and it's not even lunchtime on Saturday yet. Despite planning a lie-in, I was wide awake at five-thirty, partly because that's when I've been setting the alarm during the week and partly because the sun was shining brightly through the thin curtains. I tried to go back to sleep, but it was obvious by six that it wasn't going to happen, so I got up. I was in the supermarket by seven and back from the laundrette by eleven, and I literally have nothing else to do until Monday morning. The caravan is still clean from my blitz last weekend, but I've run the vacuum cleaner round and given the bathroom a good scrub anyway. I was tempted to attack the little patch of wasteland outside, but I don't have any gardening equipment and I don't really want to spend any more money than I have to right now. I can't even use up some time with ladder training, as I did the course last night to take my mind off Deborah and the various ways I'd like to engineer her demise.

Thinking of the ladder course reminds me of the piece of paper with Noah's address on it in my bag. I fish it out and stare at it for a while, while I try to decide what to do. Practising going up and down ladders is a long way from my idea of a fun weekend, but sitting in the caravan of shit, bored out of my mind, isn't terribly appealing either. At least I'd have some company if I was at Noah's, but I don't want him to think I'm needy. I'm paralysed with indecision as I knock up a salad for lunch. It's just after midday, so strictly speaking it's too early, but it's something to do.

By the time I've finished eating and cleared up, I can't stand it any more. With a growl of frustration, I pull on my boots and plug Noah's address into the navigation app on my phone. Around twenty minutes later, I find myself on his street. Even if I didn't have the number, his house would be easy to spot because it's the only one covered in scaffolding. It's a traditional, red-brick terraced, house with a big bay window on the ground floor and two windows above. There's a small, paved front garden with a low wall and a door set back on the right-hand side. I can't see Noah anywhere on the scaffolding, so I walk up to the front door and ring the bell. A few seconds later, he throws open the door and beams.

'Ella! This is a surprise. Have you come to play on my scaffolding?'

'One ladder-trained project manager reporting for duty,' I reply with a salute.

'You'd better come in then,' he says, standing to one side.

As soon as I enter the hallway, it becomes clear to me that this project is far more than just a light refresh. The hallway walls have been taken back to bare brickwork and a quick glance into the front room reveals the same state of affairs there. The staircase is missing, so the only access to the first floor is via a ladder. Noah leads me to the kitchen at the rear, which has definitely seen better days.

'I was just fixing some lunch,' he explains. 'Do you want anything?'

'I've eaten already, thanks. This is quite the project. Are you doing it all yourself?'

'Pretty much. The idea is to sell it on for a profit and then buy another one and do the same. This is the third one I've done, and I plan to be mortgage-free by number five. I like these houses because, unlike the ones we're building, they have a bit of character. Ashford is like a tree, have you noticed?'

'No, what do you mean?'

'All the new developments are on the edge of the town. It's how it's always been. So it's like the rings of a tree; you start with the newest houses on the outside, and the closer you get to the centre of the town, the older the properties get until you hit the real charmers. I picked this one up at auction as a probate sale. It's basically solid, but needs modernising.'

'I've seen people like you on *Homes Under the Hammer*,' I laugh.

'It's a sound concept, as long as you know what you're doing and you keep the budget under control. Thankfully, I've got a lot of connections through my job, so I know where to get help when I need it.'

'What's the plan?'

'Keep the period features as far as possible, but bring it up to date sensitively where I can. So, for example, the decorative tiles on the floor in the hallway will stay, as will the cast-iron fireplaces. But the staircase was completely rotten, so I've got a mate making me another one. I'm re-wiring and re-plastering throughout, which is why the walls are all stripped back. I'm also going to extend the kitchen into what's now the bathroom and rejig the layout upstairs to make room for a bathroom up there. I'm going to lose a bedroom to do it, but the value of the house will still go up because people really don't like downstairs bathrooms now.'

As he explains his vision, he's assembling a doorstop sandwich filled with ham, cheese, pickle and salad. It looks delicious, and I'm slightly regretting my early lunch. I can't help noticing that the fridge is both modern and well stocked and, when I glance through the open door into the equally dilapidated-looking bathroom at the back of the house, I notice a toothbrush, toothpaste and shaving equipment arranged neatly by the basin.

'Are you *living* here?' I ask him, as he takes a large bite. I have to wait a few moments before he replies.

'Of course.' He seems surprised by the question. 'Why?'

'Isn't it difficult? Where do you sleep?'

'Upstairs, where do you think?' he laughs. 'Do you want to see? It can be your first ladder of the day.'

Without waiting for an answer, he puts down his sandwich and bounds over to the ladder, climbing it effortlessly until he's out of sight. By the time I reach the bottom, he's leaning over from the landing and grinning.

'Up you come,' he calls. 'This is a nice easy one. It's fixed in place at the bottom and the top, so it's no harder than a standard loft ladder.'

'I lived in a flat. We didn't have a loft ladder,' I reply as I reluctantly start to climb. That's not strictly true; I'm hiding the fact that Mum and Dad's house does have one, but I never needed to use it because Dad's always considered the loft his domain. However, Noah is right. I do the safety checks I learned on the course, and this is about as well tethered as a ladder can get. I'm still feeling a bit shaky once I reach the top, though.

'Here, let me help you.' Noah takes my hand to support me as I step off the ladder onto the safety of the floorboards. Despite shaking hands with him when we first met, I'm acutely aware of the physical contact this time. His hand is so different from Lee's; it's rugged, whereas Lee's was buffed and manicured to perfection. Noah's hand feels incredibly masculine in a way that Lee's never did. I feel a strange urge to just carry on holding it, allowing my thumb to explore the contours of his palm, but Noah is thankfully oblivious to the effect he's having on me, and releases me as soon as I have my footing.

'OK, so the main bedroom is at the front,' he tells me as he leads me through the doorway. Like the rest of the house, the walls have been stripped back to brick, and the single mattress on the bare floorboards indicates that there probably isn't a Mrs Noah, which makes me happier than it ought to. In the corner, there's a battered armchair and a tiny, portable TV. A chest of drawers and a hanging rail on wheels complete the room.

'Suddenly, the caravan of shit feels like a five-star hotel,' I giggle.

'It's not as bad as it looks,' he replies. 'And the good thing about living on site is it keeps me focused on the renovations. Imagine the luxury when I've put fresh plaster on these walls, painted and laid some carpet. Something to aim for, right? Here, let me show you.'

I follow him back onto the landing and into the second bedroom. This is around the same size as the front room, but that's all they have in common. The walls are plastered and painted in a very delicate shade of yellow. The floorboards are still bare, but it's the first room I've seen in this house that looks even vaguely habitable.

'Another coat of paint and then I'll move in here so I can start work on the front bedroom,' he tells me. 'Come and look at this.'

He leads me out again and into what must have been the third bedroom, but is obviously going to become the bathroom, from the pipes I can see everywhere.

'Believe it or not, this is nearly done,' he tells me. 'All the main plumbing is in, I just have to get the sanitary ware, connect it all up, and then tile and plaster.'

'Wouldn't it be easier to do one job at a time? Plaster the whole house in one go?'

'It would probably be more efficient, yes, but I like to break the tasks up, otherwise it gets monotonous.' He grins. 'I don't need a project plan, before you offer.'

'Touché.'

'At the moment, all the interior work is on hold because of the repointing,' he continues. 'That is boring, but I need to get it done while the weather is good. Also, the scaffolding is costing a fortune, so the sooner I can get rid of it, the better.'

To my delight, he takes my hand again to help me back onto the ladder, but this time my eyes are drawn to his arms. I wouldn't say they were much bigger than Lee's, but they somehow seem more impressive. I think it's probably because they've come from a lifetime of hard physical work, rather than three workouts a week in the gym. At least thinking about Noah's biceps takes my mind off the perils of the ladder, so I'm in surprisingly good shape when I reach the safety of the ground.

* * *

'There's something I don't get,' I say to him a couple of hours later. He's somehow managed to coax me onto the scaffolding, and he's showing me how to remove the old mortar so he can replace it with fresh. I'm not relaxed, exactly, but I'm nowhere near as anxious as I was the first time.

'Go on.'

'When we first met, you said you were from seafaring stock. How come you're a builder and not at sea?'

He smiles. 'You have a good memory. I'll have to be careful what I tell you, I can see that.'

'Are you going to answer the question?'

'I'm not sure.'

'Because? If there's some massive family rift, and one of your siblings is likely to blow your house up, I think I'd like to know. I'm a little vulnerable on your scaffolding.'

He laughs. 'There's no family rift, I can promise you.'

'So what's the story?'

'If I tell you, you are not to breathe a word to anyone at work, do you understand? I'll never hear the end of it if you do. It's bad enough when I see my family, I don't need it following me here as well.'

'Go on. You can't say something like that and not tell me the rest.'

'OK. My family have fished for generations and, being a boy and the eldest child, I was expected to take up the reins when my father retired.'

'But?'

'But I can't do that.'

'Why not?'

'The truth is that I suffer from seasickness.'

'That's it?' I feel let down. 'Lots of people do, even people who work on boats. I saw this documentary once—'

'Yeah, but I'm not talking about normal seasickness,' he interrupts. 'I'm talking chucking up before the boat even gets out of the harbour. Just the smell of the boat makes me feel nauseous. And, unlike most people, I never get my "sea legs", so I basically keep chucking up until there's nothing left to come, and even then I keep retching until we get back to shore. I went out with my dad for a week once, and I was in such a dreadful state by the time we got back that we agreed it would be better if I found a different profession. What makes it even more humiliating is that they replaced me with my sister.'

'I thought women were bad luck on boats?'

'Exactly. It shows how bad I was that even she was preferable to me.'

I can't help but giggle. 'For someone who can't set foot on a boat, Noah is a real bummer of a name.'

He smiles. 'The irony isn't lost on me.'

As I continue scraping out the old mortar, I turn the conversation over in my mind. Lee would never have admitted to a vulnerability like that; he would have found a way to bluster his way out of it with half-truths and misdirection. Noah's honesty is both refreshing and surprisingly attractive.

21

'How's it going?' Ava asks. After a bit of texting back and forth, we've found an evening when she's not on shift to have a catch-up call.

'Amazing,' I tell her. 'I'm living in this incredible penthouse apartment, and I'm out every evening wining and dining prospective clients. I never knew the construction industry could be so glamorous.'

'Really? I thought you were just a project manager.'

'*Just* a project manager? The nerve of you! I'm pretty much running the show single-handed down here.'

'You're taking the piss, aren't you.' Frankly, I'm surprised it's taken her this long to rumble me.

'It's a fair cop. Do you want to see?' I switch the call to video mode. I've only just got in so I'm still wearing my work clothes. I give her a head-to-toe pan, taking in my make-up free face, fluorescent vest, dusty jeans and steel toe-capped boots.

'Cor, get you!' she exclaims. 'I'd better not show this to Ben; you're practically his wet dream. All you'd need is a hard hat to tip him over the edge.'

'I've got one, but I left it at work.'

'Thank goodness he's downstairs watching TV and not listening to you. This would be like one of those online chatrooms to him.' She puts on a husky, sexy voice. 'Tell me more about your hard hat. What make is it? Is it shiny? Would you like me to polish it?'

'Give over,' I laugh. 'Do you want to see my accommodation?'

'You bet. Give me the full tour.'

'Hang on. We need to do this properly.' I turn the video mode off and walk outside. 'Are you ready?' I ask.

'Absolutely. The suspense is killing me.'

I point the phone at the ground, so all the camera can see is grass, and turn the video mode back on again. Very slowly, I raise the camera, until the caravan and its scrubland garden come into view.

'No. You're kidding me,' Ava gasps.

'I'm not. Welcome to my humble abode, lovingly referred to by my colleagues as the caravan of shit.'

'For fuck's sake. Are you serious?'

'Deadly. Would you like the tour?'

'Is the inside as bad as the outside?' she asks.

'Not any more. It took pretty much the entire bleach supply of Ashford, but it's actually habitable now. I haven't got any pictures of what it was like when I arrived, so you'll have to use your imagination. It was bad, though. Trust me.'

'Worse than that dodgy place in Wales we stayed in when we were little? Do you remember that?'

'Was that the one where Mum spent most of the week chasing cockroaches?'

'That's it.'

'Yeah, it was worse than that.'

'Why didn't you just come home?' she asks, after I've

described the mattress, its stains that reminded me of the shroud of Turin, and the state of the kitchen and bathroom.

'I nearly did. I took one look at it and hightailed it to the nearest Premier Inn, fully intending to come back home the next day.'

'What stopped you?'

'Stubbornness, mainly. That and I wasn't sure how to give the keys to the site back. Anyway, the site foreman has been really nice, and he helped me bring a new mattress in and take the old one to the tip.'

'You've always been stubborn. I have no idea where you get it from.'

'Of course you don't. You aren't stubborn at all.'

She laughs. 'So the foreman is really nice, eh?' There's a provocative edge to her voice. 'This new mattress of yours, has it seen a bit of action?'

'Of course not! Quite apart from the fact that I'm never having another office romance, Lee and I have only just broken up.'

'Just two little problems there. One, you're on a building site, not in an office, and two, the relationship with Lee was dead long before you called it.'

'That's not true!'

'Of course it is. Why do you think you're able to talk about him so easily, without sobbing uncontrollably?'

'Whatever. I'm not in the market for a new man, and it certainly wouldn't be someone I worked with if I was. I've learned my lesson there. He's just friendly, that's all.'

'Is he single?'

'I don't know for sure, but I think so.'

'You haven't asked?'

'No. If I start asking too many questions about his personal life, he might jump to all sorts of conclusions and think I'm interested in him, which would be a disaster.'

'I think you're being a bit dramatic.'

'I'm not. Think about it. Let's say, just for the sake of argument, that he's interested in me. If I start sniffing around his personal life, he might take that as a green light to come on to me. I'd then have to turn him down and it would be massively awkward working with him. On the other hand, if he wasn't interested, he might think I was coming on to him and feel he needs to let me down gently, which would also be awkward, because he'd constantly be trying to spare my feelings.'

'Jeez. Talk about analysis paralysis. You could do it subtly, you know. You could find out a bit about his hobbies and then ask what his girlfriend thinks of them. Unless he's gay, of course. Do you think he's gay?'

'I haven't thought about it, because I'm not into him!' I exclaim, my face reddening as I remember my unfortunate reaction to him holding my hand.

'You so are!' she laughs triumphantly. 'I can see it in your guilty expression. So, given that you're too shy to ask him outright, what makes you think he's single?'

'He only has a single mattress in his bedroom.' I regret the words as soon as they're out.

'You were in his *bedroom*?' she shrieks. 'This I have to hear. For such a platonic relationship, beds seem to be featuring an awful lot, wouldn't you agree?'

'It's not like that,' I tell her hotly. 'He's renovating a house, and he showed me around it at the weekend, that's all.'

'So you're seeing each other outside work?'

I'm getting annoyed with her now. 'Stop reading more into everything than there is. I had to do some health and safety training on how to use ladders, and he offered his scaffolding for me to practise on.'

'Sorry, but that sounds like the plot of a porno movie.' She puts the husky voice back on. 'Come and see my scaffolding. There is a really long pole I'd like to show you. Next thing you know, he'll be round to fix your washing machine and you'll have to pay him in kind.'

'I don't have a washing machine. I have to go to the laundrette.'

Thankfully, this little nugget is enough to divert her, and she goes back into outrage mode about how Atkinson Construction are taking advantage of me. When I tell her about my conversations with Deborah, she's all for leaping into her car, driving round to Deborah's house, and shoving a few of Teddy's looser turds through the letterbox. Now that I've got her off the scent of the non-existent romance between Noah and me, I'm enjoying the conversation much more, and I'm smiling broadly by the time we disconnect.

* * *

'So, I've got my nickname. I'm Carol,' I say to Noah the following Saturday. He's managed to coax me up to the second storey of the scaffolding, where my reward is helping paint the soffits and fascia boards at the top of the house. I was seriously wobbly when I finally made it up here, but I'm slowly acclimatising and, although I'm not completely relaxed, my heart has stopped pounding. I know I've got to get down at some point, but I'll deal with that when it happens.

'I heard John calling you that. It's a good sign, means he's accepted you. Do you know how he got there?'

'Yeah, it was a toss-up between Carol and Wendy, apparently.'

'I didn't hear about Wendy. Where did she come from?'

'John's grandkids are into *Bob the Builder*, and Bob's business partner slash love interest is a woman called Wendy, apparently. Anyway, he decided that was too obvious and ditched it.'

'If we were going with *Bob the Builder* characters, I'd have called you Lofty, after the crane that doesn't like heights,' Noah laughs.

'Shut up, boat boy. Anyway, how come you're such an expert on children's TV? Is there a Mrs Noah and a brood of baby Noahs somewhere, waiting anxiously for their real-life Bob the Builder to come home?' Ava would be proud of me. This is just curiosity though, nothing more. I will confess to the occasional sideways glance at his biceps, which are flexing in a most attractive way as he moves the paintbrush, but there's no intent in it. If I've conquered my fear of heights enough to make it up here, I'll take all the rewards I can get, thank you.

'No Mrs Noah or baby Noahs,' he replies. 'My sister's children watch it and, naturally, they think I'm just like him. Anyway, tell me how you ended up as Carol.'

'Typically convoluted. He's decided that, as project manager, I'm the numbers bird, as he puts it. That led him to the TV programme *Countdown*. Do you know it?'

'I've seen it. That's the one where the contestants pick random consonants and vowels, and then have to make the longest word they can think of.'

'That's the one. There's also a maths round, where they pick a load of numbers, and then have to add, subtract, multiply and divide in order to get as close as they can to a number set by the computer.'

'I'd forgotten about that.'

'At the end, the co-presenter tells them how to do it, and she's the numbers bird. John named me after her.'

'Umm, isn't the numbers bird Rachel Riley?'

'Naturally, but this is John we're talking about, so you have to go back a few years.'

'Ah. Carol Vorderman.'

'Exactly.'

'How are you getting on with him? He's obviously softened to you.'

'Yeah, I could do without him calling me "darlin'" and referring to me as a "bird", but other than that, I think we're making progress. He was very pleased with his roof trusses when the right ones turned up on Wednesday.'

'I always thought the way to a man's heart was through his stomach,' Noah smiles.

'Unless you're John, it seems.'

'Thinking of which, it's nearly lunchtime. Are you going to come down and let me make you a sandwich, or do I have to bring something up here?'

'I'll come down. I'm supposed to be practising, remember? It's not all about you getting slave labour to work on your house.'

'Fair point. Come on then.'

It takes me an age to complete the first stage of the descent. As soon as I walk over to the top of the ladder, the distance between me and the ground becomes painfully obvious again. I can't even rely on the comfort of Noah's strong hands because he's gone down first this time. I can just about hear him calling out words of encouragement over the sound of blood rushing through my ears as I tentatively place my feet on the rungs. Every step is agony, and I have to pause when I finally reach the lower level of scaffolding, just to catch my breath and get my legs to stop shaking.

However, I'm surprised and delighted to discover that the second ladder, down to the ground, poses no problems at all, and

I perform a little victory dance, much to Noah's amusement. The house is dark and pleasantly cool inside after being in the sunshine all morning.

'Would you like a beer?' Noah asks, proffering a bottle from the fridge.

'I don't think so. The health and safety training was pretty firm about the dangers of mixing ladders and alcohol.'

'It's alcohol free.' He shows me the bottle. 'It might surprise you to learn that I have had a little bit of health and safety training myself.'

'Ha ha. Go on then. I reckon I've earned it.'

'That you have. By the time this scaffolding goes, you'll be up and down it like a pro.'

'And you'll have had hours of free labour. I'm not sure who is getting the better deal here.'

'You, obviously.' He grins. 'You're overcoming your fears and learning new skills. I ought to be charging you, really.'

'You believe that, if it helps.'

'Would you rather be spending the weekend in the caravan of shit?'

'OK, you've got me,' I laugh.

The truth, which I'm certainly not going to share with him, is that the days I'm spending with him on the scaffolding are rapidly becoming the highlight of each week.

22

'Carol, you have to come and see this,' John tells me as he barges into the site office. I've got so used to him calling me that in the couple of months I've been here now that it doesn't even register that it's not my proper name. I've got to the point where I'll respond equally happily to Carol or Ella.

'What's up?'

'They've bloody excelled themselves this time.'

'Who?'

'Williamsons, who do you think? Come with me.'

Grabbing my hard hat, I follow him outside and down to number five, one of the smaller 'Windsor' homes, which is in the process of being made watertight. The roof is on, and the glazers are fitting the windows that arrived yesterday.

'I know it's not strictly my job,' John is explaining, 'but Mike wasn't sure what to do, so he asked me, and I thought it best to come and get you.'

I understand why that might be. Mike is the team leader of the glazers, and I don't know him nearly as well as some of the others, because they only come on site for a few days at a time to fit the windows for each house when it's ready, unlike the others, who are here pretty much every day.

'We need to go up to the top floor,' John tells me as he starts to climb the ladder up to the first layer of scaffolding. I wouldn't say I'm completely over my fear of heights, but my practice weekends at Noah's have certainly helped, and I follow him up without an issue.

'Show her,' John tells Mike, who is waiting for us along with another guy from his team and a stack of window frames. Together, they lift one of them and offer it up to the opening. It's not even in place before I can see that it's too small. There's a large gap at the top.

'Stupid question,' I say to Mike, 'but before I go and call Williamsons, this is definitely where this frame is supposed to go, isn't it?'

'Absolutely, we checked them all,' he tells me. 'The ground-floor exterior doors and windows all fit fine, but none of the first-floor ones do. We wondered if they might have been mislabelled, but we've tried every frame in this opening, and none of them fit. We also offered them up to the other openings, and it was the same story.'

'What about the glazing?'

'We checked that. The glass fits the frames fine, it's just the frames that don't fit the house.'

I sigh. 'OK, leave it with me.'

'What on earth are you doing up there?' Noah's voice calls from the ground. Thankfully, this time, his tone is curious rather than furious.

'Looking at windows that don't fit. Why?'

'The trucks with the Portakabins for the sales office have just arrived, and they want to know where they're supposed to go.'

'I would have thought that was pretty clear. It's well marked out.'

'Yeah, but they're covering their backsides. They want you to tell them, so it's your fault rather than theirs if it's wrong.'

'Charming,' I mutter under my breath. 'Fine,' I call. 'I'll be down in a minute.'

'What do you want us to do with these?' Mike asks, indicating the window frames.

'I can't delay the interior works while we wait for the right windows,' I tell him. 'Can you work with John to board up the top floor openings, so we're watertight at least?'

'It means the top floor of the house will be completely dark. Not ideal,' John tells me.

'I know. We'll just have to get some lights in there so people can still see what they're doing, OK?'

'You're the boss, darlin'.' He smiles because he knows it annoys me when he calls me that.

'You are such a bloody dinosaur,' I tell him as I head back to the ladder to go and sort out my next problem. 'How on earth your wife puts up with you, I have no idea.'

'She loves me even more than you do,' he grins.

Once I'm back on the ground, I follow Noah to the site entrance, where two huge lorries have the new sales office on the back, in sections, with a crane parked up alongside them. The two show homes are now complete with the exception of furniture, which is arriving later this week prior to the sales office opening on Monday. We have two sales people starting, Deborah informed me, called Kayleigh and Breanna. I was a bit worried that she'd come down to conduct the interviews in person, but thankfully she did them online. I find it slightly odd that we haven't seen her once since I started, but nobody is complaining, least of all me.

We've had a bit of rain over the last few days; not enough to slow down the work, but enough to make the ground claggy. My boots are covered in mud, and I've learned that there's no point trying to keep jeans clean either. My current pair are sporting an impressive bracelet of mud around the ankle of each leg. At Noah's suggestion, I've invested in an ugly waterproof seat cover for the Fiat to stop me getting mud and cement dust on the upholstery, and I now have a pair of trainers in the boot, along with a bag for my boots, so I don't fill the footwell with mud either. The site office has not fared so well, and the floor is festooned with muddy footprints. I've given up trying to keep it clean, at least until the ground dries up again, anyway.

'What happened to the fear of heights?' Noah asks me, as we stroll towards the trucks. 'You were clambering all over that scaffolding like you were born to it.'

I turn to him and smile. 'I had a good teacher who helped me to overcome it,' I tell him.

'I knew I should have charged you.'

'Umm. I think you did pretty well out of it, didn't you?'

Over the last few weekends, Noah has found all sorts of jobs for me to do. Once the soffits and fascias were painted, he decided that he ought to renew the guttering while he was up there, so I've been helping with that, as well as replacing the rotten, timber-framed windows with modern, double-glazed units. To be fair, I didn't actually have a lot to do with that as Mike came and helped him with the heavy lifting, but he (deliberately, I suspect) had a tendency to leave tools he needed in his van, so I would be regularly sent up and down the scaffolding, bringing them to him. I haven't minded as it's been mostly enjoyable and I've learned a lot too. I am also getting slightly addicted to his doorstop sandwiches; they're always delicious and well-filled, plus I have to confess that I rather enjoy watching him make them, especially if he's wearing a tight T-shirt. Ava keeps telling me I should put my 'no office romances' rule in the bin and, to use her phrase, 'jump his bones'. I've made it very clear to her, every time she's brought it up, that there is no way that is going to happen, and Noah hasn't given off the slightest signal that he's interested in me anyway, but she won't let it go. I actually find it liberating, knowing that we'll never be more than work colleagues and, I hope, friends, but that doesn't stop me appreciating his physique.

I haven't heard a thing from Lee since he hung up on me the day after I arrived. That doesn't surprise me; he will have been waiting for me to make the first move, apologise to him and beg for his forgiveness. I was thinking about it the other day, and I realised I couldn't remember a single time in the whole five years we were together when he apologised to me. He doesn't take up a lot of my head space, because my days are usually flat out dealing with issues and fiddling with the schedule to try to ensure we stay on track despite Williamsons' efforts to derail us, and I'm not very good at leaving work behind me in the evenings either. On the rare occasions that Lee does creep into my thoughts, they tend to go more in the direction of wondering how I never noticed what a narcissist he was at the beginning. I will admit to being curious about whether Orchestra have done anything with the recording, but I'm not sure whether they can without corroborating evidence; although Lee seemed pretty confident they wouldn't find any, that was before Ava pulled her little stunt with the recording.

'Where do you want this office then, mate?' the crane driver asks Noah, completely ignoring me. This is the part of my job I hate the most. I've lost count of the number of people who have tried to completely overlook me in favour of literally anyone with a penis.

'No bloody idea,' Noah replies, winking at me. 'You'd better ask the boss.'

'And where is he?' the crane driver replies.

'I'm here,' I tell him.

'Oh, sorry, love. I didn't see you there.'

Of course you didn't, I'm tempted to reply. After all, five foot
four women wearing yellow hard hats and hi-vis are renowned
for blending seamlessly into the background, aren't they?

'Can you see that concrete plinth over there?' I ask him,
pointing at it.

'Yup.'

'Excellent, well done.' I can't help delivering this in a slightly
sarcastic tone. 'I'd like you to put it on that. The utilities are all
ready for you to connect up to.'

'Yeah, but which way round do you want it? If we put it down
and bolt it together, and then you don't like it and want it
changed, that's going to be a massive pain in the arse and we
haven't got the hours allocated to do it. I know what you ladies
are like for changing your minds about things.'

I'm flabbergasted. This guy makes John seem positively
metrosexual.

'Good question,' I reply, pretending to be considering this for
the first time. 'What do you think the punters would prefer,
having the front door facing the car park where they can find it
easily, or having to walk all the way round to the other side to
get in?'

'It's not my job to decide,' he tells me, folding his arms
defensively.

'Hm. It's just so difficult to choose. Which way round do you
think it should go, Noah?' I ask him, coquettishly.

Immediately, I know I've pushed too far. Noah looks deeply
uncomfortable and his cheeks redden. I realise that I've put him
in an impossible situation. If he answers, he's playing straight into

the hands of the crane driver's chauvinism. If he doesn't, he looks just as weak and indecisive as I'm pretending to be.

'Front door facing the car park,' I tell the crane driver curtly, before turning on my heel and heading back towards the site office. Noah is right behind me as I go through the door.

'Don't ever do that to me again,' he hisses once we're alone.

'I'm sorry. He was just such an arsehole. Surely it's bloody obvious which way round the office should go? He just wanted to score his little misogynistic point.'

'I get it. Don't think I haven't noticed how people are with you. But you don't have to humiliate every single person who is surprised to find a woman in charge of a building site, and you certainly don't need to drag me into it, OK? I'm one of the good guys, or at least I thought I was.'

'You are!' I tell him earnestly. 'I really am sorry. It was a heat of the moment thing, and I never meant to embarrass you, I promise.'

His expression softens. 'Up until that point, it was quite funny watching you. You were like a cat playing with a mouse. I don't think he got it, though.'

'I don't think he did either. What am I supposed to do with people like that?'

'My mum always used to say to me, when I was growing up, "Don't feel you have to die on every hill." Words to live by, I reckon.'

'That's easy for you to say. You're not the one being over-looked and talked down to.'

'No, but none of the guys who work with you every day over-look you or talk down to you, do they? He just doesn't know you.'

I sigh. 'It just pisses me off, that's all.'

'I know,' he tells me. 'And, for what it's worth, I'm sorry.'

I smile at him. He's right: he is one of the good guys.

23

'What are we working on today?' I ask Noah over our sandwiches, a few Saturdays later. The scaffolding is long gone, but we've fallen into a rhythm of me doing my own chores on Saturday mornings, and then helping him with his house for the rest of the weekend. I've met a few of my neighbours from the caravan park, and they're friendly enough, but they generally keep themselves to themselves, so Noah is still the only person in Ashford I'd call a friend. I get on well with the guys on site, but they have their own lives, so apart from a drink in the pub on a Friday afternoon, I don't see any of them outside work. It's a beautiful summer day, so I'm rather sad that the scaffolding is gone and I'll be stuck inside for the afternoon.

'I've sanded down the front door, so are you happy to give it a coat of primer?' he asks. 'I thought you'd like that, because you can be outside enjoying the sunshine rather than stuck inside with me.'

Although the bottom floor of the house is still stripped right back, the new staircase has been fitted, and a lot of progress has been made upstairs. The new bathroom is in (painted and tiled by yours truly), and the front bedroom is plastered and painted as well. The outside of the house is now looking very smart, thanks to the new windows and repointed brickwork. It still has a long way to go, but I can tell it's going to be amazing when it's done. I've learned so much from my weekends here; not only have I pretty much conquered my fear of heights and ladders, but I'm now a bit of an expert on cutting and hanging tiles, repointing, and I even know more than I probably want to about plumbing. The only thing Noah hasn't let me try my hand at is plastering, as he says that's a skilled job that takes a long time to learn, but I'm not upset about that. Watching him applying smooth layers of plaster has been more than adequate compensation.

I'm probably no more than half an hour into my work when I hear a familiar voice behind me.

'What's going on here then, Carol?'

I put down the paintbrush and turn to see John and a woman I assume must be his wife standing on the pavement.

'I'm just helping Noah, John. It passes the time,' I tell him.

'My front door could do with a lick of paint, if you're bored.'

'I'm not sure you could afford my rates.'

'Why, what's Michael paying you?'

I flush slightly.

'I thought so. Don't worry, your secret's safe with me.'

'What secret?'

'Look. If word gets round the site that you're hanging around with Michael on the weekend, there's going to be gossip, that's all I'm saying.'

'If anything like that happens, I'll know exactly where it came from, and we'll be having a chat,' I tell him, firmly. 'I'm just helping out a friend in my spare time. Nothing more to it than that.'

Thankfully, before John can go any further down this particular rabbit hole, we're interrupted by his wife.

'Ted, aren't you going to introduce me to your friend?' she asks.

Ted?

'Carol, this is my wife Roberta. Roberta, this is Carol, who project manages the site.' I notice that John is suddenly looking a bit uncomfortable.

'Oh, this is the woman you've been telling me about?' Roberta asks him, before turning to me. 'Ted's a big admirer of yours. He's always telling me about clever ways you've moved things around to keep the build on track.'

John is now full-on fidgeting, but I can't work out whether that's because she's revealed much more about what he really thinks than he'd ever let on to me, or whether it's the Ted thing. I have to find out about that.

'Has he also told you that my real name is Ella?' I ask.

'He's hopeless,' she agrees. 'I don't know a single person he actually calls by their real name, except me.'

'But you don't call him John?'

'No. He's always been my big teddy bear, haven't you, love?'

To my delight, John turns absolutely crimson and invents a reason for them to hurry away. I don't think he'll be telling anyone on site that he saw me, somehow. I'm still giggling about it when I finish the door.

* * *

'I thought we'd do something different tomorrow, if you're not busy,' Noah tells me as we're packing up for the day. I haven't mentioned the Ted thing to him; I'm keeping that as private ammunition for now.

'I don't exactly have a packed social calendar down here, as you know. After I've exchanged a couple of sentences with Betty next door about the foxes getting into her bins again, I think I'll be pretty much free. What did you have in mind?'

'I thought I'd take you on a bit of a tour of Kent. Have you actually been outside Ashford since you arrived?'

'I haven't really had any reason to go anywhere else.'

'And what sort of things do you like? Stately homes, castles, gardens?'

'All of them. I probably like gardens most, though.'

'Noted. I'll collect you from the caravan of shit at nine sharp.'

I can't help smiling to myself as I drive home. Noah hasn't been anywhere near the caravan park since the weekend I arrived, so he's in for a surprise. His house isn't the only project I've been working on in my spare time. Al and Doreen, my neighbours on the other side from Betty, are keen gardeners and were more than happy to lend me some tools to attack the patch of scrubland outside the mobile home. I've also borrowed ladders (now that I can climb them) and given the whole of the exterior a good wash so, although it's never going to be the Ritz, it's pretty much unrecognisable as the same place I moved into when I arrived.

'Bloody hell!' he exclaims when he shows up the next morning. 'Either you're superwoman, or you've been massively bored. I thought I'd come to the wrong place for a moment. I had to double-check.'

'All my own work,' I tell him proudly, gesturing at the neat patch of grass and flowerbeds that have replaced the scrubland.

'And the caravan?'

'Yup, that was me too.'

'Amazing. Right, are you ready to go?'

Oddly, I've got so used to my scruffy jeans, work shirts and boots that I found it very difficult to decide what to wear today. Normally, it would have been a no-brainer and I'd have gone straight for a dress or a skirt with a strappy top and a pair of ballet pumps underneath, but that somehow felt too 'date' like, so I've gone for a pair of shorts, T-shirt and trainers. If we're going to be walking around gardens, I figured they'd be more comfortable anyway. It's another beautiful day, and I'm quite looking forward to a bit of sightseeing.

'Where are we going?' I ask him as we leave Ashford behind and head into the countryside.

'We're starting at Sissinghurst,' he replies. 'It's one of the most famous gardens in Kent, created by Vita Sackville-West. It's only about twenty minutes' drive, but it was the first place I thought of when you said you liked gardens. Plus, there's a whiff of scandal about it, and who doesn't like a bit of intrigue, eh?'

'What sort of scandal?'

'I can't remember the name of the bloke she married, but their first home together was a house called Long Barn near Sevenoaks, where she discovered her love for gardening and created her first garden. Then, some years later, they bought Sissinghurst and she really went for it. But it seems gardening wasn't her only passion. She also had a number of affairs with both men and women, the most famous of which was her affair with Virginia Woolf. Have you heard of her?'

'Yeah, she was a famous author.'

'I'll take your word for it. English Literature wasn't really my favourite subject at school. Anyway, it seems our Vita was a bit of a girl. Or, at least, she liked a bit of a girl.' He grins wolfishly.

'And how do you know all this?' I ask him.

'Googled it last night after I booked the tickets.'

'Tell me, what is it that men find so fascinating about lesbianism?'

'What do you mean?'

'You were practically salivating about Vita just then. You never hear women talking about gay guys like that.'

'Yeah, well.' He blushes slightly and an awkward silence descends. I can see him trying to work out what to say and decide to take pity on him.

'Relax, I'm just curious, that's all. What's that?' I point to a house with a round, pointy tower at one end, topped with a wooden hood with a board sticking out of it.

'That's an Oast house. You'll see them all over the place in Kent. They were used for drying hops back in the day, but now most of them have been converted into houses.'

'How do they work?'

'Oh, come on!' he exclaims. 'You need to give me notice before you ask questions like that, so I can look up the answers. All I know is that Kent was famous for its hops, among other things, and Oast houses were used for drying them.'

'Kent, the Garden of England.'

'Exactly, although you'd struggle to see why it's called that, living in Ashford. That's why it's important to get out occasionally and see other parts of the county. Did you know Kent only has one city?'

'I didn't.'

'Neither did I,' he smiles. 'Amazing what you can find online, isn't it?'

'Lesbians, mainly,' I joke.

'Oh, look, we're here.'

Noah is right about one thing. This garden is spectacular and I take my time, drinking in the various 'rooms' as the guide book describes them. I can tell that this isn't really his scene, but he's very patient and follows me round without a word of complaint. He doesn't even seem to mind when I get carried away and grab his hand a couple of times so I can drag him over to see a particular flower or display.

'That was amazing, thank you,' I tell him as we make our way back to his van.

'There's more to come,' he assures me. 'We're heading for Tenterden next.'

'What's there?'

'A vineyard, where we're going to have lunch.'

'What, as in wine vineyard?'

'Yep.'

'I didn't know we had any of those in the UK.'

'Me neither, but then I'm not exactly a wine connoisseur. Anyway, TripAdvisor said it was nice, so I booked us in. I thought you might enjoy the wine tasting, but it was already fully booked, I'm afraid. But the restaurant had availability, and we can wander around afterwards if we want to.'

'It's probably for the best. If I drink at lunchtime, I'm likely to go to sleep.'

'We don't want that. I've saved the best till last.'

'Oh, yes? What's that?'

'Wait and see.'

Lunch proves to be quite the eye-opener. Not the food, although that is very nice, but I learn something new about Noah. I know that he makes a mean sandwich, but it's soon clear to me that he knows quite a lot more than that, as he navigates the slightly intimidating menu confidently, choosing dishes that I totally wouldn't have predicted.

'This is a side to you I haven't seen before,' I remark.

'I do love decent grub,' he admits. 'I sometimes think that, if I hadn't gone into the building trade, I'd have trained as a chef.'

'Do you regret it?'

'No. I admire what chefs do, but I wouldn't swap working environments. I get fresh air, and they get a sweat pit. I reckon I chose the right path.' He spreads a little smoked mackerel mousse on a piece of sourdough, takes a bite and groans with pleasure.

'God, this is amazing,' he enthuses. 'Try some.' He carefully breaks another piece of sourdough, spreads it with mousse and holds it out to me. I open my mouth to allow him to pop it in and he's right. It does taste incredible, but I'm momentarily distracted by the intimacy of the moment where his fingers lightly brushed my lips and I had to concentrate very hard to prevent myself from kissing them.

Our final stop of the day turns out to be a beautiful, sandy beach. It's quite crowded on this warm, summer day, and Noah has to try a few places before he finds a parking space, but it's the perfect end to a brilliant day. I buy us both ice creams, and we take off our shoes and paddle in the icy sea. As the sun starts to dip, we head back to Ashford, where we go to a different pub from the usual one and sit contentedly in the garden, sipping ice-cold beers.

'This has been the best day,' I tell him enthusiastically when he drops me back at the caravan park. 'Thank you so much.' Without thinking, I rise onto my tiptoes, wrap my arms around him and give him a kiss.

'I'm so sorry,' I stammer when I realise what I've done.

'It's fine,' he smiles. 'That was the perfect end to the perfect day.'

'Oh, was it?' I'm both embarrassed and kind of wanting to do it again. My lips are tingling gently, and I'm not sure it's all to do with his stubble.

'Yeah. A bit short, if I'm being completely honest, but otherwise good.'

'You poor thing.' I reach up and press my lips to his again, letting them linger this time.

When I pull back, it's obvious that something vital has shifted. There's an intensity in his eyes that I've never seen before, and I'm both excited and scared of it. Our eyes are locked on to each other, my heart starts thumping in my chest, and I can sense the endorphins rushing into my system. Agonisingly slowly, he moves forwards until our lips meet once more.

I'm fizzing. This is nothing like kissing Lee. This is raw and exciting, and my body takes on a life of its own, pressing harder against him as my hands dig into his back. As his arms move to encircle me in return, our mouths open and our tongues find each other, everything feels right.

This is wrong, my inner voice tells me. *This is everything you said you would never do again.*

That niggle of doubt is enough to bring me to my senses with a thump.

'I'm sorry. I can't do this,' I tell him as I break off the kiss and slip out of his arms.

Without another word, I turn on my heel and flee into the safety of the caravan, slamming the door behind me.

24

Noah is avoiding me. He's trying to pretend that everything is normal, but it's obvious he can't bear to be in the same place as me. As soon as the morning meetings finish, he's always got something urgent he needs to go and deal with, and he's stopped calling in to the office unless he absolutely has to. If I go and find him on site, he'll invent a reason to deflect me onto someone else. It's Friday morning and I'm dreading the weekend ahead; there's no way I can go round to his house until we've cleared the air, and we can't do that while he's keeping as far away from me as possible. But the truth is that I miss him terribly, and it's going to be a very long and boring weekend on my own.

'This is *exactly* why office romances are a bad idea,' I'd said to Ava earlier in the week.

'It's not much of a romance, though, is it?' she'd replied. 'Basically, you had a bit of a kiss and then you ran away. More primary school than adult channel if you ask me. I'm not surprised he's avoiding you. I would, too. For all he knows, you hated the kiss, or you actually find him repulsive. He's probably massively embarrassed, which is why he can't be around you.'

'But it's created this really horrible atmosphere. I just want things to go back to how they were. If only we'd never kissed!' I'd wailed.

'Too late for that now. Just give him some space. I'm sure it'll be fine.'

The guys all file in for the morning stand-up, and I notice that Noah comes in last, as he has done every day this week. He won't look me in the eye, and he stands at the back close to the door, so he can make his escape as soon as humanly possible. He looks a picture of misery, and I suspect my expression is a mirror image of his. The guys give their updates, but I'm struggling to focus; all I can think of is Noah and how unhappy he looks. My prediction proves correct and Noah vanishes as soon as the meeting wraps up, but John stays behind, looking a little pissed off.

'Can I help you with something?' I ask as he settles himself in the seat opposite me. His expression reminds me a little of the way he looked on my first day, and my heart sinks even further.

'What's going on between you and Michael?' he asks bluntly.

'Nothing!' I say, more forcefully than I mean to. 'What makes you think something's going on?'

'Oh, you know, just the little things. Like you being round at his house last weekend, happy as a songbird, and now you're both moping around with faces like thunder and don't seem to be able to spend more than a few seconds in the same place. I'm no mind reader, but I'd say something happened. I'm not the only one to pick up on it either. I've heard the brickies muttering, and those guys never notice anything.'

I sigh. 'It's complicated.'

'I bet it bloody isn't. You birds just like to make things complicated so we think you're all deep and mysterious.'

'Do you have any idea how disrespectful it is to refer to

women as birds?' I ask him, grateful for the opportunity to change the subject.

'My use of the English language isn't the bloody issue here, darlin'. The issue here is that something appears to have gone on between the two bosses, and the whole site is suffering as a result. So, much as I don't want to, I've got to get involved, because someone has to sort the two of you out.'

'Why are you speaking to me? You could talk to him, man to man.'

'Tried that. He wasn't having it.'

'What did he say?'

'He told me to fuck off and mind my own business.'

'Good advice, I reckon.'

'Believe me, I'd love nothing more than to leave well alone. If you two were acting like grown-ups, I would do. But you're not. So spill.'

'Fine. He kissed me.'

'What, out of the blue? Did he force himself on you, is that it? I'll have words with him if he did.'

'No, he didn't force himself on me. We had a really lovely day out, and then we ended up having a kiss at the end of it, and everything has gone wrong as a result.'

He looks dumbfounded. 'Is that it?'

'What do you mean, is that it? Didn't you hear what I said?'

'Yeah, you had a bit of a snog. So what? Don't take this the wrong way – you're much too young for me – but you're a good-looking bird – sorry, *woman* – and he's a good-looking guy. What's the problem? Was he no good?'

'It's not that. It's just that romantic relationships between co-workers are a really bad idea.'

'Bollocks.'

'What?'

'I'm sorry, but that's bollocks. Look at Eric and Derek, the sparkies. They've been together for as long as anyone can remember, and they're as happy as can be. Yeah, they bicker all the time, but it's obvious they're mad about each other.'

'Who are Eric and Derek?'

'I'm not sure I can even remember their real names, I've called them that for so long. Eric is called Paul, I think, and Derek is Richard. It might be the other way around.'

'I know who you mean now. Are they a couple?'

'Oh, yes, didn't you know? You can't hire one without the other. They go everywhere together. Anyway, this isn't about them, it's about you and Michael.'

'I can't have a relationship with someone I work with. I just can't, OK?'

'Why not?'

'If you must know, my last boyfriend worked at the same company as me. It ended really badly, and I promised myself I'd never date someone I worked with again.'

'Did the relationship end badly because you worked together?'

'Yes, kind of.'

He sighs and leans back in the chair. 'Go on.'

'He took a job with a rival company without telling me, and he did some underhand stuff to get it. Because of that, we lost the contract and I got made redundant, which is how I ended up here. There's more to it than that, but that's the gist.'

'So it actually has nothing to do with you working together, does it?'

'Have you not listened to a word I just said?'

'I did. What I heard is that he was a massive prick, not that working together was the problem.'

'But it was. If we hadn't worked together, he wouldn't have lost me my job!'

'He'd still have been a massive prick, though, and you'd probably have split up anyway when you realised. The job is incidental.'

'I disagree.'

'Fine. Let me put it a different way then. Do you know what I love?'

'Apart from disrespecting me and my sex, no.'

'Vindaloo. I bloody love a vindaloo. Every Friday, after going to the pub with the boys, I stop at our local curry house and pick up a vindaloo for me and a prawn korma for the missus. She's not as keen on the spicy stuff as me.'

I have no idea where he's going with this, but I sense he's not going to be deflected.

'A couple of years ago, me and the missus went on holiday to Blackpool, your part of the world.'

'I'm from Leeds,' I correct him.

'It's all north to me. Anyway, we went to this curry house on the last night of our break and I ordered a vindaloo, like I always do. It tasted a bit odd, but I put that down to your lot not doing it quite right, like fried Mars bars.'

'Fried Mars bars are a Scottish thing, nothing to do with the north of England.'

'Like I said, everything above the Watford Gap is the same to me. Anyway, we're on the motorway the next afternoon, and I get this sudden cramp in my stomach. Straight away, I know I'm in trouble, but thankfully we're only a couple of miles from a service station. I leave the missus in the car and run into the gents' as fast as I can, but I only just make it. I'll spare you the grisly details, but it wasn't pretty. I don't know how long I was in there before I felt safe to come out, but it felt like hours. I was all for getting back on the road to get home as quickly as we could, but thankfully the missus talked me out of that, and suggested we sit in the car park for an hour, just to make sure there weren't going to be any repeat episodes.'

I've completely forgotten what the point of all this is supposed to be, but I'm interested to see how the story ends. 'I'm guessing this was just the first round?'

'Yup. Every twenty minutes, like clockwork. I had no idea where it was even coming from by the end. Luckily it was one of those places with a hotel attached, so we booked ourselves in there, and I had one of the worst nights of my life. I honestly wanted to die.'

'I expect it was a while before you wanted another vindaloo.'

'Not at all. I was down the curry house the very next Friday. And that's my point.'

'OK. You're going to need to elaborate because I'm not with you.'

'How many vindaloos do you think I've eaten in my life? Hundreds, definitely, maybe even a thousand, who knows? And out of all of them, I've had one bad one. If I'd let that put me off, I would never have had another vindaloo, and I'd have missed out on countless Friday nights of spicy pleasure. That's what you're doing. You had one bad relationship with some knobhead you happened to work with. Guess what? Not all the men you work with are knobheads. Make better choices, rather than spouting shit like "workplace romances are a bad idea", or whatever it was you said. Does that make sense?'

'Honestly? I'm not sure. I will think about it, though, I promise.'

'Good. Well, I'm done here. All this woo-woo relationship bollocks has drained me. Sort it out, will you?'

'I'll do my best, thanks, Ted.' I give him a cheeky wink.

'Don't you bloody dare,' he growls, and disappears through the door.

* * *

As I adjust the plan yet again to try to get around the latest delivery cock-up, I think about what he's said. I am attracted to Noah, there is absolutely no doubt about that, and, from the way he kissed me, I think I can be confident that he feels the same way. Is John right, though? What if we let this 'thing' between us turn into something more, and it doesn't work out? Would that actually be any worse than the situation we're in now?

My thoughts are interrupted by the sound of a van door slamming and the engine starting. I glance at my watch and I'm horrified to discover it's lunchtime already, which means they're packing up for the weekend. If I'm going to have any chance of talking to Noah before Monday, it has to be now. I grab my hat and rush outside.

'Do you know where Noah is?' I ask one of the departing brickies.

'No idea. Sorry.'

I get the same response from the other people I ask, but I know he's still here because I can see his van in the car park.

His van. Of course!

I don't know how long I stand there, leaning against the bonnet of Noah's van, but it feels like an age, and the site is pretty much deserted by the time I spot him walking towards me. His shoulders sag as soon as he catches sight of me, and I wonder for a moment whether he's going to turn and go back the other way.

'Can it wait?' he asks wearily as he comes to a halt in front of me. 'It's been a hell of a week, and I really need to get away from here. I'm sure we can sort whatever it is on Monday morning.'

'It can't, I'm afraid. Would you mind coming to the site office with me? I'll try not to keep you longer than I absolutely have to.'

He sighs. There's so much sadness in that sigh that my heart breaks a little bit.

'Fine.'

His lack of enthusiasm couldn't be more evident as we make our way to the office. He's not quite dragging his heels like a naughty schoolboy, but it's not far off. We enter the site office and I close the door carefully behind him.

'What's up?'

'I need to apologise to you about last weekend—'

'No,' he interrupts. 'I'm the one who should be saying sorry. I got carried away. It won't happen again, I promise. Can I go now?'

'Not yet, please. I have one more thing I want to say. You see, the problem is that I'd quite like it to happen again. Right now, ideally.'

I can feel my heart banging against my ribcage with nerves. I've basically thrown myself at him; if he walks away now, I'll be completely humiliated.

'But last weekend—'

'I know. I'm sorry. You caught me by surprise, that's all. But I've realised that I do want this, if you do. I want you, Noah.'

It's all I can do not to sag with relief as his miserable face lights up. Very slowly, I step towards him and take his face in my hands, the stubble gently tickling my palms.

'I thought I'd ruined everything,' he murmurs.

'Shh,' I whisper as our lips meet, very gently. We stay like that for a while, not moving, but just kissing very gently. Every so often, I pull back and stare into his beautiful, kind eyes, before leaning forwards for more. At some point, our arms wrap around each other, then our mouths open and the kissing becomes more intense and I know, deep down in the core of my being, that this is the man I want to be with.

'We'd better get to the pub,' I gasp when we finally surface for air. 'They'll be wondering where we are.'

'Do we have to? I'm pretty happy here.'

'We have the whole weekend ahead of us.'

He grins. 'Will the weekend involve more of this?'

'I should bloody hope so.'

25

Noah and I had sex this morning. I can't really believe I'm saying that, as it was only yesterday that I kissed him. It wasn't planned or assumed, at least not by me, although I suspect he may have had other ideas. What happened was that I came over as normal and we started work on the house. Now that the new bathroom is in and functioning, Noah has hired a skip, so he was working on dismantling the old downstairs bathroom and carrying it out, while I started painting the banisters of the new staircase.

So far, so innocent. However, every time he came back through the hallway after carrying something out, he'd casually brush past me. At first, he'd just touch my back, but then his hand started dropping lower and ever so gently stroking and squeezing my bottom. Then he moved my hair to one side so he could brush his lips over the back of my neck. It was slowly driving me crazy. It's another warm day, so I'd dressed lightly in T-shirt and loose shorts. It was torture as he slowly increased the intensity. At one point, he slipped his arm around my waist while he kissed my neck, and I could take it no more, guiding his hand under the fabric of my top and bra and onto my breast. I could hear the catch in his breath as his thumb moved across my nipple.

'Enough,' I'd said, turning around and cupping his face while I kissed him. 'We're never going to get anything done at this rate. Close the front door and take me upstairs.'

He didn't need telling twice but, while I was raring to go, tugging hungrily at his clothes, he was in no rush. It was agony and ecstasy all at the same time because my body was crying out for him, but he just continued to tease with a light touch here, or a little kiss there. By the time the main event came around, he'd already tipped me over the edge once. It was so different to what I've been used to with Lee, and I mean that in a good way. Even the sex itself was totally different. Sex with Lee always came with a running commentary from him that went something like 'Oh yeah, baby, that's fantastic. Mm, yeah. Oh, yes, just lift your knees a little, oh yes, that's it, oh now we're cooking on gas, that's the puppy right there,' and so on as he pumped away, grabbing bits of me to help himself along. It was a little off-putting at first, but I learned to drown him out, and it seemed to make him happy, even if it never really did it for me.

Noah, on the other hand, was almost totally silent until the end. He was so gentle that, at times, he barely seemed to be moving at all, which made all the sensations much more intense. His eyes were locked on mine and I felt slightly uncomfortable to begin with, as if he was scrutinising me. But then I noticed the hunger in them and realised that, far from appraising me critically, he was drinking me in, and it made me feel desired and powerful. I will happily have lots more of that, thank you very much.

Afterwards, I'd grabbed my underwear to get dressed, but he'd stopped me.

'You are so beautiful,' he'd told me, in a hoarse voice I hadn't heard before. 'Can I just look at you a little longer?'

'You're pretty easy on the eye yourself,' I'd told him, running my hand down his chest. There had been the slightest sheen of sweat on it, making him shine.

'I'll tell you something,' I'd called to him later on from the shower, 'whoever tiled this bathroom really knew what they were doing!' which had made him laugh.

We're back downstairs and he's still brushing past me as he passes, but now that the sexual tension has been released, it's just nice; I'm enjoying the physical contact without wanting to drag him upstairs. Of course, if it carries on like this for the rest of the day, I'm not making any promises that things won't escalate again, but I'm under control for now.

'I don't want to presume,' Noah says to me over lunch, 'but would it be a good idea for me to invest in a double mattress, do you think?'

'The thought did occur to me while I was painting,' I reply. 'I don't want to be rude, but your house is a bit of a campsite still so, lovely as the shower is, I'm not sure I want to stay here overnight yet.'

His face falls a little.

'I'm not done,' I tell him. 'I think it would be a good idea for you to get a double mattress anyway, just in case we find we need to rush upstairs like we did this morning, but I also wondered whether you might like to stay over at mine from time to time.'

'Are you seriously suggesting that the caravan of shit is a nicer place to spend the night than my beautiful home?' He's trying, and failing, to look offended.

'The caravan of shit is delightful now, as you well know, and it has the advantage that nobody goes past.

He does look genuinely annoyed now. 'Are you ashamed to be seen with me?'

'No! Not at all, it's just...'

'It's the workplace romance thing, isn't it? You're still hung up on that.'

'A little, yes,' I admit.

'I hate to pop your balloon, but I think you'll find everyone knows already.'

'How? Why?'

'Umm, because we showed up at the pub together, looking happy after a week when everyone noticed we weren't speaking. It's not a big deal, I promise you. They'll just be pleased that things are back on an even keel.'

'But what if...'

'What if we fall out? How about we don't fall out then? I don't know where you've got this hang-up from, but we're not doing anything wrong. We're both single and free to date whomever we choose.'

'Are we?'

'Are we what?'

'Single.'

A smile spreads across his face. 'I guess not. Not any more, anyway.'

* * *

'Tell me about the workplace romance thing,' he says to me as I'm preparing dinner for us on Sunday evening. After a bit of negotiation, he's agreed to give the caravan a try, and I'm a little nervous. The sex bit will be good, I know that, but being in the same bed as him all night is another big step we seem to be taking very quickly. What if he snores? What if I do, but Lee never noticed? He was always a pretty heavy sleeper.

I explain the rules that Orchestra had about workplace romances, and how Lee and I had to stay under the radar even when we lived together.

'How does that work, though?' he asks. 'Surely people saw you arriving together and worked it out?'

'We didn't arrive together. On the rare days that we were both going to be in the office, he would drive in and I would take the bus.'

'Sorry, are you seriously telling me that he wouldn't even drive you in? What kind of man lets his girlfriend take the bus when he's going to the exact same location? He could have made up a story about picking you up on his way in if you didn't want them to know the truth. It's weird enough that your employer gets to dictate who you can and cannot date, but when your boyfriend won't even give you a lift to work, that's proper fucked up.'

'I get it when you say it like that. It seemed normal at the time.'

'Hm. Are you up for a challenge?'

'I'm not sure. What do you have in mind?'

'I'd like to give you a lift to work tomorrow morning.'

'I don't know,' I tell him. 'Isn't that being a bit provocative?'

'Who would we be provoking, exactly? As I told you yesterday, most people will have worked it out on Friday, and I can guarantee that none of them will care. Those who do will probably be happy that everything is back to normal and they don't have to walk on eggshells around us any more. Do you trust me?'

'Of course I trust you. I'm not in the habit of getting naked with people I don't trust. It's just a big step, that's all.'

'So going to bed with me was an easy decision, but going to work with me is a big step that you need to think about?'

I consider what he's said as I start to assemble the salad to go with the steaks I bought to soften the blow that he's staying with me rather than the other way around. Rationally, I know that what he's saying is true, but I've become so used to keeping my relationship under wraps that it seems dangerous to be so open, somehow. I decide to put it out of my mind for now and deal with it in the morning. Noah seems to sense that he's gone as far as he can with this one, and also lets it drop.

'Can I ask you another question?' he says some time later. He's washing up, and I'm standing behind him with my arms wrapped around his chest. We both know what's going to happen when the washing up is done, and I am looking forward to it immensely.

'Of course.' I nuzzle the back of his neck and silently wish he'd just leave the dishes because the barely detectable scent of his shower gel is putting disturbingly graphic pictures of water cascading over his naked body into my mind and getting me more than a little hot under the collar.

'I'm going to visit my parents next weekend. How would you feel about coming with me?'

I'm totally unprepared for what he's just said, and it actually makes me a little uncomfortable. Although I know Noah pretty well, the romantic part of our relationship is still very new. If the tour of Kent and our first kiss was, say, step one, and going to bed was step two, meeting the parents has got to be step five or six. Noah is definitely jumping the gun on this one.

'Oh, wow,' I say, gently detaching myself from him. 'It's quite soon. Are you sure you want to be introducing me to your family so early? What if they hate me?'

'Why would they hate you?' He seems genuinely puzzled.

'I don't know, but it happens, and it would make things awkward, don't you think?'

'Is this all about your previous boyfriend, like the workplace romance thing?'

'No. Lee's parents loved me.'

'And mine will too, I'm sure.'

'I don't know, Noah. This all seems to be going very fast.'

'Hey, no pressure at all. If you're not ready, that's fine. We can do it later. I suppose I'm just keen for them to meet this amazing woman I'm dating.'

'Dating?' I can't help but laugh.

'What would you call it, then?'

'I'll take the amazing woman part, thank you, but I think I'd phrase the dating part differently. Dating implies wining and dining, rather than painting and tiling, which is how we've spent most of our time together so far. How about "Hey, Mum and Dad, this is Ella, who I coerced into working on my house for free under the false pretence of curing her fear of heights and then lured into my bed"?'

'I don't think I lured you. If I remember correctly, it was you that suggested we went upstairs.'

'Technicalities!' I argue. 'I was sorely provoked by some underhand foreplay.'

'Oh, you poor thing,' he laughs. 'I don't seem to remember you minding. In fact, I'd describe you as an active participant.'

'I was probably just going with the flow.'

'I think we're getting off topic.' He smiles. 'Of course you don't have to come if you think it's too soon. I suppose I just didn't like the idea of a whole day without you in it, and I admit that I'd quite like to show you off, but I don't want you to feel uncomfortable.'

He turns back to the sink to carry on washing up. Feeling

reassured that he's not pressurising me, I move behind him again, and my hands somehow find their way under his belt and end up resting provocatively on the waistband of his underpants.

'I'll think about it,' I tell him as my fingers slip underneath the elastic. 'Now, about this underhand foreplay and the question of who lured who.'

'OK, OK. I give up,' he groans. 'I just have one more argument for the defence, while I have enough willpower to resist what you're doing.'

'And what would that be?' I ask. From what I've just found, logic should be way beyond him by now. I'm not sure I'd be able to frame a particularly coherent argument myself, if I'm honest.

'I did buy you lunch.'

'That you did. Well done,' I tell him, as he turns and starts lifting my top.

26

Noah was right. Although I was sure we would be hot gossip all over the site, our joint arrival the following morning appeared to be a compete damp squib. Part of that was because we were pretty much the first to arrive so Noah could unlock the site, but even the occupants of the few vans that were waiting to be let in when we arrived couldn't have seemed to care less. John grunted, 'Morning, Michael, morning, Carol,' and that was the only acknowledgement we got. I'm not stupid, and I'm sure that the rumour mill was feeding the information that Noah and I were together to all those who didn't already know, but nobody seemed bothered by it at all.

I, on the other hand, still have a problem, which is Noah's invitation to meet his family. I've been thinking about it for most of the week, but I haven't come to any firm conclusions. Noah's been really patient and not said anything more about it, but I know he's expecting an answer soon. I did briefly toy with asking John what I should do, but one lengthy, curry-based intervention is more than enough for me, even though I have to admit he was spot-on with the first one. My decision is made harder by the fact that I can't quite put my finger on the cause of my reticence. Of course Noah's family will want to meet his new girlfriend, and I'm curious to meet them too. I suppose it's just the slight awkwardness that he seems to feel about his inability to join the family firm. I don't think I could just sit silently if they were mean to him about it. Also, despite what Noah seems to think, I still feel that it's awfully early in our relationship to be meeting each other's families. What if they reveal all sorts of embarrassing secrets about him? Are we solid enough to weather that, or would I be completely put off? I know we all have embarrassing secrets from childhood, but what if he was the kind of child who liked to torment kittens or something? I'm pretty sure he wasn't, but you know what I mean.

By the time Friday comes around, I know I have to give him an answer.

'Noah,' I say to him as we're locking up the site. 'What would this meeting your family thing involve?'

'What do you mean?'

'Is it having a meal with them, for example, or staying with them for the whole weekend?'

To my relief, he laughs uproariously. 'I love my family to bits, but even I couldn't spend a whole weekend with them, so there's no way I'd inflict that on you.'

'Why not?'

'Firstly, because the concept of a "weekend" doesn't really exist when you're fishing. It's incredibly heavily regulated in terms of what you're allowed to catch and how much, so it's pretty much a seven-day-a-week occupation, either at sea, filling in all the paperwork, or maintaining the boat. So, while I'm sure we'll be fed, we'll definitely have to sing for our supper. The reason I chose this weekend is because the boat isn't at sea, and the planned maintenance is largely painting, which I know is up your street.'

'What is it with your family and forced labour?' I ask. 'Or do I have a boat-related neurosis that you're planning to cure, despite me being unaware of it?'

He does at least have the decency to blush a little. 'Sorry. They're just not "put your feet up, have a cuppa and tell us about yourself" people. There will be cups of tea, and conversation, but everything revolves around the boat, and the boat comes first.'

'OK, what's the second reason?'

'Sorry?'

'You said "firstly", which implies there should be at least one more reason.'

'I'd have thought the second reason would be obvious.'

'Enlighten me.'

'I might want you to myself for a large part of the weekend, if you don't have other plans.'

'Oh, yes?' I smile flirtatiously at him.

'Yeah, the banisters need a second coat of paint,' he grins.

'You really know how to make a girl feel like a princess,' I laugh as I climb into his van. 'What happened to my predecessor? Did she come to her senses and run away, or did you just wear her out?'

As I say this, I realise I actually don't know anything about his relationship history. 'Tell me about your previous girlfriends,' I ask him as he starts the engine and turns in the direction of the pub.

'Why?'

'It helps me to understand you. Are you the kind of guy who goes in for serious, long-term relationships, or is there a string of broken-hearted women out there that you've casually tossed aside after a month or two? I need to know what I'm getting myself in to.'

'The first one,' he tells me after a pause. 'In fact, there have only been two serious girlfriends. I did have a few flings in my early twenties, but I don't think any of them got to the point where there would have been broken hearts.'

'Tell me about the serious ones.'

'The first was Megan. Her parents lived on the same street as mine. We became friends in primary school and, when we hit puberty and the hormones kicked in, we were naturally drawn to each other. I think, in retrospect, we were both worried about putting ourselves "out there" and so we were like a kind of safe space to experiment with what sex and sexuality meant for us.'

'Did you love her?'

'That is such a good question. I thought I loved her at the time but, looking back at it, I think it was more of a really intense friendship with benefits.'

'How did it end?'

'It became clear that we were heading in different directions. She was much more academic than me, so she was always going to go to university. I never had any ambitions like that. So, she went off to study English Literature, and that was the end of us. She started going out with some guy off her course, and married him a few years ago. They've got a baby now, Mum tells me. She's a teacher in Essex somewhere. Her parents still live down the road, but I haven't seen her for years.'

'What about the second one?'

'Leanne.'

'Yes?' I prompt when it becomes clear that he's not going to elaborate.

'Sorry, I'm just trying to think how best to describe her. Some-where between "force of nature" and "whirlwind" is probably as close as I can get. She's one of those people who is just completely comfortable in their own skin and totally uninterested in what other people think of her. I'd never met anyone quite like her, and I was mesmerised by her. We went out for three years.'

'And how did that one end?'

'Things started to unravel when I realised that she was just as uninterested in my views as anyone else's. Whenever we had different opinions, she'd just shut me down or belittle me, and I started to resent her for it. Once my family realised that I was having second thoughts, they revealed what they really thought of her, and that kind of sealed our fate.'

'Why, what did they say?'

'My mother called her, and I quote, "a mouthy little bitch".'

'This is the same mother you're dragging me to meet? Are you sure this is a good idea?'

'Are you a mouthy little bitch? I haven't seen that side of you.'

'No, but my anxiety level just went up a few more notches.'

'They will love you, trust me. What about you?'

'What about me?'

'I've told you my history. Now it's your turn.'

'Three serious relationships, no flings,' I say. 'The first one was Damien, in secondary school. We went out for two years and I lost my virginity to him, so that was a big thing.'

'And how did that end?'

'Badly. I broke his heart.'

'How?'

'He was a lovely guy, but he lacked oomph, and that started to frustrate me. He was a bit like a puppy, permanently eager to please, and I wanted someone who would step up more. He cried when I told him it was over, and I felt like an awful person for ages.'

'Who came next?'

'Sean. I met him in my first year of university. He was the total opposite of Damien. He was a bad boy, and I think I was attracted by the danger after drippy Damien.'

'Harsh.'

'But probably true, at least in part. Anyway, that ended the way all relationships with bad boys end, in flames.'

'Sounds intriguing.'

'How can I put this? He was reckless, he drank heavily and took a lot of drugs. He was wickedly funny when he wasn't high or drunk, but the times when he was lucid became fewer and farther between, and eventually, the university lost patience with him and threw him out. He didn't seem to mind, he just carried on living in his student house and partying harder than ever. In the end, I couldn't take it any more. To be honest, I'm not sure he really knew who I was by the time we split up. He died of an over-dose a year after I graduated.'

'Wow. That must have been hard for you.'

'Yeah. I wondered whether I should have stayed, whether I should have tried to help him. I was pretty messed up for a while, but my sister, Ava, rescued me. It took a while, but she helped me to see that there was nothing I could have done. He was hell bent on self-destruction, and it would only have been worse for me if I'd stayed until the bitter end.'

'And then there was Lee,' Noah says.

'And then there was Lee,' I agree.

'Don't you think it's odd that he hasn't tried to get you back?'

'It's not his nature. If I know him, he's convinced that I'm going to fail down here, so he's just biding his time until I go crawling back, begging for forgiveness. Either that or he's moved on already.'

'He sounds like a charmer,' Noah observes.

'He's not all bad, but I've come to realise that he is a narcissist. The centre of Lee's world is always going to be Lee. I need more than that.'

'Plus, he never taught you how to hang tiles.'

'You're right!' I laugh as we pull into the pub car park. 'What on earth did I see in him?'

27

In the end, I had nothing to worry about. Noah's family were lovely and I got on particularly well with his sister Rachel, who has skippered the boat since their father allegedly retired last year. I say allegedly because, even though he no longer goes to sea, he still acts like he's in charge. Rachel reminded me a bit of Ava; she has the same no-nonsense attitude to life, and I picked up early on that she's very good at completely ignoring her father when she disagrees with him. Noah wasn't exaggerating when he said that everything revolved around the boat; even Rachel's husband James, a solicitor with no apparent interest in fishing, was pitching in, and I felt a bit sorry for Noah, who spent most of the day looking decidedly queasy even though the boat was tied up and not moving at all.

'It's the smell as much as the movement,' he reminded me when I asked about it. 'I just have to catch a whiff of diesel oil and fish and I want to puke.'

The only people who weren't on board doing something were Noah's mother (a formidable woman called Pat) and Rachel's two children who, at three and five years of age, were considered too young to help out. They stayed onshore under the watchful gaze of their grandmother. Thankfully, she seemed to like me as well, and Noah was certainly in a good mood when we got back into the van to head home.

'They definitely loved you. I told you they would,' he'd sighed contentedly as we left Ramsgate behind us.

'There's one thing I don't get,' I'd replied. 'I don't want to sound grasping on your behalf, but that boat must be worth quite a lot.'

'Yes.'

'Is it fair that Rachel gets all of it? Shouldn't some of it come to you?'

'You're assuming my family owns it.'

'Don't they?'

'No, of course not. The finance company owns it.'

'Oh, OK.'

'I like that you were coming in to bat for me, though. The only thing my parents actually own is their house, and I hope they'll be in it for a long time. You can rest assured that, if there's anything left after we've paid for whatever care they might need later, Rachel and I will split it fifty-fifty.'

'I liked her. How did she and James meet? They're like chalk and cheese.'

'He helped her with her divorce. Her first marriage was to this complete tit called Owen, who I suspect thought he could use her to get his hands on the boat and, more importantly, its quota. Thankfully, she saw through him before he could do any real damage and hired James to make sure he didn't get any rights over the boat in the settlement. The rest, as they say, is history.'

* * *

Although it's only a few weeks after the trip to meet Noah's parents, autumn seems to have arrived with a bang and the temperature has dropped significantly. We're getting some floodlights delivered today in time for the clocks changing, but the weather has generally continued to be kind, so we're making good progress. I'm humming happily to myself as I wander across to check how much of our latest delivery is actually of any use. My eye is caught by Kayleigh, one of the sales people, leading a couple across from the sales office to the 'Eton' show home.

'What else are you looking at?' I hear her ask them.

'We've been viewing a couple of properties in Singleton,' they reply.

'Oh, so you're looking at second-hand houses as well?' She sounds very slightly dismissive of the idea. 'Don't get me wrong, there's nothing wrong with a second-hand house, but you don't get to stamp your own identity on them in the same way as you do on a new build, do you know what I mean? Here we are.'

My ability to eavesdrop is cut off as the door closes behind them, but I can't help giggling about the concept of a second-hand house. I'll store that one away to use on Noah later.

'How's it looking?' I ask Steve, the head sparky, who is checking over the rolls of electrical and internet cabling that were delivered a couple of hours ago.

'Do you know, it's what we ordered. To be fair, it's hard to get electrical cabling wrong, but I wouldn't put it past them to find a way. I saw Super Mario from the plumbing team earlier, and apparently even the sanitaryware for number seven is correct. Williamsons are obviously having a good day.'

'Great stuff. All we need are the bricks for number three, and we'll be onto a winner.'

I'm not telling anyone, but I'm actually on track to hit one of my milestones and earn a bonus. I don't want to jinx it, hence my silence. If the bricks arrive, and they're the right ones, we'll have everything on site that we need to hit it, so I've got my fingers and everything else crossed.

No sooner have I indulged the thought than my mobile starts ringing in my pocket. I spot the number and my spirits plummet.

'Hello, Ross. How are you?'

'I'm OK, thanks, Ella. Listen, I'm calling about your bricks. It's bad news, I'm afraid.'

'I don't want bad news, Ross, I want bricks. What time are they arriving?'

'They aren't. Sorry.'

'What do you mean, they aren't?'

'They were supposed to arrive here yesterday, but they hadn't turned up by the end of the day, so I chased the factory this morning. I don't know what to tell you, Ella, but they swear blind that they never got the order, so they haven't manufactured them. I managed to find the paperwork and tore them off a strip, so they're going to expedite the process, but the earliest we'll be able to get them to you is two weeks from today. I'm really sorry, Ella, but it's out of our hands. I can't even try another factory, as they're the only people who make these particular bricks.'

Fuck. I should have known something like this would happen. There goes my bonus, along with my good mood.

'OK. Well, I guess there's nothing to be done. Deborah is off today, but I'll call her in the morning and let her know.'

'Thanks. I really am sorry, Ella.' His voice drips with insincerity, and I mouth a couple of obscenities after disconnecting the call.

I need to be alone for a few minutes to vent some of my frustration, so I head straight back to the site office. Unfortunately, Noah is in there doing some resource planning so I swallow the stream of invective that I had prepared, settle at my desk and bring up the plan instead, even though I'm certain I can't save this one.

'You look like you've just swallowed a wasp,' Noah observes. 'What's up?'

'I've just had Ross from fucking Williamsons on the phone, and the bricks we need for number three won't be here for another two fucking weeks,' I bark.

'Why not?'

'The factory never got the order, apparently.'

'Hm. How much do you trust Ross?' He seems annoyingly unperturbed by my rage.

'I wouldn't trust the little shit as far as I could throw him, but I can't see how it benefits him to lie to me about this.'

'Here's another question. Do you know which factory the bricks we use come from?'

'No idea. Should I?'

'I think you should, because it's one of the many mysteries of the Bitch Queen.'

'Tell me more.'

'When the council grants planning permission for developments like this, one of the things they consider is sustainability.'

'Right.' I'm not sure where this is going, but I am sure Noah is leading up to a point.

'I happen to know that one of the conditions of planning permission was that the bricks had to be a particular style, sourced from Kent. I also know that the factory that was chosen is in Sittingbourne.'

'And you're telling me this because?'

'Because, if I were you, I'd want to double-check that our friends at Williamsons hadn't shat on us again. You know, just out of interest.'

'You suspect the cock-up might be at their end?'

'What do you think?'

'I think it's worth finding out a bit more, you're right. Do you know the name of the factory?'

'As it happens, I do.'

A few minutes later, I've dialled the number.

'Kent Bricks, Colin speaking, how may I help?'

'Hello, Colin. This is Ella from the Atkinson Construction site in Ashford. I've just had a call from our suppliers, Williamsons in Leeds, to tell me that there's been a mix-up with the orders, and you can't supply the bricks we need for two weeks. Would you happen to know anything about that?'

'I wouldn't off the top of my head, sorry,' he replies. 'Do you know what type of brick it was?'

'I don't, I'm afraid. I gather the planning permission specified a particular type, but Williamsons dealt with all of that.'

'No problem, I can look up the order history easily enough. Are you OK to hold for a moment?'

'I wonder whether you're right,' I say to Noah as 'Pachelbel's Canon' plays tinnily down the line to me. 'This doesn't sound like the kind of outfit to lose an order. They sound much more clued-up than Williamsons do.'

'Hi, Ella, are you still there?' Colin's voice enquires a minute or so later.

'I am.'

'It's a bit odd, this one. We were expecting the order and the bricks are ready, but we had a call from someone at Williamsons saying that you were running behind schedule and asking if we could hold on for a couple of weeks. Does that help?'

'It certainly does,' I tell him, grimly. 'Out of interest, if I can get the paperwork cleared, how quickly could you get them to us?'

'Do you have a haulier lined up?'

'I don't, I'm afraid. Are there any that you use regularly?'

'I'd call Gavin at Sittingbourne Logistics if I were you. He's done all your deliveries so far. If he's got the lorries and the drivers, you can have them as soon as you like.'

'When you say, "as soon as I like", what do you mean?'

'I think you'll struggle to get them on a truck today, but I'd be surprised if Gavin couldn't get them to you tomorrow.'

'Thank you. I'll give Gavin a call and get back to you.'

'Well?' Noah asks as soon as I disconnect the call.

'Williamsons *is* fucking us over,' I tell him angrily. 'They called and delayed the order! Not only is there no shortage of the bricks we need but, get this, they've been coming direct from Sittingbourne to here all along.'

'Of course they have.' He looks nonplussed. 'Where else would they go?'

'Williamsons have been charging us haulage from Leeds on the invoices.'

'Really?'

'Yes. So that looks like a fat bung going in someone's back pocket, doesn't it? I wonder if Deborah knows.'

'What are you going to do?'

'I'm going to talk to Gavin and get my bloody bricks.' I bash the number that Colin gave me into the phone and, after a few rings, Gavin answers.

'Colin's right,' he tells me once I've explained the situation. 'There's no way I could get them to you today, but I can probably jiggle the schedule and get them to you tomorrow afternoon if that's any use?'

'That's brilliant, thank you, Gavin. Let me just get the paperwork squared, and I'll call you back to confirm.'

Noah is looking surprisingly uncertain when I hang up the phone.

'How are you going to sort this today when the Bitch Queen isn't available?' he asks.

'I'm going to try an experiment,' I tell him. This latest fiasco has planted a nasty thought in my head, and I'm going to try something risky to see if I'm right. I don't have the next number I need stored, so I have to do a bit of internet searching to track it down.

'Atkinson Construction, Abby speaking. How can I help?'

My mind is instantly cast back to the day of my interview and the young woman who let me in. This is Christopher Atkinson's daughter, and I remember the way she looked at Deborah. At the time, I thought it was odd, but now I think that she may have been on to something.

'Hi, Abby, it's Ella from the site in Ashford. You probably don't remember, but we met briefly when I came for interview.'

'Of course I remember you!' Her voice is warm. 'How's it going?'

'Not great. Is your father around, by any chance?'

'Yeah, he's here. Do you want me to put you through?'

'Please.'

It doesn't take me long to explain the situation to Christopher, leaving out my suspicions, and ask his permission to place the orders with the factory and haulage company directly.

'Of course,' he replied. 'Just get them to send the invoices to Deborah, and I'll explain to her what's happened. I'm impressed with your resourcefulness, Ella. Well done.'

As soon as I'm off the phone to Christopher, I confirm the order with Colin and Gavin, and they assure me that the bricks will be on site before 3 p.m. tomorrow. There is just one more job to do.

'Williamsons, Ross speaking. How may I help?'

'Hi, Ross, it's Ella.'

'Oh, hi, Ella. What's up?'

'You know the order for the bricks that you were telling me about earlier?'

'Oh, yes. I really am sorry about that. I've had another word with the factory, to see if there's anything that can be done, but they've assured me that's the fastest they can get them to you.'

You've got to hand it to him, he does lie smoothly.

'It's really not a problem, Ross,' I tell him in my sweetest voice. 'I've found an alternative source, so I'm cancelling the order.'

There's a long pause before he comes back. 'I'm sorry, I don't think I heard correctly.'

'I said I'm cancelling the order, Ross. I've found a local supplier who can get the bricks to me tomorrow.'

'That's impossible!' He's sounding rattled now. 'The only factory that produces that brick is the one I spoke to. If you're thinking of using some sort of substitute, I need to warn you that the planning department will never allow it. Does Deborah know about this?'

'Not yet, but Christopher Atkinson approved the change, and it's the same brick, so I think the planners will be OK. You have a good evening now, won't you?'

As soon as I hang up, I grab Noah's hands and drag him on a little victory dance around the site office, singing 'Ding Dong, the Witch is Dead' from *The Wizard of Oz* at the top of my lungs.

28

I'm barely through the door of the site office the next morning when my phone rings. It's Deborah.

'Good morning, Deborah,' I answer cheerfully. 'Did you have a nice day off?'

'Cut the crap.' Her voice is pure ice. 'I've just come in to a message from Ross at Williamsons, saying you've cancelled the brick order and placed it with another supplier?'

'That's right. He told me a load of bullshit about how the factory had lost the order, but when I called the factory to check, they told me that Williamsons had asked for a delay. If I'm to hit my milestone, I need those bricks, so I talked to Christopher and he said it was OK to get them direct.'

'Christopher isn't in charge of the Ashford site, as you well know,' she hisses. 'I am, and I take an extremely dim view of you going behind my back in this underhand manner. You should have waited and talked to me. Anyway, luckily for you, we can still put it right. I need you to cancel your new order and reinstate the one with Williamsons. In the meantime, I'll have a chat with Ross and see whether we can get the bricks to you a bit quicker than he said yesterday.'

'I can't do that,' I lie. 'They're already on their way.'

Her voice is low and dangerous. 'You find a way to cancel that order, or else.'

'Or else what?' The blood is pumping through my veins now. I'm determined not to back down.

'Or else you'll regret it.'

'I'm not cancelling the order, Deborah. Williamsons clearly told me they couldn't get the bricks, but Ross was lying. You weren't available so I went to Christopher, who gave me the OK to get them direct from the factory. I've done nothing wrong, and I need these bricks to arrive today to hit my milestone.'

'You stupid little bitch!' Her voice has now risen by about an octave and she's practically screaming at me. 'Can't you see that there are more important things in the world than your bloody milestone? I have a delicate contractual relationship with Williamsons that goes way beyond your site, and you're putting that at risk. Cancel the order.'

'Frankly, Deborah, I don't really give a shit about your delicate contractual relationship. It's bollocks. They're taking you for a ride. Did you know that they're charging you haulage from Leeds on bricks that only come from Sittingbourne?'

I've obviously landed a blow, because there's a pause before she replies, and her voice sounds a little less sure of itself.

'You clearly know nothing about business,' she blusters. 'There are swings and roundabouts, and ways of presenting accounts that are more advantageous than others. I'm fully aware of what Williamsons are charging, and there's nothing under-hand going on. Now, are you going to cancel the order or not?'

'I've told you. I can't cancel it as it's already on its way.'

'In that case, you leave me no choice. I'm terminating your

contract with Atkinson Construction with immediate effect on
the grounds of gross insubordination. Please hand your keys in to
the site foreman and ask him to contact me to confirm that you've
done so. I'll expect you to have vacated your accommodation by
the end of the day.'

'You can't sack me!' I exclaim. 'I've done nothing wrong!'

'You've done plenty wrong. Your insubordination is grounds
enough, but you've also jeopardised the whole company.'

'Hang on a minute, Deborah...'

'Goodbye, Ella.' The phone goes dead.

I'm speechless. I knew she'd call, and I knew she'd be pissed
off, but I never considered that she might actually sack me. I sink
into the chair behind the desk in a daze.

'Carol, I know we've got the morning meeting in a minute, but
I wanted to catch you quickly before,' John tells me as he comes
into the site office a few minutes later. 'The architrave for the
dining room in number thirteen is five mil too short. Dave
reckons he can get around it with a bit of filler in the gap, and the
punters will never know, but I wanted to check with you first.'

'Honestly, John? I have no idea. Apparently, I don't work here
any more.'

Before he gets a chance to reply, Noah bursts through the
door.

'What the fuck's going on, Ella? I've just had the Bitch Queen
on the phone ordering me to take your keys off you.'

'Yeah, I know. She fired me.'

'Why?'

'She demanded that I cancel the order with Kent Bricks. I
refused to back down, so she sacked me.' I hand him the site keys.
'Here you are. I'll drop the caravan key in once I've cleared it out.'
I push past him, automatically grabbing my hard hat, and march
in the direction of my car. Now that the sales office has opened,

the staff car park has been relocated to the other end of the site, so I have to walk past all the houses to get there. I can see the various team leads heading towards the site office for the morning meeting, and a few of them look confused to see me walking the other way, but thankfully none of them say anything.

'Wait!' Noah's voice calls from behind me, but I don't change my pace. A few seconds later, he's alongside me.

'What are you doing?' he asks.

'I've been fired, Noah. It's over,' I tell him, bitterly, as the tears finally start to flow.

'You don't know that. Give her an hour or two to calm down and I'm sure she'll see sense.'

This is enough to stop me in my tracks and I turn to face him.

'You know that isn't going to happen as well as I do,' I say. 'I thought I had her this time, I really did, because I dotted every I and crossed every t when I bypassed Williamsons, but I underestimated her badly. Nothing anybody says or does will persuade her to change her mind. Now, if you'll excuse me, I have a caravan to clear.'

'Where will you go?'

'I don't know. Home, I guess.'

He looks absolutely crestfallen. 'But what about you and me?'

'I don't know,' I tell him honestly.

'I do. Why don't you bring your stuff over to my place? There are loads of building sites around here, and I'm sure one of them must be looking for a project manager. You'll get a better job in no time and you can stay as long as you like.'

I consider what he's said. 'Are you asking me to move in with you?'

'Umm, yes. I guess I am. Look, I've never met anyone like you, and I think we've got something special. If you go back north, I'll do whatever I can, but I'm not sure how easy a long-distance relationship is going to be in practice. So yeah, why don't you move in?'

'What if I don't find another job straight away? I don't have another redundancy package to keep me going, Noah. I've been sacked. My pay stops now and I don't have enough of my last package left to pay you rent.'

'I didn't say anything about charging you rent.'

'So you'd let me move in and live with you for free? Eat your food, use your gas and electricity?'

'Yes, if that's what it takes to stop you leaving.'

I gaze into his eyes. There is so much love and kindness there, and I would love nothing more than to grab all my stuff from the caravan and drive straight to his house. But one of us has to be realistic about what that would mean, and it doesn't appear to be him.

'That's a lovely idea, it really is,' I tell him through my tears.

'Great, I'll come and help you move. I'm sure the others can get by without me for a bit.'

'I haven't finished. It's a lovely idea, but I can't take you up on it.'

'Why not?'

'Because it wouldn't work, for all sorts of reasons.'

'Such as?'

'OK, let's say I do this and move in with you. It would be lovely to begin with and I'm sure we'd be really happy, but there's only so long that you'd be able to tolerate me freeloading before you started to resent me. I don't want what we have to go there.'

'I couldn't ever resent you!'

'You say that now, Noah, and I know you mean it, but when we're six months down the track, I'm still unemployed and you're the one paying all the bills, it would be a different picture.'

'I'd be happy, even if you were unemployed for two years.'

'See it from my perspective then. How do you think I'd feel about being reliant on you for everything and not having my own income? Would that make me happy?'

'I don't see what difference it makes. What if you go home, and you don't get a job?'

'It is different, because they're my family.'

'So you're saying that it's OK to sponge off your parents, but not off the man who loves you?'

'Please don't say that, Noah. You're just making this harder.'

'But I do. I love you, Ella, and I'll do whatever I can to make you happy. You love me, don't you?'

This just makes the tears flow faster. 'It's not about whether I love you or not. It's about—' I dry up.

'What? Tell me.'

'We should never have done this,' I tell him baldly. 'I knew office romances were a bad idea, but I let myself fall for you anyway, and now look at the mess we're in. I don't belong here, Noah. I don't belong on a building site and I don't belong in Kent. I know you would do anything to keep me here, and I love you for it, but there's no future for us if we're not equals, and we can't be equals if I'm relying on you for handouts. If you love me like you say you do, then you'll do the right thing and let me go.'

* * *

I have no idea how I managed to get back to Mum and Dad's without having an accident, because I cried. All the way. I was still crying when I got here, and I'm now sitting in my old room sobbing my heart out. All my stuff is still in the car, but walking away from the man I love, clearing out the caravan and the long drive have emptied me and I just have no more energy for anything. I should never have applied for the stupid job in the first place, as I'm much worse off in a lot of ways than before I started. I'm unemployed, again, but without the reserves I had when Orchestra made me redundant. I've got to go through the painful process of trying to find another job, again, with a broken heart to boot. Despite all that, I can't regret meeting Noah. He'll never know how much I wanted to accept his offer, but in the end, I promised him that we'd keep in touch and I'd apply for other jobs in the south so we could hopefully be together. It was enough to get him to step back and let me go, but I think we both know the chances of me moving back down to Kent are minimal.

I'm distracted by a ping from my phone. It's a message from Noah and my heart breaks all over again. I don't know if I can bear to read it. Eventually, I wipe away the tears so I can at least see what he's written.

Did you get home safely?

I tap out a reply.

Yes, thank you. Are you OK?

I can see he's typing. It's after five, so he'll be at home, sitting in the chair in his bedroom. I can see it so clearly, and I yearn to be there with him. His reply makes me feel like the worst human being in the world.

I've been better. You?

I consider how to reply for a long time, but in the end I decide to be honest.

I've been better too.

29

This was a bad idea, I've come to realise. Yes, Noah might have ended up resenting me, but being stuck at home with Mum and Dad's platitudes is far worse. If I had a pound for every time they told me that I will get over him, there are plenty more fish in the sea, and variations on those themes, I'd be able to retire and move back south. Ava is also trying to help, and printouts of various job vacancies she thinks might suit me keep getting shoved through the front door. I can't cope with any of it. Having said that the chances of moving south again were pretty much nil, I have secretly started scanning the vacancies in Ashford and applying for anything I think I have even the remotest chance of getting, including a vacancy for a shelf-stacker in one of the supermarkets. None of them have come to anything so far.

I haven't heard any more from Noah. I've lost count of the number of times I've read his messages, and I still cry every time I look at them. I spend hours each day thinking about him, what he's doing and how the house is coming along. I miss him so much, I have a permanent ache in my gut, and my appetite has deserted me.

'Try to eat a little more, love,' my mother is urging as I push the lasagne we're having for tea round my plate. 'You're looking awfully thin. You need your strength, now more than ever.'

She's not wrong. I've lost over half a stone in the two weeks I've been home. If ever you need a sure-fire weight-loss programme, a broken heart is it. Unless you're a comfort eater, I suppose.

I did have a very snotty email from Deborah a couple of days after I'd got home, detailing the hour and date my pay was stopped and asking where she should send my P45. She also couldn't resist putting the boot in by writing,

I'm sure it doesn't need to be said, but we will not be able to supply you with a reference.

I sent her my address by return, but there's no sign of the P45 yet.

When Mum finally gives up trying to cajole me into eating more, I retreat to the relative safety of my bedroom. We're definitely regressing; at one point, she even suggested that I, 'just take three more mouthfuls,' which is what she used to say when I refused to eat my vegetables as a child. My mobile phone is on my bedside table, and I notice that I have a missed call from an unknown number. Thinking it might be one of the companies I've applied to getting back to me, I press to return the call.

'Ella, is that you?' the unmistakeable voice of Christopher Atkinson answers after a couple of rings.

I don't know what to say. Only Deborah's voice would be more unwelcome right now. Why on earth would Christopher Atkinson, CEO of the company that just fired me, be calling?

'Are you there? Please don't hang up,' he continues.

'I'm here. Is this about my P45? Because I haven't received it.'

'It's not. I, umm, need to talk to you about something. I wondered if you would be prepared to meet me.'

'Christopher, you do know that I don't work for you any more, don't you?'

'I know that Deborah tried to fire you,' he tells me. 'But I haven't processed the paperwork yet, and Deborah is, er, leaving the company soon. This would all be a lot easier to explain face to face, if I can persuade you.'

What to do? On the one hand, I want nothing more to do with Atkinson bloody Construction, but I'm curious about Deborah leaving, and that's enough to sway me.

'What did you have in mind?'

'There's a pub in East Morton that has a very good reputation. The Farmer's Arms, I think it's called. I've been meaning to go for ages, but the opportunity has never arisen. Would you consider meeting me there for lunch tomorrow? It will be on me, obviously.'

OK, now I'm in a really difficult position. Christopher isn't to know that he's talking about the pub that Lee's parents own. How would they feel about seeing me? Would it all be massively awkward? At least Lee won't be there on a midweek lunchtime, I suppose, but it's not ideal.

'I'm sure there must be somewhere more convenient for you,' I tell him. 'I could come to the office if you prefer.'

'I think I might be wanting a break from the office. I have what I suspect will be a difficult meeting in the morning, so a change of scenery and a pub lunch will be very welcome. Shall I book a table for twelve-thirty?'

He's not going to be swayed, and if I'm going to learn anything about the sudden departure of my nemesis, I realise I'm going to have to go along with it.

'I'll see you there,' I say.

'Excellent. I'll make the booking now. See you tomorrow.'

* * *

In my eagerness not to keep Christopher waiting, I actually arrive at the Farmer's Arms around twenty minutes early. I decide to sit in my car until he arrives, but that plan implodes when Lee's brother Nathan appears, carrying a crate of empty bottles to the bottle store, and spots me.

'Ella!' he exclaims when I wind down the window. 'What are you doing here? You're not stalking Lee, are you?'

'No, what makes you say that?'

He looks a little uncomfortable. 'Umm. Lee told us that you didn't take the break-up particularly well.'

Of course he'd have reframed it. I should have known.

'Did he now? What did he say?' I ask.

Nathan is starting to fidget. 'He said you were really upset, that you were crying and begging him to let you stay, but he knew he had to do it as it was the right thing for both of you.'

'So if I told you that's totally untrue and I actually finished with him?' I suggest.

He ponders for a moment. 'That would make an awful lot of sense, now I come to think about it. I never saw you as the hysterical type. So what are you doing here then?'

'I'm meeting my ex-boss for lunch and I'm a bit early.'

'Well, come and wait for him at the bar at least. Mum will be delighted to see you. I don't think she believed a word of Lee's story from the beginning.'

I follow him inside and it's like stepping back in time. Nothing has changed. Why would it, I suppose? Nathan offers me a glass of wine, but I turn it down and opt for a Coke instead.

'Ella, what a lovely surprise!' Lee's mother envelops me in her trademark hug, as if I were still her son's girlfriend.

'Hello, Kate. How are you?'

'I'm fine, thank you. What brings you to this neck of the woods? Were you looking for Lee?'

'No. He's at work, isn't he?'

'Ah.' She looks a little uncomfortable. 'I've got to go, but Nathan can fill you in. Lovely to see you. Are you eating with us?'

'Yes, I'm meeting my ex-boss for lunch.'

'Family discount, Nathan, OK?' Kate instructs as she bustles off.

'What was that about?' I ask Nathan.

'I probably should have mentioned,' he says, looking a little bashful. 'Lee works here now. Don't worry, we'll keep him away from your lunch. He's in the restaurant today, so if you and your ex-boss are happy with a table in the bar, he'll never know you're here. Why are you meeting your ex-boss anyway?'

'I'm not sure yet. It's a complicated story. Why is Lee working here?'

'That isn't a complicated story, but it does take a little while to tell properly.' He leans forward and lowers his voice conspiratorially. 'It seems that treachery doesn't pay.' Nathan's eyes are sparkling with thinly concealed delight. He's a terrible gossip, and this is obviously a big story for him.

'What does that mean?'

'What was the name of that place where you both worked?'

'Orchestra.'

'That's right. So, do you remember that he left Orchestra rather suddenly for one of their competitors?'

'Harmony. It's engraved in my mind. That little stunt cost me my job, didn't he tell you?'

'No, sorry. So there he is, all happy at Harmony, when his new boss taps him on the shoulder and drags him into a meeting room. I don't know the full ins and outs of it, but it seems someone at Orchestra had found proof that he'd been up to no good, and that Harmony could potentially be implicated. He swears blind he did nothing wrong, but Harmony couldn't get rid of him quickly enough.'

'They sacked him?'

'They did.'

I feel a pang of guilt, remembering the recording that Ava sent in. I try as hard as I can to keep my face neutral.

'But why is he here? He always swore he'd never work here,' I ask.

'Ah. So, after he got the push from Harmony, things unravelled fairly quickly. He's a typical sales guy, Lee, so he's got good patter and had little trouble securing interviews. But, and this is a big but, there was an issue with the references. Harmony weren't going to give him one, given that they'd slung him out to avoid a scandal and possibly a court case, and Orchestra certainly weren't going to, as he'd done the dirty on them. So, imagine you're interviewing this promising-sounding candidate, and then he reveals that not just one, but two of his most recent employers are not prepared to vouch for him. Bit of a red flag, isn't it?'

I'm reminded of my snotty email from Deborah. At least Orchestra would still give me a reference, I think. I make a mental note to contact them and check.

'I can see that would make things difficult,' I say to Nathan.

'Indeed. And, on top of that, he's got his posh car and the swanky apartment you were living in to pay for. With no income, that all crashed and burned fairly spectacularly. It was only Dad's intervention that stopped him from getting evicted by the bailiffs. I don't know how much Dad had to lay out to stop him getting a serious black mark on his credit rating, but given the late-night discussions I kept stumbling into, I think it's a lot. So, he's here until he pays back what he owes them and gets back on his feet.'

'Poor Lee.'

'Why are you saying that? It sounds like he did the dirty on you as well.'

'He did, but I wouldn't wish that on him.'

'Well, him moving back here made someone's day,' he smiles, 'so it's not all bad.'

'What do you mean?'

'Do you remember Rosie, who also works here?'

'I do. She had a massive crush on Lee, I seem to remember.'

'She's got her claws well and truly into him now. Are you OK hearing this?'

'Yes, Lee and I are ancient history and, as I told you, I was the one that finished things between us. Are he and Rosie together then? I would have thought she was too timid for him.'

'You're right. It's funny really, because when he was mister big, with his flash car and everything, she was in awe of him and barely said a word to him. Now that his circumstances are, shall we say, "reduced", that's all gone and she doesn't think twice about giving him a piece of her mind. Between you and me, I think she's quite good for him. Not that you weren't, of course.'

'He won't stay here for long, though, will he? He's bound to have a plan.'

'Oh yes,' Nathan laughs. 'He's never short of plans, that one. What he's short of are the means to execute them. After the reason for his lack of interview success dawned on him, he decided that he was better suited to being an entrepreneur and has come up with all sorts of business ideas. Unfortunately, all of them so far have required significant investment. He doesn't have any money, the bank won't touch him with a barge pole, and

Mum and Dad have made it abundantly clear that they've spent all they were prepared to on bailing him out.'

'What about Rosie's parents? Knowing Lee, he wouldn't have thought twice about approaching them.'

'Right again. He tried to get them to invest in a second-hand car lot idea, but I don't think they had the kind of sums that Lee was looking for and Rosie nearly ripped him a new one when she found out he'd asked them.'

'I'm struggling to imagine that.'

'Like I said, the fact that he's no longer the rich guy with the flashy suits has made her bold.'

'And you're loving all of this, I'm sure.'

'I wouldn't say I'm loving it, because he's my brother even when he's being an arse, but it's certainly more peaceful around here without him swaggering around being the big shot. I think this might be your man.'

I turn and come face to face with Christopher Atkinson and, to my surprise, he has Abby with him.

'I'm so sorry we're late, Ella,' he tells me. 'It's been a bit of a week and my morning meeting went on longer than I'd antici-pated. Have you got a coat with you? I thought it might be nice to sit outside. It's such a beautiful day and I feel like I could do with some fresh air after being stuck in the office this morning. It also means I can tell you what this is all about without us being overheard.'

30

'That's much better,' Christopher sighs after his first big mouthful of the guest IPA. 'I won't lie, it's been a tricky few weeks.'

I'm not sure how to respond, or even what he wants, so I remain silent. After another large mouthful, he leans forward and lowers his voice.

'Tell me honestly, what do you think of Deborah?'

'She wasn't the easiest boss I've ever worked for,' I reply as tactfully as I can.

'Fucking nightmare, more like,' Abby murmurs. 'I always hated the bitch.'

'I'm well aware of your opinions on the subject, thank you, Abby,' Christopher admonishes her. 'Ella, would it help you to express yourself more openly if I told you that the reason Deborah has left the company is that I dismissed her this morning?'

So that was his difficult meeting. I'd love to have been a fly on the wall for that one. I am shocked, though; they seemed very close when I went for interview. Once again, I try to keep my face neutral.

'I can see you're surprised,' he continues. So much for my neutral expression. 'The truth is that some anomalies came to my attention a few months ago, and I've been looking into them with the help of a private investigator and a forensic accountant. When she tried to terminate your contract, a number of things came to a head very quickly. I'm sorry it's taken me this long to get in touch, but I needed to go down to Ashford last week and I didn't think you'd be interested in a conversation while Deborah was still on board.'

'You say she *tried* to terminate my contract, but I can assure you that she was pretty clear about it. She definitely fired me.'

'There's a small problem with that,' he smiles. 'It's my company, and I do the hiring and firing, not her. So, as far as I'm concerned, you're still an employee on the payroll. If, after this meeting, you decide you don't want to continue working for me, I'll quite understand and we'll come to an arrangement, but I hope what I have to tell you will persuade you to stay.'

'Please hear him out,' Abby chips in, obviously worried that I'm going to give him a piece of my mind and storm off. Part of me is tempted, but curiosity gets in the way. We're interrupted by Rosie wanting to take our food order, and she doesn't look at all pleased to see me. Once we've chosen and she's stalked off towards the kitchen, Christopher leans forward again.

'What do you know about haulage?' he asks.

'I know trucks turn up and deliver stuff, but I haven't thought about it in much more detail than that, I'm afraid.' I do know more than that, but I'm keeping my cards close to my chest for now.

'OK. Most haulage companies charge based on distance,' he tells me. 'For a forty-four-tonne articulated lorry, which is what we mainly use, that's generally just shy of three pounds per mile. Bear with me, there is a point to this. Leeds to Ashford is around two hundred and fifty miles by road, so you're looking at something in the region of seven hundred and fifty pounds in haulage fees to bring a full load from Williamsons down to your site, plus extra if the driver needs to stop overnight on the way. I gather, from talking to your site foreman, that a lot of your deliveries were incorrect?'

'Yes. It was infuriating, because I kept having to adjust the project plan to allow for the fact that the goods we needed hadn't turned up. When I first started, I phoned Williamsons to complain, and they just said the goods had been unloaded so they were my responsibility. Then I tried to check them before they came off the lorry so we could send the wrong stuff straight back, but Deborah tore me off a strip for that.'

'I bet she did. You were interfering with her little scam.'

'I'm sorry?' I didn't see that one coming.

'Atkinson Construction has always concentrated on the north of England because that's where we're based. Expanding into the south was very much Deborah's idea, which I bought into because she persuaded me that the profit margins would be better. We've got two sites in the south: your one at Ashford and the other at Broadbridge Heath, near Horsham. Here's where it starts to get interesting. The deliveries you received weren't completely wrong; they were simply destined for the other site.'

'I don't get it.'

'Neither did I to begin with. What did Deborah tell you to do with the incorrect items?'

'She arranged for them to be collected and, some time later, the right stuff would turn up.'

'Did you ever ask what she was doing with them?'

'No. To be honest, I wasn't that interested. I just wanted the right materials. I was focused on doing whatever I could to keep the project on track.'

'That reminds me of another question. How many of your milestones did you hit successfully?'

'I nearly hit the last one, but we had the debacle with the brick delivery, and then Deborah sacked me, so that was the end of that.'

'I asked the Broadbridge Heath project manager the same question, and he gave the same answer. You are the only two project managers who haven't hit any of the milestones but, according to the accounts, you were paid the bonuses for all of them. You're also the only two who were under Deborah, so I think we can guess where that money went. Anyway, you were getting materials destined for Broadbridge Heath and they were getting yours. We managed to get copies of the invoices that the haulage company sent to Williamsons. What they show is that the goods were being moved directly from one site to the other. So, a truck would collect your incorrect items and take them straight to Broadbridge Heath, and vice versa.'

'That makes sense, if that's where they were supposed to be. It would have been better if they'd gone to the right place first time around, though.'

'Indeed. But the invoices from Williamsons to us showed much higher figures than the hauliers had charged them. We worked out that, instead of passing on the actual charges, they were billing us for bringing the load all the way back to Leeds, and then from Leeds to the other site.'

I decide to reveal what I know. 'They were doing the same with the bricks,' I say. 'They were coming direct from Sitting-bourne, but the invoice showed Leeds.'

'Yes, we saw that too. Given the number of deliveries, it will have added up fast. We don't have the final figure yet, but it's well into the tens of thousands, possibly even more.'

'But how would that have benefited Deborah?'

'Good question. If I tell you that Deborah is divorced but kept her ex-husband's surname, and that her maiden name is Williamson, does that give you a clue?'

He obviously sees the penny dropping from the look on my face, and continues. 'Gus Williamson, the owner of Williamsons, is her brother. Ross is her nephew.'

'Bloody hell.'

'It gets worse. We don't know this for sure yet, but we think the reason she kept her married surname is because the investigator found a Deborah Williamson with a criminal record.'

My mouth drops open.

'Funnily enough, she was done for embezzlement.'

'What are you going to do?' I ask.

'We're working on that. Assuming she is the same Deborah Williamson, another criminal charge would be the best outcome, but it's possible that the police won't want to pursue it. If they don't, we'll sue Williamsons for every penny they have. Either way, Deborah, Gus and Ross are going to regret this, don't worry about that.'

'When I rang you, to ask whether I could source the bricks directly, did you know what was going on then?' I ask.

'I had a pretty good idea. I'm sorry I couldn't tell you at the time, and I feel dreadful that you got caught in the crossfire like that. However, we were interested to see what she'd do. If it's any consolation, trying to get rid of you only tightened the noose around her own neck.'

I can't help but feel a grim sense of satisfaction.

'Can I revise my answer to your first question?' I ask him, suddenly.

'Absolutely.'

'I'm with Abby. Deborah was a nightmare from the start and I hated her.'

'Which brings us onto the final piece of the jigsaw. I'm going to be honest with you, Ella, and tell you that I was not in favour of hiring you. It's nothing personal; you just didn't have any experience of construction.'

'I was a little surprised to be offered the job,' I reply.

'However, Deborah insisted that you were the one she wanted. She gave me this long spiel about how important it was to have more women in the industry, that your skills were transferable, and also that you were prepared to accept a significantly lower salary than someone with more experience. She promised me faithfully that she'd keep an eye on you and support you if you were struggling.'

'She has a very funny way of being supportive,' I observe, making Abby snort with laughter.

'I'm afraid she saw you as an easy target. She was counting on your lack of experience to ensure her little scheme continued to go undetected.'

'So, when I started demanding we check everything...'

'Yes, she wouldn't have liked that at all.'

'What a bitch,' I sigh, and Abby giggles again. 'There's one thing I don't get,' I continue, switching my attention to Abby. 'When I came for interview, I noticed the way that you looked at Deborah when she walked into the room. You'd obviously sussed her, but I'm guessing you didn't say anything to your dad. Why?'

'I tried, believe me,' she replies. 'But, by the time I realised what she was really like, she had Dad eating out of the palm of her hand. We had a massive row and I was forbidden from saying anything more about her.'

'Not my finest hour,' Christopher agrees. 'But she never gave me any reason to doubt her. Whenever I was around, she was a model of efficiency and kindness. We were also,' he blushes, 'having a bit of a clandestine relationship.'

'It wasn't that bloody clandestine,' Abby retorts. 'It was obvious what was going on, and she told me more than once that she could make things very difficult between you and me if I didn't toe the line.'

'She duped me there too, it seems. After Abby's mum died, I reckon Deborah saw that I was lonely and exploited it. Thinking of relationships, tell me about you and Noah.'

I blush furiously.

'I thought as much. He's obviously holding quite the candle for you too.'

'I'm sorry,' I mumble. 'I know office romances are a bad idea...'

'Mine certainly was!' He laughs bitterly. 'But, if you'll permit a little meddling from a man who ought to know a lot better, I think he's a keeper. Do you know what happened on site after you left? Why I had to go down there?'

'No.'

'I've never come across anything like it, and I've been in this industry for a long time. As soon as they'd unloaded your brick delivery, you know, the one Deborah objected to so strongly, they all walked off site.'

'I'm sorry?'

'The whole workforce downed tools in protest at your dismissal. Deborah got a call from Kayleigh in the sales office saying that everyone had left, and she and Breanna were being evicted from the office because Noah was locking up the site. I've never heard Deborah properly lose her cool before, but it was volcanic. Of course, she insisted to me that she would get the situation under control, but I decided to intervene and go down there myself. She didn't like it, but I pulled rank.'

Christopher has to break off because Rosie appears again, this time delivering our food. Her facial expression is still mutinous, and I just hope she hasn't spat in it.

'Mm, this is delicious,' he comments, after a couple of bites of his steak and kidney pie. 'Anyway, I went down there and met Noah and this fellow called John. They were very clear with me about you, Deborah and Williamsons. They couldn't speak highly enough of you, but the other two didn't come across so well. They referred to Deborah as "the Bitch Queen". Are you familiar with that term?'

'Oh, that is just too good,' Abby laughs.

'There's little love lost between the guys on site and her,' I comment.

'But they have immense loyalty to you. That says a lot. Noah wouldn't let me leave until he'd fired up the computer and showed me your project plan, which I will admit was very impressive. So here's the pitch. Would you consider going back down there and continuing? In return, I will increase your salary to the market rate for your position and give you a greater say in the sourcing of materials. Before you answer, you might like to know that I took the opportunity to view a few other sites down there, and I'll definitely be making a long-term commitment to more projects in the area, so I'd like you to consider becoming a permanent member of the team as well.'

'That depends. Will I be working for you, or are you looking to replace Deborah with someone new?' I ask.

'Good question. You'll be working with me initially, but I can't run the company on my own; there are too many moving parts, so I need help. However, I've learned my lesson and my new associate will be someone I know I can trust implicitly. I've already decided who it will be, and I hope you'll work very well with her once she's up to speed.'

'It's me,' Abby tells me.

'And this is the very last thing I want to ask you before you give me your decision,' Christopher continues. 'Abby has grown up in the business, but she's never experienced construction at the sharp end. We were talking about it on the way over, and she's asked to come and spend some time with you, learning the ropes. What do you think?'

I consider his proposal, but I'm fairly certain I know what I'm going to do. He's fired the Bitch Queen and offered me everything I could have asked for, and there's no way I can turn down the offer after the effort that Noah, John, and everyone else on site went to. I feel quite emotional when I think about them all walking off site to support me.

'I think we can make that work,' I tell him.

31

Christopher is initially bemused when Rosie refuses to bring him a bill, so I take pity on him and explain my relationship with the owners.

'Why didn't you tell me?' he exclaims. 'I would have chosen somewhere else if I'd known.'

'It's fine,' I reassure him. 'They wouldn't have given us the family discount if they weren't pleased to see me.'

I still have half a glass of Coke when they leave, so I tilt my head up towards the sun and enjoy the warmth on my face. I'm going to see Noah again, and the thought makes me want to burst with joy.

'Are you waiting for me?' a familiar voice asks.

'Hello, Lee. Nathan told me you were working in the restaurant today. I wasn't expecting to see you.'

'Oh, really?' He's sneering unpleasantly. 'You turn up at my family's pub, and you honestly expect me to believe you weren't hoping to see me? Why else would you be here?'

'I had a meeting with my boss, and he suggested having it here. I tried to put him off, actually.'

'Oh, spare me the bullshit, Ella. What do you want?'

I study him for a moment. I can see he's tried to maintain his suave appearance, but there are definite cracks showing. His eyes have lost their sparkle, and I'm amazed to see that he obviously hasn't shaved for a day or two. His expression is oddly triumphant, and I realise that he genuinely thinks I've come here just to see him.

'I don't want anything, not from you anyway,' I tell him mildly. 'I'm just finishing my drink and then I'll be on my way.'

'Good,' he spits. 'I'm with Rosie now, so if you were thinking of trying to win me back, you're going to be disappointed.'

I struggle not to laugh. He really is something else.

'I heard,' I tell him as I swallow the last of my drink and stand up. 'I hope you two will be very happy. I have to go now. I have a building site in Kent to run and an amazing man is waiting for me there. Goodbye, Lee.'

I can sense his eyes on me as I stride away, and I can't help smiling.

As soon as I get home, I send a message to Noah. I would have done it from my car in the pub car park, but I didn't fancy another confrontation with Lee, so I hurriedly started the engine and drove away. I type:

The Bitch Queen is gone and I am reinstated!

I stare at the screen for a while, waiting for the ticks to go blue, but he must be away from his phone or in the middle of something. I'm nervous; despite Christopher's assurances, I'm not sure how Noah is going to react. I do know that I'm prepared to do whatever it takes to put things right with him, though.

Mum and Dad are out, and I'm desperate to share my news with someone, so I wander over to Ava's house. After the traditional fussing over Teddy, we settle in the kitchen and she puts the kettle on.

'I've still got the job,' I tell her, grinning. 'I am officially un-fired, with a substantial pay rise, and they've made me perma-nent as well.'

She pauses. 'Is that good news?'

'Yes, why wouldn't it be?'

'What about that woman who made your life so difficult?'

'Deborah? She's gone. Christopher fired her this morning.'

'Hang on. She fired you and then Christopher fired her? That's a lot of firing, don't you think? What was his reason for reinstating you? You don't think he's secretly in love with you, do you? Might be worth checking. I expect he's worth a bob or two.'

'Stop it! I can't tell you the details, I'm afraid, because it's all confidential, but gross misconduct on Deborah's part probably sums it up.'

'Are you taking over her job?'

'Absolutely not. I'm going back down south tomorrow to pick up where I left off. Turns out I'm quite good at this whole construction thing. Christopher's looking at other sites in the area, so it sounds like I'm going to be busy.'

'I hate to rain on your parade, but I assume he'll be replacing Deborah with someone. What if you don't get on with them?'

'I reckon it will be OK. I already know who it is.'

'Oh, yes?'

'Abby, his daughter. She's really nice, and she's coming down for a few months to get some experience of what happens on site. I think we'll get on just fine.'

'And what about Noah? Have you talked to him?'

'No, not yet. I've sent him a message, but he's obviously busy.'

'How do you think he'll feel about seeing you again, after you fled?'

'According to Christopher, he's still keen, so I'm pinning my hopes on that. He and John, the head chippy, organised a walkout in protest at my dismissal.'

'Really?'

'Yup. That doesn't sound like he hates me, does it?'

'One final question. Are you sure this is what you want?'

'Yes, definitely.'

'Then I'll cross everything for you.'

'Thank you. I've also got some other news, actually.'

It's over an hour later when I leave her house, having filled Ava in on Lee's fall from grace. She was absolutely delighted, and completely unrepentant about sending in the recording, although I am still a little conflicted about it. Her view is that he got everything he deserved, and hopefully he'd learn some important lessons from his experience. Thankfully, Mum and Dad are a bit more positive about my reinstatement than Ava was, probably because it meant I'd stop moping around their house. I'm loading up the car in preparation for the journey tomorrow when my phone finally pings with a message from Noah.

Are you coming back then?

OK, so not as ecstatic as I'd hoped. My spirits drop a little as I type out my reply.

Yes, tomorrow.

The ticks go blue straight away and I can see he's typing, but I'm now consumed with doubt. What if Christopher read the situation wrong, and Noah doesn't want to see me after all? Maybe the walkout wasn't anything to do with me. Maybe it was just a general protest against Deborah. His reply, when it arrives, is cryptic.

Is there anything else you'd like to tell me? Now would be a good time...

How am I supposed to respond to that? After a good ten minutes of indecision, I decide to go all in and tell him the truth about how I feel. If he rejects me, that's probably no more than I deserve.

I love you.

His reply is immediate.

I know. I love you too. I'll see you tomorrow. xx

* * *

The contrast between my first journey south and this one couldn't be more marked. Where I was uncertain then, and everything looked unfamiliar, I feel like I'm coming home this time. The closer I get to Ashford, the more impatient I feel, and I have to keep a close eye on the speedometer. I'm practically howling with frustration when I get stuck in a long queue to pass an accident that's been moved to the hard shoulder, but I eventually reach the site a little after three. I'm so hyped up that I manage to get my hi-vis vest in a tangle, and I lose a couple more precious minutes sorting it out, before I march up the site towards the office.

'Wotcher, Carol. Nice to see you back!' John calls from the roof of one of the Windsors, I forget the number.

'Thanks, John. Do you know where Noah is?' I yell back.

'He's at the show home. Apparently, one of the punters used the bog in there. The water hasn't been turned on yet, so it's causing a bit of a problem.'

'Nice.'

'I know. It's all bloody glamour, this job.'

Thankfully, I'm spared the evidence of our potential home-owner's evacuation, as Noah comes out of the show home front door just before I get there.

'You. Site office. Now,' I growl at him. I just have time to register the surprise on his face before I turn on my heel and practically sprint to the office.

'Welcome ba—' is as far as he gets before I've pinned him to the wall and planted my mouth on his.

'I'm so sorry about everything,' I tell him when we come up for air.

'I knew you didn't mean it. Or, at least, I was pretty certain,' he smiles.

'How?'

'Your face gave you away. Promise me one thing.'

'What?'

'Never take up poker.'

I laugh.

'Shall we try that conversation again?' I suggest. 'See if it goes the way it should this time?'

'OK. I love you, Ella.'

'And I love you too, Noah. How do you fancy skiving off for the rest of the afternoon?'

'Will I get in trouble?'

'Oh, yes. Lots, I should imagine.'

'Sounds fun. Lead the way.'

32

SIX MONTHS LATER

'Hurry up! We can't afford to be late,' Noah yells up the staircase. The house is finished and he's already accepted an offer, so we're off to the auction to bid on another run-down dump, allowing us to go through the whole renovation process again.

'Mm, you look nice,' he says, holding out my coat as I walk down the (beautifully painted) staircase in a skirt and blouse. Although we seem to live our lives in scruffy jeans and tops, Noah reckons we need to look like 'ordinary punters' at the auction. His view is that, if we pitch up looking like builders, people will cotton on to the potential of the property when we start bidding, and it might drive the price up. I think it's all mumbo-jumbo, but I'm happy to go along with it for his sake.

I am excited, as I've never been to a house auction before, but there's a part of me that also feels sad about selling Noah's beautiful home and starting over with another wreck. It's not just that it's also been my home for the last three months; it's that there's so much of our story embedded in this house. Wherever I turn, there's a reminder, whether it's a memory of climbing the scaffolding when I look up at the front of the house, the tiles in the bathroom, or the staircase. Even though the kitchen is unrecognisable, with sleek units and lots of natural light from the bifold doors that open onto the garden, I can still remember the old layout with the bathroom at the back and Noah making one of his ludicrous sandwiches in the grotty kitchen. The buyers are a couple with a young family, and I try hard to think positively about how much they will enjoy living here.

'Do you know where you're going?' Noah asks, as he folds himself into the passenger seat of the Fiat. Even though he normally moans like anything about travelling in my car, it's all part of his bizarre psychological game today, so the van is staying behind.

'I've put it into the satnav, but if you're going to contradict it all the way like you usually do, I'll turn it off.'

'I don't contradict it!'

'Uh-huh? You believe what you want.'

As we pull out of the parking space, the disembodied voice tells me to turn right at the end of the road.

'Why is she taking you that way?' he queries. 'I'd go left if I were you, and then head for the outlet centre. What?'

'You didn't even let her get to the end of the road. You're getting worse, I swear.'

'It's not my fault if she doesn't know where she's going.'

'Just turn her off and direct me. You know you're going to do it anyway.'

'It's a fair cop, boss. Did Abby get off OK?'

'Yes. Her dad collected her. He was down to sign the paper-work for the new site anyway, so it made sense.'

'John and Roberta are really going to miss her, I think.'

'It was kind of sweet, though, wasn't it? They made quite a convincing surrogate family. Imagine if she'd met someone while she was down here? I can easily see John doing the whole "what are your intentions" speech.'

When Abby first came down, the plan was for her to move into the caravan of shit. I'd already moved in with Noah, so it seemed like a good solution. John, unsurprisingly, took one look at her and started muttering darkly about the 'birdifying' of the construction industry now that there were two women on site. Kayleigh and Breanna appeared not to count, due to them being 'sales birds', who didn't have anything to do with the actual building work. In typical John fashion, it was all talk, and he and Abby quickly formed a strong bond. When he invited her over for dinner one Friday and Roberta heard that she was on her own in the caravan, they ended up insisting that she move into their spare room, and Roberta mothered her to death until the day she left.

'Before we get to the auction house, there's something I need to tell you.' Noah's voice is suddenly serious.

'What?'

'The buyers dropped out earlier this week. The agent rang to let me know on Tuesday.'

'Oh, no. I'm so sorry. Why didn't you tell me?'

'I've been thinking about what to do. You really love this house, don't you? I can tell.'

'I do, a little,' I admit. 'But I'm trying to be rational about it. I know you have to sell it.'

'Not necessarily. In fact, I've been thinking that we might keep it.'

'Really? But what about your plan? You know. Buy, renovate, make profit, rinse and repeat.'

'We can still do it. It means going back to the beginning, mortgage-wise, but that's not the end of the world. This house is special, though, isn't it? It's the first one we did together, and I'm surprised to find that I don't really like the idea of other people living in it.'

'Are you sure?'

'I think so. There will always be houses, but this one is our home.'

'Our little space to argue about whose turn it is to put the bins out,' I tease.

'Exactly.'

I glance across at Noah and smile. I can't believe I ever told him that I didn't belong here, because the truth is that I don't belong anywhere else.

ACKNOWLEDGMENTS

Thank you so much for reading this book. Writing a book set on a building site has come with all sorts of challenges, including having to learn more than I ever thought I would need to about roof trusses! I need to say a huge thank you to Anna Parfitt, who replied to my enquiries about brick factories in Kent with such enthusiasm and knowledge, even offering me a factory tour. I hope I've done your wisdom justice.

I want to say a massive thank you to the amazing Boldwood team. Working with you is an absolute joy. I want to call out Hannah, Cecily and Emily in particular. Thanks for your patient editing, which required the manuscript to go back and forth a few times. Caroline, thank you for stepping in to look after me as well. Of course, writing the book is only the first step, and I want to say thank you to Nia, Jenna, Amanda and all the team for the amazing work you do connecting my books with readers.

Mandy and Robyn, once again you have done great work as my alpha and beta readers, and I want to say a big thank you to both of you for that. To my family, who are so supportive and make space for me to write, thank you to you too. And, of course, to our dog Bertie, who enables me to make space in the day to walk and plot.

MORE FROM PHOEBE MACLEOD

We hope you enjoyed reading *Love at First Site*. If you did, please leave a review.

If you'd like to gift a copy, this book is also available as an ebook, hardback, large print, digital audio download and audiobook CD.

Sign up to Phoebe MacLeod's mailing list for news, competitions and updates on future books.

https://bit.ly/PhoebeMacLeodNews

Explore more heartwarming romantic comedies from Phoebe MacLeod.

ABOUT THE AUTHOR

Phoebe MacLeod is the author of several popular romantic comedies. She lives in Kent with her partner, grown up children and disobedient dog. Her love for her home county is apparent in her books, which have either been set in Kent or have a Kentish connection. She currently works as an IT consultant and writes in her spare time. She has always had a passion for learning new skills, including cookery courses, learning to drive an HGV and, most recently, qualifying to instruct on a Boeing 737 flight simulator.

Follow Phoebe on social media:

 twitter.com/macleod_phoebe
 facebook.com/PhoebeMacleodAuthor
 instagram.com/phoebemacleod21

Boldwood

Boldwood Books is an award-winning fiction publishing company seeking out the best stories from around the world.

Find out more at www.boldwoodbooks.com

Join our reader community for brilliant books, competitions and offers!

Follow us
@BoldwoodBooks
@BookandTonic

Sign up to our weekly deals newsletter

https://bit.ly/BoldwoodBNewsletter

Ingram Content Group UK Ltd.
Milton Keynes UK
UKHW040248210723
425530UK00001B/1

9 781804 262924